TERMINAL LIFE

TERMINAL LIFE

A Suited Hero Novel

Richard Torregrossa

Oceanview Publishing
LONGBOAT KEY, FLORIDA

ISBN: 978-1-60809-120-1

Published in the United States of America by Oceanview Publishing, Longboat Key, Florida
www.oceanviewpub.com

10 9 8 7 6 5 4 3 2 1

PRINTED IN THE UNITED STATES OF AMERICA

It is better to be violent, if there is violence in our hearts, than to put on the cloak of nonviolence to cover impotence.

—Mahatma Gandhi

TERMINAL LIFE

CHAPTER ONE

Luke jogs up the subway steps and catches a glimpse of his reflection in a store window. His suit is freshly cleaned and pressed, his shoes polished, his shirt crisp despite the summer heat. The dimple in his necktie required three attempts to get the symmetry just right, but it was worth it. He thinks to himself that he looks and feels quite well for a man who doesn't have long to live.

The job interview is set for one o'clock, but he is kept waiting for twenty minutes until Shelly, the director of human resources, is able to see him.

His suit seems to be as much a candidate for employment as he is, for he sees, at times, her glancing at the smooth roll of his lapels, his rectilinear white pocket square, the way his trousers drape when he crosses his legs, and the sliver of white sleeve that contrasts with his Glen plaid jacket, all intended effects that follow the law of angles.

Shelly seems both puzzled and impressed. Puzzled in that she does not quite understand the sartorial fine points that have created the force of the suit's gravitas, its crafted geometry, its arresting statement of order, its monochromatic subtlety.

She will never be able to see that we are all on our way to becoming someone else and his suit is his vehicle, a discrete entity, a bulwark against chaos, a whole and not an array of disconnected accessories.

She rudely answers the phone in the middle of their conversation as if he is not even in the room. Zaftig and curvy, her confident body language makes it clear that she finds her girth empowering, a useful substance over her trim and lithesome colleagues. Her black dress with white polka dots has a plunging neckline that shows off her plump breasts and an alabaster neck around which she wears a black beaded necklace with a gemstone pendant.

She fixes her elbow on her desk so that her arm stands straight up like a phallus, showing off her sizeable wedding ring and gold wedding band encrusted with diamonds. She rotates the rings with her thumb, a habitual gesture that has an element of preening about it.

Luke listens to her conversation because it is impossible not to listen.

"Tampons! Exactly!" She giggles and glances at him as if suddenly remembering that he is present but present in some deeply insignificant way.

It is a bright summer afternoon, the view panoramic from the fifty-first floor of this Midtown office building. The window blinds divide the abundant sunshine into shards as sharp as glass and they seem to cut rather than lightly shine on her.

He has no plans for the afternoon, nowhere to go, no one to see, just back to the streets, back to the shelter. The job has no practical interest to him because he is not here for a job. He is here for another reason, the best opportunity he's had since his breakdown, since the murder of his wife and the disappearance of his seven-year-old son, a first step toward finding the truth, the truth that is being kept hidden from him.

White clouds scud across an arresting azure sky. They are soft and vaporous as if they have emanated from a genie's lamp. Luke is comfortably seated in the plush chair across from Shelly's desk, rolling his MetroCard over his fingers like a card shark. He does this carefully because he has sharpened one edge of the MetroCard with a razor blade.

Shelly finally concludes her phone call and offers a half-hearted apology that is really no apology at all.

"Oh, I'm sorry. Now, where were we?"

"We were nowhere," he says and gets up to leave. "That was discourteous and unprofessional, behavior that reflects badly on the company as well as on you. We are concluding this interview."

Flustered, her mouth falls open and forms a vacuous moue. Her lips are full and her red lipstick is as thick as cake icing. She is taken aback by his insolence, his flouting of her authority, until she sees the cold look in his eyes, the stalwart stance of the man in the smart suit before her.

Clearly, she senses the imminence of danger, of something awful happening if she makes the wrong move. Her composure vanishes, her confident demeanor turns to nervousness and fear. No longer does she feel protected by her girth, her diamond ring, and the job title that makes candidates fawn and grovel before her.

She puts her hand on the phone as if on the handle of a weapon. Her expression makes her thoughts easily readable. He might be loony, the kind who would do her harm. She must call security.

"I'm sorry," she says again, starting to pick up the phone.

But it is too late.

He slashes her neck with the sharpened edge of the Metro-Card. The gesture is so quick and surgical that it makes a perfect incision—so perfect that it seems not to cause pain nor even draw blood at first, just surprise, but when the blood rises to the surface, it comes fast and fluidly. She presses her hand to her neck, but the blood oozes through the interstices of her fingers. Droplets fall onto his résumé.

The blood is deceptively profuse, but she will be okay, for the compression of her hand on the incision will stave off the flow. But the look on her face is one of shock and fear and surprise and confusion and that was his intent. That was his assignment. Mission accomplished.

CHAPTER TWO

He leaves her office, shutting the door behind him, and calmly walks past the receptionist. "Have a good day," he says. She nods, smiles perfunctorily.

The elevators are unavailable, all on different floors, so he takes the staircase to the suite below. He is aware of the security cameras and avoids them by ducking his head. He is also aware of the landscape of cubicles manned by workers who are transfixed by the lambent light of their computers. They do not look up. They do not pay him any mind. Still, he keeps his head down until he is on the elevator. In the palm of his hand is his Metro-Card, a concealed weapon. He is surprised when the elevator doors open and there are no security guards to accost him.

But as soon as he turns the corner, two appear. One is beefy, tall, and dark-skinned, a Puerto Rican, and well fed; his stomach hangs over his belt. The other one is white, perhaps Irish, with red hair and freckles, pale and pasty with a neatly shaved head that is oddly lumpy. Both are holding walkie-talkies. He appraises them quickly, reads their name tags. Brandon and DeShawn. They have been aroused from the boredom of inaction, but just barely, and their expressions clearly reveal that they are bovine, slow-footed, dull, feckless. He keeps walking and that's when the Puerto Rican security guard confronts him by holding up his hand, a signal for him to stop.

"Hey, Brandon! DeShawn!" He greets them cheerfully, as if

they're friends, and they pause, struggling to recognize the stranger. This makes his assault all the more unexpected.

He grabs DeShawn's hand, rolls it back and to the left until he hears a slight crack and then jerks it forward as his knee rises up to strike his solar plexus. DeShawn coughs, sputters, and tries to catch his breath. Luke brings an elbow down into the center of his back, which causes him to drop to the floor.

Brandon is frozen, confused, scared. He clumsily reaches for something on his belt—pepper spray or a baton, but he fumbles, and the leg that felled DeShawn, without touching the ground, juts out like a spear into Brandon's kneecap. It makes a sound like the snap of a dry twig. Brandon crumbles to the floor and grabs his leg as if it might fly apart. In one fluid movement they have both been disabled.

Luke pauses briefly, ready for some kind of manly retaliation from at least one of them so that he can preempt it, but they both remain in a polyester heap, gasping, groaning, so he walks slowly to the revolving doors that open onto the street, sidesteps a few onlookers who have not comprehended what has happened because they are too distracted by the text messages streaming into their smart phones. By the time they realize what has happened, Luke is gone, long gone.

CHAPTER THREE

The sidewalk is teeming with pedestrians and Luke blends easily into the eddying crowd. He casually walks two blocks to the subway near Bryant Park, where the throng is thicker, and uses his MetroCard for the purpose it was intended, to pass through the turnstile.

McKenzie is waiting for him on the subway platform, but he does not have the rest of the money. Luke grabs him by the throat and pushes him against the wall.

"She ruined me, that bitch," says McKenzie. "It was a fling, that's all."

"Yeah, yeah, I heard it all before. Everybody's got a hard-luck story," says Luke. "Tell it to your priest."

"Fired me after eighteen years of loyal service. I lost everything. I'm broke. Not a dime in my pocket."

"That's what you get for cheating on your wife."

"Everything, man. I lost it all."

"You've still got your life," says Luke, holding the Metro-Card to his neck, "but you'll lose that too unless I get the rest of my money. See that train coming into the station? How'd you like to take a tumble onto the subway tracks?"

Luke grabs his arm and forces him through the crowd to the edge of the platform.

"All right, all right. I'll get you your money."

"Let me have your watch."

"It's the last thing of value I own," says McKenzie in protest, but strips it off and gives it to Luke. He tries to wriggle free from Luke's grasp but Luke subdues him by incising his arm at a pressure point; his sharpened thumbnail draws a nipple of blood. Almost anything can be made or used as a weapon—everything from a towel to a toothpick, one of the many skills he learned as a Navy SEAL. Improvisation is the key to survival, in combat or on the streets.

The train rumbles into the station. The crowd ebbs and flows and McKenzie, glistening with sweat, looks around to find that Luke has vanished. He is as relieved as he is surprised.

Luke boards the downtown Q train and returns the Metro-Card to his wallet with more care than is usually associated with this act, like returning a gun to its holster. He will need it again, for it has taken him exactly where he wanted to go.

CHAPTER FOUR

He knows that the security cameras will contain images of him that will be used by the police. The information on his résumé is mostly false, but he assumes there's enough information on it for the police to track him down if they care to, but he knows that they have bigger crimes to pursue, for this is a city full of big crimes. Big crimes and overworked cops.

But it doesn't matter anyway. He doesn't really care because according to Dr. Ornstein, an oncologist at the VA Hospital, he has cancer, Hodgkin's lymphoma, the classic type—nodular sclerosing Hodgkin's lymphoma to be exact.

The symptoms that prompted him to see Dr. Ornstein were fevers that would come and go for no known reason, night sweats, weight loss, and a lump on his neck above his shirt collar that was painless but annoying. The lump turned out to be a swollen lymph node.

Dr. Ornstein ordered a CBC—complete blood count—that revealed the number of red and white blood cells, platelets, and the amount of hemoglobin (the protein that carries oxygen) in the red blood cells. He also performed an excision biopsy on the lymph node and concluded that the cancer was in its very early stages and could be cured with treatment, but Luke declined.

A year, maybe less, is enough time to accomplish what he needs to accomplish and that is really all he cares about and that is why he often visits the intersection of Flatbush and Nostrand Avenues where Uncle Paulie has one of his many locksmith

shops, all nifty money-laundering operations. He knows this because he used to work there before he went into the military.

But it has an even greater significance. This is where his wife,
Crissy, was killed in what was reported to be a robbery.

Luke had been against her working for Uncle Paulie. It had
been one of their worst quarrels. It was a job, she argued, and
a good job, better than any she could find. It was local, in
Brooklyn, and she wouldn't have to make the long trek into
Manhattan by subway. She hated the subway. The stifling New
York City subways, old rattletraps, filthy, overcrowded, dangerous, and filled with straphangers who looked like they all
needed a good jolt of antidepressants and a shower.

The pay was good, too, a lot better than a minimum-wage
job, the only kind she could find. She'd be a manager, increase
her bookkeeping and computer skills. She'd be based in the Nostrand Avenue store, but she could manage the other stores with
weekly visits.

Moreover, Uncle Paulie agreed to a flexible schedule that
would allow her to come and go so that she could take Jack,
then five, to school and pick him up. Crissy's family lived in
Brooklyn, too, so they could look after Jack when she was busy
at the store or worked late. Here, she had a support network
and she and Jack could have at least a semblance of a family life
while Luke was away for long periods. How could he deny her
that?

"So why is Uncle Paulie being so good to you?" he'd asked
her.

"He's family."

Luke snarled at this because Crissy didn't know the half of
it and she never would now.

"He's a mobster."

"Yeah, I know, but who isn't around here? And who better
to have my back than him while you're away?" she said, her

voice rising in irritation as if it was his fault. "I'm alone. This is the best I can manage. For us. And money's tight."

He understood her anger, insistence, and frustration, and all of her points were well taken, so he backed off, let her have her way.

Still, he had a bad feeling about it. But what could he do? He was thousands of miles away on deployment in Afghanistan and had no idea when he would return home.

He should have been firmer. Yes, at least in hindsight, he should have been firmer. It haunted him as if her murder was all somehow his fault. As irrational as it might sound, maybe it was. He couldn't shake the notion and the guilt was too much for him to bear. When he heard the news that she had been shot in the face in a robbery, he had already been suffering from post-traumatic stress disorder and it pushed him over the edge, nearly to the point of a psychotic break, eventually landing him in the VA psych ward, pumped full of meds.

He was unable to sleep. His mind raced, often with suicidal thoughts, but then he would think about Jack, his towheaded little boy who had just turned six and sent him drawings of his school teacher and the park where he played, which only made him feel cowardly. How could he abandon him? But the pain was too intense. He couldn't bear it. He just did not want to live.

Emotionally numb, paralyzed with depression, plagued by blackouts, hyperarousal, irritability, and bursts of uncontrollable anger—often directed at himself—he attempted suicide. Clumsily, in a daze, his hands so shaky he botched it. A nurse noticed him trying to slit his wrists with a pen. He had barely punctured the skin before she grabbed it away from him as if he was a naughty schoolboy defacing the classroom wall.

They upped his meds. Discussed shock treatment. Still, he felt emotionally dead, hopeless, inert, a failure as a man and unworthy of fatherhood. He couldn't take care of himself, so how could he take care of Jack?

Eventually, he was released, sent home, where he languished, damaged, unable to function, so he checked himself into a shelter, trying to pick up the pieces.

Now, staring out the window, he wonders how long he has been here. A year, maybe more, maybe less; time seems elastic; days seem like months, months seem like days, but he thinks about only two things: revenge, for the culprits were never found. This makes him wonder. This makes him wonder about a lot of things, things he needs to know, things he needs to resolve, put to rest, bury, kill, vanquish, avenge. He also thinks about Jack, now seven, growing up without him. They must reunite. They will reunite. For the first time since his breakdown he feels stirred to action and in his mind a kind of healing is taking place.

CHAPTER FIVE

So far, his visits to Uncle Paulie's locksmith store on Nostrand Avenue have not yielded the result he would like, but he is patient. He knows that he will run into Uncle Paulie sooner or later, and Uncle Paulie will be very surprised to see him alive and well—perhaps not so well but very much alive.

He returns to the shelter and packs his clothes. It is a dangerous place, but he feels safer here than on the streets because the danger is not hidden the way it is on the streets. The danger is so apparent that he finds comfort in that. And, of course, he has the suit, the carefully cared for suit. Every morning Mark Mohr, an arthritic former wrestler who ran a dry cleaning store before drugs got the best of him and he lost everything—his business, his family, his friends, his house, and a good deal of his mind—cleans and presses his suit in exchange for protection from the bullies, thieves, and mental cases that prey on those unable to defend themselves.

Luke sleeps in his suit, more out of necessity than choice. The deranged denizens who dwell here are so petty that they will steal anything, including shoelaces if not the shoes themselves, so he is ever vigilant.

He has devised a special way of sleeping in his suit so that it does not wrinkle. It's pretty simple, but requires the kind of discipline that perhaps one only learns in the military. He sleeps like a corpse in a casket, hands folded over his chest, legs straight, jacket and trousers pulled taut, legs extended, and his mind focused in a Zenlike concentration to resist any temptation to toss and turn. No easy feat, but he has mastered it, so that when he wakes in the morning he looks as crisp and well kempt as a Wall Street banker.

But he knows that tonight they will try to steal his suit. The gangs prey on the weak but they are amateurs, for they cannot tell the weak from the strong, the smart from the dumb. He sleeps in a maze of mattresses, some stained, but his is always clean. At about two a.m. he is attacked. They attempt to steal the suit off his back. He knows who they are even in the dark because he has been watching them watching him. Stalin, Lenin, and Hitler, he calls them.

But his suit is too smart for them. They do not understand its power, its fasteners and clever clasps, binding buttons and secret side adjusters, its stubborn adherence to his person, its loyalty and history, their shared intimacy, and so they are befuddled, frustrated. They can no more steal his suit than they can steal his skin.

And this makes them angry, so they thrash him. Not severely, but just enough to inflict noticeable bruises. And this is what he wants. It is a test to see if he can feel pain again, for he has been numb, dysphoric, for a long time. Since his recent losses, he has been immune to physical pain, hardly alive. He could have fought them off easily, because he has the skills, but with each blow it is as if he is coming back to life, a kind of Christlike resurrection, an almost religious ecstasy.

But the assault will not be without reprisal and it too will serve a purpose. It will be a kind of practice run for bigger and better acts of vengeance. It will test his skills, exactly like they were tested during the confrontation between the two feeble security guards. Is he still sharp? Has he lost his edge? He wants to know. He wants to know if he can return to his previous level of martial expertise.

The next day he relates the incident to Mr. Jenkins, his social worker, in a casual manner, not because he wants to but because Jenkins gasps when he sees him and says, "What the hell happened to you?"

"The shelter is not much of a shelter." It is more of a jest than a complaint, but Jenkins does not laugh.

"Do you want to see a doctor?" asks Jenkins. "You look hurt."

"No," he says. "My suit is fine."

"I'm not worried about your *suit*. I'm worried about you. Why do you stay in that shelter anyway? You must have friends, family. I know you have some Navy money put aside."

"My choice."

Dr. Barr, his psychiatrist, is also concerned when he sees him.

"You might have a concussion," he says, "broken bones. I'll make an appointment."

"I've seen enough doctors. It looks worse than it is."

"I might adjust your medication. You seem a little too calm."

"We're fine."

"Let's talk about Jack."

"I still want to find him, now more than ever," says Luke, suddenly emotional, trying to stifle the quiver in his voice. "I want to raise him, but I'm afraid of being a single father because I don't think I'd be any good at it now, not in my condition, not without Crissy. Despite my military heroics, I'm afraid. I'm a coward."

"I thought we were past these feelings of guilt and self-loathing."

"Not yet, but I'm getting there. Let's just say I'm starting to assert myself."

Dr. Barr looks at him warily. "Violently?"

"You don't miss a thing, do you, Doc?"

"There are no easy answers. I know that, but these violent urges. Direct them into—"

"I know. Something positive." Like finding Crissy's killer.

"What are you going to do now?"

"Keep moving."

CHAPTER SIX

He leaves Dr. Barr's office and takes the subway into the city and gets off at Lexington Avenue. McKenzie is waiting for him at Raffles Coffee Shop. McKenzie looks haggard but less nervous, undoubtedly because he has the rest of Luke's cash. Luke puts the envelope in his coat pocket and pats him on the cheek.

"Pleasure doing business with you," he says, "but be careful who you jerk around. I'm a sweet guy. But the next guy might not be."

"Can I have my watch back?"

Luke laughs. The guy's got balls. Luke picks up McKenzie's sandwich and takes a bite, a big sloppy bite, wipes his mouth, and dumps the sandwich onto the table. "You've got to be kidding," he says, shaking his head.

Then he walks to Madison Avenue and enters Busconi's, a tailoring shop he has long patronized. It is soothingly lit, cool, and smells of polished wood and cinnamon, fine wool and fabrics, and strong coffee.

He enters the foyer with its dark paneling and leather club chairs. Sample fabric books are stacked on a mahogany table by the window. The décor is like a gentleman's club, and he sits down and picks up a magazine. He knows the staff and they know him. Kelly brings him his usual, a double espresso. She is an attractive young woman, sincere, polite, friendly, and the musical sound of her bracelets lifts his spirits. He likes it here. He smiles, thinking that soon he will walk in and order a new suit.

"The suit is fine. A bit soiled, but we'll take care of that," says Haskell, a lanky man in his early sixties with his sleeves rolled up, a tape measure draped around his neck, and hair mottled like moss on a rock. Haskell has been his tailor for many years, during the good times and the bad. "But what the hell happened to *you*?"

Relieved that the suit is intact, he returns to the shelter and sees his attackers mulling about by a trestle table ringed with coffee cup stains and donut crumbs. They smirk. They think they have acted with impunity. He watches television with the usual assemblage of down-and-outers in the recreation room, patiently waiting for midnight, when everybody will be asleep. He approaches his attackers singly. Hitler is first and the easiest target. He waits until Hitler falls into a blubbering unconsciousness.

It was easy to find and trap the roaches. They are all over, but he set his traps in the alcove near the microwave. He picked the two smallest but liveliest of the bunch, then quietly makes his way to Hitler's filthy corner strewn with ratty sweatshirts, plastic bottles, and a brown paper bag that held a knife until it was surreptitiously removed by him. He has it in his back pocket.

The mouth expulses sour air vaguely redolent of cheap wine and rattles his unshaven jowls. Luke drops the roaches into the gaping maw and with one adroit motion seals it shut with a precut piece of duct tape. Then he finds Stalin and Lenin, also asleep, and with his yellow-and-blue MetroCard slashes their throats. He is surprised by his agility, his deftness, and is glad that he has stopped taking the antipsychotic medication that made him feel dazed, lethargic, inert, suicidal.

Ninjalike, he weaves back to his bed, retrieves his duffel bag, and shakes Suggs, also a former Navy SEAL whom he met in the psych ward at the VA Medical Center in Brooklyn where they were outpatients, both being treated for PTSD. Suggs, his skin as dark as weak coffee, is often mistaken for an African American. Although it annoys him, he exaggerates his resentment for comic effect. He was born in Grenada. "The Island of Spice," as he likes to say, "but I'm twice as nice. And I'm brown, not black. Nothing against the brothers, but I'm a Grenadian American."

They became friends, but Suggs hadn't fared as well as Luke. His PTSD was severe and he resisted treatment, choosing to disappear into the bottom of a bottle, walk the streets in a mental haze, another crazy on the streets of The Greatest City in the World.

But Luke was always there for him, often finding him passed out in the gutter, his clothes tattered, a bloody tooth on the ground where he'd collapsed on the hard pavement from alcohol poisoning or malnutrition. People walking by him with no regard, like he was offal to be avoided, but this was a veteran, this was a man who had fought for his country. Hadn't he earned their regard, their concern, their compassion?

But what did they know? What did they care? They were late for work, late to pick up their kids from soccer practice, late to the dentist, late to that new Italian restaurant that opened on Columbus Avenue they'd heard so much about. They had lives, no time for a destitute man on the streets.

Luke, though never in the best shape himself, managed to get him to homeless shelters, church charities, hospitals, anyplace where he wouldn't freeze to death in the winter and could receive decent care, a hot meal, medication. Suggs never stuck around, though. He'd wander off. And keep wandering. But Luke would always find him, for he never wandered far.

Suggs is startled, ready to fight.

"Hey, hey," whispers Luke. "It's me. Calm down."

"Luke?" says Suggs.

Rubbing the sleep from his eyes, Suggs is relieved to see a friend and not a foe trying to rape or steal from him. "Did you do the deed?"

"Yeah. Gotta move. I'll be in touch. Stay off the booze. I'll be needing you."

"When?"

"Soon, soon."

"I'm not going anywhere. As for the booze, well—Where you going, Luke?"

But Luke is gone before Suggs finishes the question, before the lights flick on and the commotion begins. Keep moving, Luke tells himself. Just keep moving.

CHAPTER SEVEN

Luke rides the subways for what's left of the night, purposely lingering at the most dangerous stations at the most dangerous times, between two and four a.m. Surprisingly, the busiest stations are the most perilous—Penn Station, Grand Central Station, 125th Street, 23rd Street, and Broadway.

Penn Station tops them all, so that becomes the locus of his journey. He rides the Q train to the last stop in Astoria, dozing off and on with his duffel bag tucked between his legs, and encounters a few sleepy passengers, a few rowdy toughs, drunk and laughing stupidly, blighted with tattoos. He glares at them, but they are too involved in their own palaver to be provoked.

It seems to him that when you are looking for trouble you can't find it. Not only can't he find trouble, the people he meets are friendly. Rebecca, a nurse still in her scrubs, sits across from him. Even though she slumps in her seat, her eyes red with fatigue, she starts a conversation. It's the suit, of course. Disarming, respectable, it makes him appear safe, harmless, even attractive.

"I waited for this train forever," she says. "It seems it takes longer and longer to get home every night. They've cut service."

He nods sympathetically.

"You work the night shift too?" she asks.

"Yeah, you could say that."

"I thought I wouldn't like it, but I do. I like having some

daytime to myself. The only thing I don't like is taking the train at this hour."

"I wouldn't worry."

"Well, here's my stop. Have a good night."

"I will. You too."

He takes the Number 2 train to the end of the line and then returns to Penn Station where he buys a cup of coffee. He boards an empty 5 train heading south. The coffee is too hot to sip, so he blows on it and watches the wisps of steam rise up and disappear.

The doors open at the next stop, and two black men in their thirties enter. One wears a do-rag, the other a wool cap, and Luke thinks a wool cap in this cloying heat? What is he thinking?

Both are wearing jeans that are slung so low they are practically around their knees. Luke, of course, is wearing his tailored suit, specially cut with the armholes smaller and higher than usual. The seam of the shoulder is not in the center; it's in the back, allowing the durable cloth to remain on a slight bias, which gives the coat greater flexibility. Both the coat and the trousers are hand sewn and made of high-quality medium-weight wool and a touch of silk to give it additional tract. All of these details allow for greater ease of movement, essential features for his purposes.

The men are glassy-eyed and boisterous, and swing on the stanchions. They laugh in bursts as if they're tweaking or drunk or both. The one in the red-and-green do-rag stares at him and he stares back. It is a kind of contest, but he does not look away.

"Problem, motherfucker?"

"No problem," says Luke with a baiting grin. "Just minding my own business."

"Keep it that way." He elbows his friend and they snicker.

"Are you lost?" asks Luke.

"Lost? You the one's lost."

"I think you and your girlfriend got on the wrong train."

"Ha! This dude's the dope. Funny fucker in a fine suit." He pulls out a knife.

"How'd you like that suit air-conditioned?"

"Shouldn't you and your girlfriend be robbing a convenience store or at home watching the highlights of the Knicks game? They lost, you know. To Boston."

"Yo, man, this dude's asking for it."

In a threatening saunter, they move toward him, shoulder to shoulder.

He thinks this is just too easy.

"What's in the bag, man?"

"A million dollars."

"You're fucking with us, ain't you?"

"You think?"

"We'll mess you up. You and that nice suit of yours."

"I'm a man of the cloth."

Could they be that stupid? He's holding a hot cup of coffee, the steam still wafting off the top of the lid.

"You're tough guys, aren't you?" says Luke. "You can handle a little good-natured kidding, right? But let me make a suggestion. I'd put that knife away because it'll look awfully stupid sticking out of your ass."

They make their move and he tosses the hot coffee at them. They are scalded, blinded, stunned, as if they thought he'd put the coffee down to fight them, but mostly they are angry, very, very angry.

He grabs hold of the handrail and lifts himself up. Springing forward, he kicks them both in the chest and they fall backward into the seats across the aisle. But they are only momentarily dazed and the one in the wool cap lurches to his feet, rubbing his eyes.

A swift inside reverse crescent kick to the side of his head knocks him off balance. He tries to recover but is tripped up, snagged, comically entangled in his own pants that have fallen around his knees while Luke moves effortlessly, cleanly, his suit abetting and not obstructing his mobility.

The attacker with the knife slashes wildly and inaccurately. A true tyro. Luke steps into, instead of away from, the slashing motion and, now perpendicular to his assailant, simultaneously strikes one blow to his bicep, one to his wrist. The arm goes numb and the knife drops to the floor. Luke hits him square in the face with his elbow and it makes a sound like a baseball bat hitting a fastball square on.

Blood squirts from a pulpy broken nose. His friend is up and on his feet, but not for long. A snap kick to the stomach and a crippling roundhouse kick to the right kneecap knocks him down. Luke picks up the knife and places it in his back pocket, his second knife in a week. He's becoming a collector of fine cutlery.

But he is happy to see that, unlike the security guards, they are still full of fight, inept but spirited. They come at him swinging. He deflects their punches easily enough, then throws more kicks and punches to their bodies, followed by a series of well-placed jabs—straight punches—that bloodies their faces.

They receive the blows with stalwart defiance, but then he delivers the coup de grâce—a tandem of vicious right crosses that nearly knocks their heads off their shoulders. Next, he makes his signature mark, really just a nick, on their throats with his MetroCard.

He has refrained from using lethal techniques that could have ended the fight in a matter of seconds because, after all, this is just practice, another test of his abilities, long dormant. No need to kill anybody. Yet.

He is pleased. It was all muscle memory, and he wishes the fight would have lasted longer, but they have had enough and stagger to the safe end of the subway car. He follows them, but the train stops and the doors open and they bolt.

He tries to sleep on the uptown local but he is too pumped with adrenaline, so he just rides the train, enjoying his newfound vitality, regained confidence, and what feels like an almost divine rebirth. He doesn't know exactly where he is but he notices a man in a porkpie hat and shiny two-toned shoes at the other end of the subway car observing him. When Luke glances at him, he quickly looks away, buries his head in a newspaper. He has seen this man before, he thinks, and he wonders if it is just a coincidence or a kind of hallucination, a side effect, from abruptly withdrawing from his medication.

CHAPTER EIGHT

From a deli window across the street from Uncle Paulie's lock-smith shop on Nostrand Avenue, he can see the dour uniformity of the rush-hour commuters in their lockstep march disembarking from the B34 bus and their descent into the fetid subway. It is a muggy morning, overcast and gray, and they all look dispirited, like prisoners being sent to some subterranean penitentiary. He remembers being one of them.

He walks the streets near Brooklyn College and a few hours later he hears a horn honk. It's honking at him, and he knows that finally his plan has succeeded. He ignores it, pretends he doesn't hear it, keeps moving. A big, black Lincoln Navigator gleaming from front to back with a grille like a set of shark's teeth pulls up alongside him and the passenger's window slowly glides down.

"Hey, Luke. *Luke!*"

It is Uncle Paulie. Luke acknowledges him with the expected expression of surprise.

"What are you, deaf?"

They say that pets resemble their owners. Luke thinks cars resemble their owners. Uncle Paulie is barrel chested with a set of large, shiny white teeth—caps, no doubt—and he is dressed in black. He is very clean and well groomed, a persnickety man in every way. It's hard to determine where his vehicle ends and he begins.

Luke swings his duffel bag over his shoulder, walks to the open window, and leans in.

"You come back from the dead or something?" asks Uncle Paulie.

"Something like that."

"Get in."

They drive around the block looking for a parking space. Uncle Paulie is very particular about where he parks. He must park among vehicle owners who share his same fastidious concern for their cars. If he sees a car parked askew or sloppily it is a sign that the driver is careless, and a careless driver might ding or scrape or damage Uncle Paulie's vehicle in some small or big way and he will not park near it.

"What a coincidence, running into you. I'm hardly ever in the old neighborhood anymore. The store here practically runs itself. I've got a great manager, Laura. Lucky to have found her. Easy on the eyes too." Luke nods and Uncle Paulie repeats, "Quite a coincidence, eh?"

"Uh-huh." Luke smiles ambiguously.

"I've been looking for you. We've all been—concerned."

"Yeah."

"So what's with the duffel bag? You joining the Navy again?"

"No, the circus."

"Wiseass. At least you've still got your sense of humor. So where you living?"

"Just bouncing around."

"I heard about your breakdown after . . . after Crissy's. . ." Uncle Paulie cannot finish the sentence. His eyes become shifty, his demeanor uncertain. "Must've been rough. I don't know what I'd do if anything happened to Marie. She's my rock. Coming up on thirty-five years of marriage. But we're proud of you.

Iraq. Afghanistan. The Medal of Honor. Special Ops. I know you saw some things." Uncle Paulie pauses, hoping Luke will volunteer insider information, a combat story, a heroic tale, a dramatic description of a top-secret Special Forces mission, but Luke remains silently scornful. It's just not something he talks about, ever.

But Uncle Paulie is nervously chatty. "So," he says, uncomfortable with the silence, "why don't you come stay with your aunt and me until you get back on your feet? I've even got a car you can use, Stevie's old Mustang."

Luke smiles again, though this time wryly. Keep your friends close, but keep your enemies closer, eh, Uncle Paulie? Luke expected the offer. So far his plan has worked flawlessly.

"Awfully generous of you."

"You working?"

"Looking."

Uncle Paulie gives his suit the once over, nods approvingly.

"Still a whiz with computers? Could use you. I've got a guy. Bangs me for twelve hundred dollars every time he touches the thing. Although he does handle our entire network."

Uncle Paulie is usually not this loquacious.

"You could work in the store with Laura. I could use a man. Business is good. I don't know what the hell happened to this neighborhood, but it's filled with dumb asses who lock themselves out of their cars and houses. I've got a bunch of repeat customers. I should offer one of those frequent customer discounts. Ha!" Uncle Paulie laughs heartily at his own joke, pats his stomach as if the vibrations pleasantly soothe his digestion. "But the real money is in security systems. Crime does pay, you know."

Finally, after circling the block about ten times, Uncle Paulie, dissatisfied with the quality of parking spaces on the street, drives into a parking lot and greets the guy in the booth like they are old friends. Luke concludes that this ritual is one of Uncle Paulie's many quirks.

They enter the store and Laura is behind the counter. Uncle Paulie walks in with an added swagger, a mode of behavior to impress Laura, though it is somewhat diminished when he must hitch up his pants because his belly pushes them down.

Laura is more than pretty. She is striking with luminous blue eyes and high cheekbones framed with tussled blond hair. When their eyes meet there is a *frisson*, a moment of connection, of immediate attraction, but she is shy and turns away. He senses that she, too, has suffered some kind of loss or betrayal that has wounded her deeply, that she is not what she once was, that she has lost a measure of confidence, trust, direction. The wounded recognize this in each other.

"Hey, beautiful," says Uncle Paulie in a blustery manner that Luke remembers well. "I want you to meet my nephew." She nods, nice to meet you, and returns to her paperwork. She has a lovely smile that is modest and sheds a warm light.

Uncle Paulie heads straight for the till, counts the cash. "You guys are going to be working together. You'll be in good hands, Laura. Luke here is a karate expert, a regular Bruce Lee, and former Navy SEAL, a Special Forces hotshot. Did two tours in those fucked-up Middle Eastern countries."

He is trying to use Luke's accolades to make himself sound like a big man and Luke resents it, but lets it go, and tries to catch Laura's eye again.

Uncle Paulie turns to Luke. "Did I tell you? Neighborhood's gotten even worse. After Crissy, the Arab owner of the deli across the street got held up too and took a bullet between the eyes for a couple of hundred bucks. Family runs it; nice people. Family sticks together. Like the Italians. His brother and his sons and nephews work it now."

Luke has seen the crude but oddly touching spray-painted memorial on the brick-lined side of the store.

"We got held up last February again," continues Uncle Paulie like a lawyer trying to make a case that this kind of thing happens all the time. "Two guys came in hiding shotguns in long coats. They didn't get much, but they scared the shit out of Tony, a big muscular guy. I can't help laughing. Spent all his spare time in the gym. Lot of good it did him. He quit. I didn't want to hire a woman, but Laura's got more balls then he'll ever have, so to speak." He winks at Laura, an attempt at flattery, charm. "So I'd like to have a guy like you around. We've got better security now. Put it in after Crissy . . ." He cannot finish the sentence as if an unexpected impulse of guilt has stricken his tongue. "We keep the door locked. We close early. And some of the smarter street rats know better than to mess with us; it's the dumb ones we gotta watch out for, the desperate druggies. We've also got surveillance cameras—the very ones we sell. Ironic, isn't it?"

A customer walks in. Laura makes him a key. Then she returns to her bookkeeping.

"So, Luke. Do you want the job or what?"

Luke hesitates. He doesn't want to appear too eager. But then Laura looks up from her desk with that lovely smile and their eyes meet again and he says, "Sure. Thanks, Uncle Paulie."

CHAPTER NINE

During the ride to Staten Island, Uncle Paulie is oddly quiet. He seems to be turning over the same thought in his mind. He even seems a little worried.

Luke wonders if he's having second thoughts.

When they cross the Verrazano Bridge, Uncle Paulie asks if he needs anything. Luke says he does. Could he stop at an electronics store?

"You broke? You need some dough?"

Luke is not broke; he's banked all those Navy paychecks when he was in the psych ward, but he says, yes, he is broke, and Uncle Paulie peels off a few hundred dollar bills from a wad that would choke a porn star. The more indebted he becomes to Uncle Paulie, the weaker Uncle Paulie will think he is. They stop at Best Buy, the electronics store.

"I'll wait here. You go ahead. Take your time."

Luke sees Uncle Paulie on his cell phone in the reflection of a car window. Uncle Paulie has the same nervous look on his face. Luke enters Best Buy and picks up a few things—a laptop computer, three prepaid cell phones, a MiFi device, a transmitter, a router, a memory card, a splicer, speakers, headphones, some odds and ends—then returns to the car. Uncle Paulie is still talking on his cell phone but cuts the conversation short when Luke opens the door and climbs aboard.

"You buy out the whole store?"

They drive to the residential area on the eastern end of Todt

Hill, the highest natural point in the five boroughs of New York City and the highest elevation on the entire Eastern Seaboard from Florida to Cape Cod. Luke has studied the area, for he knew this day would come. What amuses him most is that the name Todt comes from the German language word for "dead."

Uncle Paulie's house resembles a cross between the White House and a medieval castle. It is at the end of a cul-de-sac, the grandest residence in a neighborhood that is one of the most affluent in all of New York City.

Armed security guards stand behind a tall gate. They recognize the car and the wrought-iron gates swing open wide. They nod respectfully to Paulie. Paulie waves, smiles the smile of a man who feels he is ably protected, safe, perhaps invulnerable.

The eight-thousand-square-foot house, almost half of which is being renovated, sits on three and a half acres of land. It is private, secluded. Two dumpsters are filled with debris and parked in the rear of the house. Tradesmen wave to Paulie, their work boots crunching on the gravel and stone breezeway as they push cement mixers.

Uncle Paulie surveys his property and is not pleased. At least a dozen empty window frames are covered with plastic.

"Damn," he says. "I knew it. The new windows aren't here yet. That's what you get when you import things from Italy."

Uncle Paulie shows him around. He is particularly proud of his classic car collection housed in a climate-controlled garage that is almost as large as the house.

"Just got that Bugatti," says Uncle Paulie, his chest swelling with pride, "but the Ford Galaxy is my favorite. Maybe not worth the most, but—"

Luke takes note of everything, things that his uncle does not necessarily point out. The barbeques near the Olympic-size swimming pool are large enough to cook an entire steer. The huge propane tanks, camouflaged behind shrubbery, are like submarines in drydock and fuel the elaborate outdoor cooking facilities and fire pits. There's a riser and a stage with a canopy. Uncle Paulie has hosted weddings here for as many as two hundred and fifty people.

The Esso gasoline pump in the garage is a vintage model, probably from the sixties. And surveillance cameras are like watchful eyes at the entrances and exits, but Luke notices that there are weak points in this costly and elaborate security system.

"You'll love this," says Uncle Paulie. "I'm installing motion sensing laser-pulse rifles."

"Are you expecting an attack by aliens?"

"Worse."

Behind the house is a meticulously maintained garden and lawn, woodlands and a high ridge lined with tall elm and oak trees. There are also two fountains, a patio, a putting green, a swimming pool, and another garden surrounded by a fence and tall trees that cast long shadows across the stippled pool waters. Despite these lush amenities, it seems to Luke that it is more like a fortress than a home. And for good reason. Uncle Paulie has a lot of enemies.

They enter the house through the garage and are greeted by Uncle Paulie's wife, Luke's Aunt Marie, a middle-aged woman in a cashmere sweater with the sleeves pulled up to her elbows. Her coiffure is a perfect helmet of dyed blond hair, her makeup fresh and not overly done, and although she is no longer as svelte as she used to be, the lines of a shapely figure are still visible.

Although she tries to hide it with a warm embrace, she is unnerved by his arrival.

"Look at you," she says, wringing her hands. "Not bad, not bad at all. Still the sharp dresser. A little thin, though. A couple of home-cooked meals and we'll get you shipshape. This was short notice, but I've got your room all ready. Come in, come in. Sit down. Tell me. What have you been up to?"

Luke absentmindedly rolls his MetroCard over his fingers, a skill he has mastered. His dexterity is such that the card goes back and forth, back and forth, seemingly on its own. But he is focused on his aunt's neck. It is a long, very graceful neck.

She continues talking. Or rather interrogating him, although he hasn't answered any of her questions.

"Where have you been hiding?" she asks. "Are you working? Paulie tells me you might be working for him again. Is that so? Is it too cold in here? Paulie likes it like a meat locker. I can turn it up. Should I turn it up?"

The room temperature must be around fifty, Luke thinks. Another one of Uncle Paulie's quirks.

"Honey," says Uncle Paulie, "enough with the questions." He turns to Luke. "How about a drink? Scotch? That'll warm you up. Good. Honey, get us a couple of scotches, will you? And make mine a double. My sciatica feels like somebody's sticking a knife in my leg."

Uncle Paulie always has expensive scotch, single malt. He watches his wife pour it from a cut-crystal decanter into glasses on a tray like a penny-pinching bar manager.

She is a confident woman who has been through a lot—a philandering husband, one screwball dead son, whacked because he fucked with the wrong people, another one in rehab, and the youngest, a lazy parasite who does whatever his father tells him to do. He runs their telemarketing business, a front for their most lucrative operation, an illegal prescription drug manufacturing and distribution racket that involves a sophisticated online network, among other things.

But his aunt is not one to be rattled. Today, though, she does not seem like herself. She spills a few drops of Glenfiddich, and

Uncle Paulie rolls his eyes. "Marie," he groans, "that stuff ain't cheap."

The smell of scotch and Uncle Paulie's cologne creates a Proustian moment for Luke, but a very unpleasant one, and it makes him gag. His mind reels back to the time when he'd come home from school and knew Uncle Paulie had been there just by the peculiar scent that lingered in the air. His father, Uncle Paulie's brother, never knew about the secret affair. The visits were regular, Tuesdays and Thursdays.

Although it's been years, Luke remembers it as if it was yesterday. Even at the time, Luke knew what was going on, but it never reached his consciousness, at least not fully, until much later when his father figured it out, that his own brother was fucking his wife, and his parents' arguments became epics of physical and psychological violence that drove his father to drink and his mother, who ironically was never much of a drinker, to overdose on pain meds and vodka shortly thereafter. Luke had just turned sixteen. He blames it all on Uncle Paulie.

"So," says Aunt Marie, handing Luke a glass, "what are your long-term goals?"

She must know, but he says matter-of-factly, "Keep moving."

"Keep moving? Doesn't sound like much of a plan." Aunt Marie's tone is light, almost tender, as if she wants information but not at the cost of annoying him. She wants him calm, pliable, and he plays along.

"You've always been goal driven," she says. "I'm sure you've got big plans."

"I'm gonna find out who killed Crissy and where my son is."

The ensuing silence is tense. Aunt Marie visibly stiffens.

"I know it's painful, honey, but you've got to let that go. It's not that I don't understand your loss. We all do. But finding Crissy's killer, if that's what you plan to do—nothing good can come of it. Let the police handle it."

"It's a cold case," says Luke. "The police aren't doing anything. Small crime, big city."

"Your son's with Crissy's parents. You must know that. And from what I've heard, Jack's doing fine."

"Where are they?"

"That I don't know."

Liar.

"Are you sure you're up to taking care of Jack after all you've been through?"

Luke levels a stern, hostile look at his aunt. "He's my son." But, truthfully, he does not know what he should do about Jack. Sometimes he thinks he'd be better left where he is, with his in-laws who are providing a safe and loving environment for him, one that Luke doubts he can replicate. Maybe there's a compromise somewhere.

"Oh, of course, of course," says Aunt Marie employing a conciliatory tone, a conciliatory smile. "If we can help in any way."

"All right." says Uncle Paulie, putting a period on the chatter. "A toast. Good to have you back."

"Good to be back," says Luke, and he means it, but surely not in the way Uncle Paulie means it. For the first time that day they exchange looks that are truly meaningful.

CHAPTER TEN

"That was great, Aunt Marie. Thank you," says Luke, pushing his plate away. Spaghetti Bolognese. He hasn't eaten this well in a long time. But he feels gorged and doesn't like the feeling. He does not want to get soft; he wants to stay lean, hungry, sharp.

The meal, the setting, the warmth of a home instead of a shelter brings back memories. Memories he'd rather not revisit, memories of Jack opening his favorite Christmas present, a new set of Lego blocks, and the excited look on his face, his eyes filled with surprise and gratitude, that innocent sense of wonder. "Thank you, Daddy! Thank you!" A voice with a distinctively high timbre that still echoes in his ears.

And the time when Jack was just learning to read and they walked by Radio City Music Hall on Sixth Avenue in Manhattan and he asked why there was such a big radio across the street.

Luke pensively stares out the window into the darkness, at the black shapes on the ridge of the hill behind the house looming like sentinels, vigilant and ghostly. He feels Crissy's spirit close and warm but at the same time feels the eternal distance between them. It is a strange, unsettling feeling that he cannot resolve. It makes him want to go back to the shelter, hide away, but that is a luxury he cannot afford. He must stay here until he finishes what he has started. Until he can once again embrace Jack with the love and the care he deserves.

"Is there anything the matter, dear?" probes Aunt Marie.

"I just want to—" but stops, shrewdly realizing that he cannot confide in these people.

Uncle Paulie and Aunt Marie exchange concerned looks. If anything, they are a team, he senses, united in a bond that, despite their marital troubles, goes back decades, and it is deep, loyal, irrationally strong, for the human heart is cryptic.

"So," asks Uncle Paulie, "you want to watch some TV, shoot a game of pool?"

"No, thanks. I think I'll take a walk and then turn in."

Luke visits the guardhouse and chats with the security personnel who are all impressively armed. Then he reconnoiters the rear of the house, again noting its most vulnerable points. The night air is fragrant and a little muggy. He walks by the Olympic-size swimming pool and sees himself dimly reflected in the still waters. He is not sure he likes what he sees.

Then he returns to the house and takes the stairs to the second floor, enters his room, and places the merchandise he bought at Best Buy on his bed. He boots up his computer, a cheap laptop, and plugs in the MiFi. He hears the TV on downstairs, Aunt Marie doing the dishes. They'll be up soon, so he must act quickly. It's been a while since he's done this, but it doesn't take long. He bugs their bedroom with a few simple pieces of equipment. It all comes back to him like he did it yesterday and this pleases him, yet another sign of his resurrection. Later that night, he listens in on their conversation.

"I told you not to bring him here," says Aunt Marie heatedly. "He knows. He *knows*, Paulie."

"I'll handle him. He's a punk. He thinks highly of himself. He always has. That's his weakness. Medal of Honor winner. Big Fucking Deal. Ends up in the psych ward."

"He's out of his mind."

"He can't do us any harm. I've got him right where I want him. *Here*."

"He gives me the creeps."

"Marie! Stop it. It's all planned. Don't worry your pretty little head."

"I've heard that before."

"Billy Dee, the private detective I hired to find and follow him, told me he's got cancer, refuses treatment. He's a dead man either way. So, nothing to worry about."

"He has what?"

"Cancer."

"What kind?"

"Hodgkin's lymphoma."

"That's curable, in its early stages anyway."

"Doesn't matter. At least in his case. He's refused treatment. The kid's got a death wish."

"Cancer? And he won't accept treatment? He really is crazy."

"He's got a death wish ever since Crissy died."

They exchange guilty looks. Luke cannot see this, but he can sense it.

"There's nothing more dangerous than a man with nothing to lose," says Aunt Marie.

"You're watching too many episodes of *The Sopranos*."

"I still think it was a mistake to bring him here, into our *home*."

"I gotta take care of this loose end. Better to have him close where I can keep an eye on him. Plus, I've got a plan that will put him to good use, something nobody is better suited for. I'll kill two birds with one stone. Him and Mark Fister."

"But the FBI, the DEA are still—"

"Marie!" Uncle Paulie's tone is firm enough to shut her up for the night—and raise his blood pressure.

Luke wonders if Billy Dee was the black guy in the porkpie hat and natty brown-and-white spectator shoes that crossed his path on more than one occasion. He's a little surprised that they know so much about his recent activities. He went to great pains to stay under the radar.

But it's okay. It puts him on high alert. Everything he suspected about Uncle Paulie must be true. It's always good to have confirmation. And it's nice to see that he also has not lost his touch with improvising basic electronics to suit his needs.

He falls asleep easily, but wakes a few hours later wracked with muscle cramps, fever, and chills, symptoms of Hodgkin's lymphoma. He knows them well. They are painful, but physical pain is easy for him to endure, far easier than the burden of loss he is carrying. And they serve another purpose. They impute in him an urgency, even a kind of paradoxical strength, a reminder that his time is limited to exact the revenge that weighs heavily on his mind.

CHAPTER ELEVEN

He likes working with Laura. She's pretty and helpful and he brings her coffee and she brings him coffee and they joke about the customers locking themselves out of their cars and houses and generally have a good time together. She notices his suit straight off, but it takes a few days for her to ask him about it.

"Why are you always dressed up?"

"Sometimes a suit is just a suit, sometimes it's a necessity. For me, it's a necessity."

She doesn't understand and he regrets his obtuse response. It doesn't matter, doesn't matter right now anyway. Soon she'll understand.

Today she seems jittery, not herself. It seems everybody in his presence sooner or later contracts a case of nervous agitation.

"What's the matter?" asks Luke. "You look like you've seen a ghost."

She glances toward the window.

"There's this guy. He's Russian. He keeps hitting on me. He's always spying. In fact, he's circling the block right now."

"Want me to have a word with him?"

"Christopher, my friend, will be here soon. He's always late."

"Up to you."

"I don't want any trouble. And I'm sure you don't either after what you've been through."

"So you know?"

"Everybody knows. It was horrible. I know what you went through. Must still be going through hell."

It's closing time. The light is fading, but he can still see Laura's shadowy stalker. Laura totals up the register and they lock the doors behind them. Luke draws the security gates; they make a loud clanking noise.

It's a clear night. The stars are out, gently pulsating. The air is soft and warm. He is about to ask Laura if she would like to sit outside somewhere and have a drink or a coffee. He is surprised at this impulse, an admission of his loneliness that feels somehow shameful, as if he's betraying Crissy. This new stirring of feeling inside of him is yet another hopeful sign of his resurrection, but he resists it, suppresses it. He does not want to be vulnerable again, not in this way, ever.

"There he is," she says.

"I'll walk you to your car. Take my hand."

Luke thinks this will discourage him, but it does the opposite, it makes him brazen. In a thick Russian accent, he shouts from the window of his car, an old Chevy convertible with the top down. "Laura! Hey, pretty baby! Sexy Laura." He lights a cigarette, blows smoke. "Laura! Oh, Laura."

Luke sizes him up. He seems a little buzzed, slightly drunk. His arms are muscular, tattooed, his head is shaved, a soul patch sprouts under a moist, simian lip, and his eyes are glassy with an arrogant glint. Unshaven, with bushy eyebrows, and a prominent forehead, he is ugly in a memorable way, a face Luke will not forget.

Luke tells Laura to wait here.

"Don't," she says, but he can tell that she wants him to act.

"I'll be nice."

"He's trouble."

Luke can feel her nails dig into his arm.

"I'll be nice. Very, very nice."

But she will not let go of his arm. She is truly afraid, almost irrationally scared, faintly trembling. Luke gently unclasps her hand and takes a step toward the Russian, but she jerks him back.

"You're really scared of this character, aren't you?"

"He's got a gun."

This only sharpens Luke's interest. It will make a nice addition to his burgeoning weapons collection.

Luke gently guides her into the doorway and then walks into the street.

"C'mon, pal," he says, waving his hand for him to come closer. "Back up, back it up. Let's talk." Luke wants him in full view of the surveillance cameras because he knows exactly what is about to go down.

The Russian puts the car in reverse and steps on the gas hard as if he's crushing a rodent, causing the tires to screech and gravel to spit from the crumbling macadam. He jams on the brakes, stopping in front of Luke, and gets out of the car, rattling off a series of unintelligible sentences, but it is clear that these are not well-mannered introductions.

"Look. I don't want any trouble," says Luke, holding up his hands to signal that he is no threat. "Just leave the girl alone, okay? She's not interested. What's your name?"

"I am Alexei," he says in a Godlike declaration. "Who the fuck are you? Her father?"

Luke steps closer in preparation for what will likely happen next. "I'm just a friend," says Luke. "Now get back in your car, Alexei, and go back to Sheepshead Bay and crawl back into your bottle of Smirnoff, okay?"

Alexei's face turns so red Luke thinks that blisters will appear. Then, rather predictably, Alexei pulls out a scuffed hand-gun, a 9mm, an old Ruger that'll probably jam, and points it in Luke's face.

"Everybody's a tough guy," says Luke, shaking his head.

"Fuck you."

"Pull the trigger, tough guy," says Luke. There is still a dark place in him that hopes he will.

"Fuck you."

Luke draws a deep breath; all of the muscles in his body relax, uncoil. He smiles, for it is so much easier to disarm a man holding a gun than a knife.

He wants the moment to last, for he feels, once again, a renewed sense of well-being, of bodily warmth, but he knows that it will be over quickly.

In one swift, deft movement he grabs the stock of the 9mm and turns it to the right so that it is perpendicular to Alexei. With his right hand he uses the inside edge of his forearm, the ulna, to strike Alexei's wrist. The combined movement breaks Alexei's finger that is wrapped around the trigger, and the Ruger is easily taken away from him. Now Alexei is the one looking down the barrel of a gun, his own gun.

"Now get in your car and drive away, and I don't want to see you around here anymore. Got it?"

Alexei, holding his finger, walks toward the car, but it is a feint, a trick, that works for the moment. Luke tucks the gun in the belt of his pants, thinking Alexei is no longer a threat, but Alexei rushes him. Luke whips out the gun and shoots him in the calf. He could've shot him in the kneecap, crippling him, causing him to walk with a limp for the rest of his life, and maybe he should have. Yes, he has a feeling he should have.

"You fuckin' shot me!" Alexei bellows, more out of surprise than pain.

"You're very perceptive."

"I kill you, you son of bitch. I kill you!"

"Somebody beat you to it."

But there is no fight left in Alexei for he hobbles to his car and makes a U-turn, tires screeching, and very nearly gets T-boned by a car driving in the opposite lane.

Luke, knowing exactly where the surveillance camera is, expertly plays the law of angles again. With his back to the camera he makes a throwing motion pretending to get rid of the gun, but he actually conceals it in the palm of his hand and then tucks it into his belt, making sure that the point at which the gun would leave his hand is out of camera range. When the tape is replayed, all it will show is what will look like Luke tossing the gun away.

He returns for Laura, whose arms are crossed tightly across her chest.

"What the hell did you do that for?" she snaps, clearly displeased with his feat. "Are you trying to be my suited hero or something? You didn't have to *shoot* him. You'll have the whole Russian Mafia after you. *And* me."

Now there's a nice thought, thinks Luke.

CHAPTER TWELVE

After lunch at the deli, Luke walks back to the store to find Uncle Paulie and his minions, most notably a familiar face, the man in the porkpie hat and polished spectators, and two men in dark suits, NYPD detectives, gathered around a dusty television screen in the back room watching the tape of his confrontation with Alexei.

They're drinking Bushmills and eating peanuts. They replay the same scene over and over, sometimes in slow motion, trying to catch every detail, enjoying it like a John Wayne movie.

"How'd you do that, kid?" asks Uncle Paulie. "How'd you take the gun away from him like that? And without getting shot? By the way, meet my friends, Detectives Heman and Fallon. And this is my associate, Billy Dee."

For the first time, he regards Billy Dee, who does not smile—who hardly reacts at all, save for returning a glance that is dispassionate, yet not unfriendly, just an absence of any real feeling, revealing a kind of cold neutrality.

"Yeah," says Detective Heman. "Pretty smooth."

"Impressive," says Detective Fallon warily, as if he doesn't really mean it.

"Basic self-defense," says Luke. "Nothing fancy."

"But did you have to shoot him?" asks Detective Heman, chuckling.

"Of course he did," says Fallon. They both laugh.

"Am I in some kind of trouble here?" asks Luke. He doesn't

care if he is, but he wants to hear their answer to see where he stands, to see what it might reveal about them.

"Not at all," says Uncle Paulie.

"Well, thanks to your Godfather here. We could look at it another way, but Paulie has convinced us that you had good cause," says Fallon. "The law is on your side. The Ruskie pulled a gun on you. You disarmed him, and when he rushed you, you had every right to defend yourself—even if it was with his own handgun!" This elicits more appreciative chuckles. "But I'd watch out. Those Ruskies love revenge, especially when their pride is hurt."

"So do I," says Luke under his breath. "So do I."

"But what happened to the gun?" asks Uncle Paulie.

"I threw it away, as you can see on the tape."

"Yeah, we saw that but we couldn't find it," says Detective Heman leveling a skeptical stare at Luke.

Laura is at her desk, listening to every word, but she has been aloof to him all morning and she is clearly not thrilled with the conversation, especially when it turns convivial. She does not laugh when the others laugh.

"Okay," says Uncle Paulie, "I've got to take care of some business with these gentleman. We'll be done in a minute."

This is Luke's cue to leave them in private and return to his station in the front of the store. In his peripheral vision he sees reflected in the glass partition Uncle Paulie handing each detective an envelope, which they slide into the breast pocket of their jackets. Then they exit with a friendly wave.

"Next time shoot him in the balls," says Fallon. "Teach those Ruskies a lesson."

Billy Dee also exits, but his departure is more discreet. No jokes, no chatter, just a nod and he's out the door. Luke walks to the window and glimpses his black Lincoln Town Car and most of its license plate number.

"Luke," calls Uncle Paulie from the back room, "come here for a second."

"Sorry to cause you trouble," says Luke offering a disingenuous apology.

"You can obviously still handle yourself," says Uncle Paulie. "I've got some other work for you if you're interested."

Luke knows exactly what he means and it's got nothing to do with being a locksmith. "I'm all ears," says Luke.

CHAPTER THIRTEEN

They sit in a booth in the back of a Brooklyn bar called The Saint's Lounge, no doubt an ironic name because there are no saints here, only sinners. Uncle Paulie slouches at an angle, half his body leaning against the wall, the other half against the booth cushion, an awkward position to ease the pain of his sciatica. One hand rests on the top of the seatback, the other holds a rocks glass. He squirms, tosses two Tylenol tablets in his mouth, like a kid eating Skittles, then washes them down with a gulp of scotch.

"Damn sciatica. That's what happens when you get old."

He exudes a curious mixture of malted barley and cologne. He is, as always, neatly dressed, his hair recently trimmed and combed back, revealing the full features of his ruddy face.

The room is empty, quiet, still. It is late afternoon, and the light outside is hazy. Uncle Paulie sits in shadow, deepening shadows that make him recede, almost disappear. The outline of his person is merely adumbrated, incorporeal, yet the force of his presence is still strong, maintained by the sharp glint in his eyes. His gaze seldom wavers. His two bodyguards are stationed nearby. Billy Dee is at the door, and Christian, a swarthy bulldog of a man with thick dark hair and a snarled lip, is at a table by the window.

Luke has taken off his suit jacket. It hangs on a hook at the end of the booth. It is like an ally, a presence watching over them.

Luke already knows what Uncle Paulie wants him to do. It is a hit, a kill, or as Uncle Paulie likes to call it, an assignment.

"The thing is that he doesn't scare. My guys have tried. Make it look like an accident. Or just kill the fucker," says Uncle Paulie, "I really don't care. He's jeopardized my whole operation. And more."

Luke is curious. *Which operation?* Uncle Paulie has so many, but he doesn't inquire. He just listens. He wants to appear disinterested. Uncle Paulie continues.

"The thing is the fucker's impossible to get to. That's something you're good at."

"Not interested," says Luke. "You know I'm through with all that."

"Yeah, yeah, we've all said that at one point. Name your price?"

"Not interested in money."

"Everybody's interested in money."

"The only thing I'm interested in is finding Crissy's killer and reuniting with my son."

Uncle Paulie rolls his eyes. "Kid, put it behind you." His tone is more like a threat than avuncular advice. Again Luke takes note of his uneasiness when he mentions Crissy's death. He finds it reassuring.

"We've been over this," says Uncle Paulie. "Revenge won't bring her back."

"But it'll bring me back."

"You do this assignment for me, and I'll do all I can to help."

"Not interested, but I'll hear you out."

"Mark Fister," says Uncle Paulie. "He's a chemist."

"You want me to off a chemist?"

"Do not underestimate him."

"Sounds like you want him out of the picture real bad. What about those detectives, Fallon and Heman? I want to see the files on Crissy. The police report, evidence, notes on the investigation. Can you set it up? They're on your payroll, right?"

"We've been over this. It was a robbery gone bad. They were a bunch of punks. Probably dead or in jail by now anyway. I'm sorry for your loss. I know what it did to you, but this is worth big money to me. And to you too. It'll give you a chance to start over anywhere you like, and you'll be helping family."

Helping family? The irony grates on Luke. He musters enough self-control to hide his pique and smile agreeably. Now's the time, thinks Luke, to try a gambit. "If you won't help me," says Luke, "I'll just have to find them myself."

Suddenly, Uncle Paulie's expression changes. There's a slight tension around his mouth, a nervous, twitching eye. His gaze narrows and he shifts uneasily in his seat. He knocks back the rest of his scotch, says, "That's a mistake."

CHAPTER FOURTEEN

Luke watches Laura take aim and fire. They've tried a variety of firearms at the range today—a Smith & Wesson .38 Special, a Taurus 605 .357 Magnum, a Ruger P512MKIII, and his personal favorite, the one he used when he was a Navy SEAL, a Sig Sauer P228 9mm.

Her stance is firm, her technique curiously competent for someone who claims she's never fired a handgun or any weapon for that matter, but when he hits the switch and a pulley brings her target to him, he thinks a blind person could've performed better.

"Not bad, not bad at all. Some shots actually hit the target," he says teasingly. There is something suspicious about her manner as if she's faking her ineptitude. "Are you sure you've never shot a handgun before?" he asks.

She shakes her head and says, "First time. Just look at the results."

He has a feeling that she could have been more accurate if she'd wanted to, but he keeps it to himself. They go to the Kings Plaza Diner for an early dinner. Then they linger over coffee.

"What can you tell me about Billy Dee?" he asks.

"I just go to work and mind my own business."

"What have you heard about Crissy? You think it's what they say?"

"That was before my time."

"Aren't you worried about suffering the same fate?"

"I'm a single mother. Divorced. I share custody with Jonathan's father. It's amicable; he pays child support, but I still need to work. Paulie gives me a flexible schedule so I can pick up Jonathan, my son, from school, spend time with him. The store is close to my apartment so I no longer commute into Manhattan. It works for me. I'm getting by and that's more than I could've said a year ago. Had to depend on my parents, live with their remarks about my bad choices, particularly marrying my ex."

"And your boyfriend?"

"He's just a friend. Nothing serious."

"So this is our first date then?"

"You take a girl to a shooting range on a first date?"

"Dinner and movie. How cliché," says Luke.

"You're such a romantic."

"You know Paulie's into all kinds of other stuff, don't you?"

"What's with all the questions? I think we better go."

"As you like."

Driving to her apartment, he notices they're being followed.

"You can just drop me off," she says.

"Look. I'm sorry about all the questions. It's just that—"

"I know. It's Crissy. You're still grieving. Just drop me off."

"That wouldn't be gentlemanly and this neighborhood doesn't look all that safe anymore. I grew up around here. Back then it was safe, but now—well, you've seen it as much as I have. It's changed for the worse."

Luke walks her to the door and apologizes again, though he really doesn't mean it. He merely wants to maintain cordial relations with her so that he can pump her for information.

"I think we got off on the wrong foot," he says.

"You're on the wrong foot. I think you need . . . time. Good night. I can see myself in, thank you."

Despite her protest, he walks her to the front door. She pauses and sternly looks at him, a mixture of pique and dimly concealed attraction. He's tempted to embrace her, but thinks better of it. She seems slightly disappointed. Her mixed signals intrigue and puzzle him.

"Can I see you again?" he asks.

"I don't think so. Let's just be friends. We work together."

"Not for long."

"Not for long?"

"Gotta keep moving."

She enters her apartment, shuts the door behind her, and he hears the metal clicks of multiple locks.

Then he walks back to his car and drives down Flatbush Avenue when he notices again that he's being followed. This could be fun, he thinks, and feathers the brakes, causing the tailgating car behind him to jolt and swerve.

They play this little game for a while until he decides to up the stakes. He jams on the brakes and comes to a screeching, sudden stop, causing the car behind him to crash into the rear of the Mustang.

He gets out and inspects the damage.

"Now, now, look what you've done," he says, wagging a finger.

The driver is dazed but not hurt, save for a bloody lip and a gash on his Neanderthal forehead. Three more cars pull over to the curb and suddenly five guys surround him. One limps forward and says, "Remember me?"

Indeed he does. It's Alexei, the one he shot in the leg. But this time he's brought his Russian pals with him.

"The Smirnoff Gang. What took you so long?"

"We've been busy."

"How's your leg? Hope you have good medical coverage?"

"You are the one who's going to need good medical coverage."

Luke sizes up the five Russians, their positions, their body language that tells him who will be aggressive, fainthearted, and the most skilled. Alexei no doubt will strike first, emboldened by the support of his little ensemble.

And he's right.

Alexei throws the first punch, and Luke makes no effort to avoid it because he knows that it'll draw the others in who are ready to pounce. It's a pretty good punch and stings a little, but the pain only heightens his senses. It makes him feel stronger, not weaker, and he responds with two swipes of his MetroCard, slicing a tiny X into Alexei's throat, a kind of warning, but he keeps on swinging.

Luke then hits him with a dropkick to his chest that sends him reeling. He follows with a sidekick that knocks him out of the circle and into a lamppost. The others rush him, but they are tentative. They clearly have no training as group fighters. And not much guts.

He sidesteps the first one, holding out a straight arm that hits him in the throat. Momentum sends this stout Russian up into the air and flips him over backward. The third one is stopped by a snap kick to the solar plexus, an upper cut, two jabs, and a savage right hook.

The fourth one wields a lead pipe, swings it in an arc, but Luke blocks it, and then wraps him up in an arm hold. A slight movement snaps his elbow, causing him to yelp like a kicked dog. Luke rips the pipe from his grasp and uses it to crack his skull and sweep the feet out from underneath the third. It all happens very fast, and Luke is pleased with his efficiency, but disappointed in their lack of skill.

"Now," says Luke, "if you don't want your heads bashed in, open up the trunks to all of your cars."

They are as obedient as children. Luke inspects each car until he finds what he suspects is there—a cache of weapons. In the trunk of the third car, he hits the jackpot. There's a duffel bag that contains a .40-caliber Glock, eleven .40-caliber magazines, silencers, six high-capacity rifle magazines, plastic explosives, two machetes, eight knives in various sizes, five tasers, six sets of brass knuckles, two expandable batons, a dozen handcuffs, and one Uzi.

"Were you fellahs planning on invading a country?"

He sees one of the Russians reach into his belt. Luke says, "Go ahead. Make your move and see how far you get." The Russian removes his hand, returns his arms to his side. Luke strikes his kneecap with the lead pipe.

"You've got all this stuff and you come after me with a lead pipe? That's insulting," says Luke. "I don't suppose you have a license for any of this, so I'll just have to take it off your hands."

Luke puts the duffel bag in the backseat of the Mustang.

Police sirens wail, but before they arrive Luke is gone. Dragging a rear bumper that sends sparks into the darkness, lighting up the night like a fireworks display. He watches it in the rearview mirror and is amused, but gets off at Bay Parkway and kicks the bumper until it falls off. No need to attract unnecessary attention, especially from the police.

The Mustang limps back to Staten Island. As the Mustang noisily pulls into the driveway, he sees Uncle Paulie standing in the doorway shaking his head.

"I'll be needing another car," says Luke, purposely testing Uncle Paulie's patience. There's really no reason for Uncle Paulie to tolerate him unless he has an ulterior motive. Could just be Mark Fister. Could be something more. Could be something less, but he doubts it.

CHAPTER FIFTEEN

The next morning Uncle Paulie, his face colored with a ruddy hypertensive glow, hands him a set of car keys and Luke drives to the Saint's Lounge in Paulie's son's old Porsche, hoping to find Billy Dee, but Billy Dee is not there and nobody knows when he'll be back, so Luke nurses an Italian beer, a cold bottle of Peroni, no glass.

Luke hears the jingle of car keys. Then the door opens and in walks Billy Dee. Billy Dee is not surprised to see him. Luke asks, "Can we talk?"

"Sure."

Billy Dee, unlike Uncle Paulie's other flunkies, is black and has an air of independence. He also has intelligent eyes. A natty dresser too, he's wearing a leather jacket, a maroon Italian knit shirt, pleated trousers, white-and-butterscotch two-toned shoes, and a snap brim hat. His brown skin has a healthy sheen, a re vealing quality, Luke thinks, for it is the product of self-discipline, of a man in control of himself, a man who is not ruled by his vices, if he has any. But what the fuck is a man like this doing working for Uncle Paulie? Something isn't right with this guy.

Luke does not expect to get any useful information from Billy Dee. After all, he's Paulie's employee, but Luke knows that the way he refuses to cooperate will say a lot about him.

"Did you know Crissy?"

"Are you taking a survey?"

"Who killed her?"

"Dunno."

"I'm gonna find them."

"Good luck."

"Luck's got nothing to do with it."

"And guess what?"

"What?"

"If I find out you're holding out on me I'm gonna come back here and kill you."

Billy Dee doesn't react; he remains expressionless, betraying no emotion. Clearly, he knows more than he lets on.

"Would you like a drink, an espresso, some advice?" he asks.

"I should be going." Luke moves to the door, but Billy Dee partially blocks the entrance. It's a sort of stand off. Luke must go around him. Instead, he walks forward, veers slightly, but they still brush shoulders.

"Stop by anytime. Sorry your visit was in vain."

"Me too."

But this is not true. It has been a fruitful visit. He has seen something in Billy Dee's manner that has told him a lot. Like Laura, he suspects that Billy Dee is more than he seems.

CHAPTER SIXTEEN

Sipping a coffee, Luke walks the aisles of the deli across the street from the locksmith shop. He comes here often and chats with Abdal, the Arab owner, and his sons. They are hard working and friendly. And, of course, they share a common tragedy, the one Uncle Paulie told him about. Abdal's brother, Fikri, was shot dead in a robbery.

The far aisle of the store is lined with windows that offer an unobstructed view of the locksmith shop. Luke stares at the shop and imagines what happened on that November night at dusk when Crissy was behind the counter and two men in long coats that concealed pump-action shotguns entered, asked for cash, and then shot her in the face.

At least that's the way he imagines it from the bits and pieces he's gleaned, a common robbery, except for the fact that they shot her. Why? Makes no sense. She would not have resisted. He doesn't even know if they got any cash. And they were certainly wearing masks and hoods so there was no way she could positively identify them, just offer a description of their general shape and build, which would be fairly useless.

Particularly suspicious is Paulie's lack of success in finding them. A mobster of his rank could have easily put the word out on the street and some snitch would've dropped a dime on the killers within an hour. Also suspicious: the CCTV tape was removed and never found.

"You look sad today, my friend," says Abdal, standing behind the counter packing groceries into a brown bag, the very counter where his brother was shot and killed. "Sadder than usual."

"It's the coffee. I know you make it fresh every day, but this stuff could burn a hole in a skillet."

"You certainly drink enough of it. You are thinking about Crissy again. Always Crissy. And you stare out the window at the shop as if you hope to see her, something you have done dozens of times. You are a strange man, Mr. Luke, a strange man, but I understand. She was a very lovely woman. We liked her a lot. She made us laugh. And we miss her too."

"Was there anything else different about that night?"

"As I have told you many times, she seemed nervous. Didn't stay to chat, which was unusual. Perhaps she was worried about you, my friend. You were in the gravest danger, and she told us that, but as it turned out, she was the one in danger."

"Why?"

"I do not know."

Abdal's son, Basir, is restocking the shelves in the middle aisle. He is sixteen years old, alert, mischievous, and defiant. He has cut his hair into a spiky asymmetrical shape, as is the fashion with kids his age. This enraged his traditionalist father, who beat him.

The next day Basir came to work after school slightly bruised but with his hair unchanged. His father threatened to beat him again, but Basir refused to change his hairstyle to conform to his father's wishes. His father, however, was pleased and proud. "That boy has spirit and nothing can break it. He will do well in the world."

Basir is fascinated by Luke's suit. He asks him questions about it, many questions, intelligent questions. He wants one just like it. He thinks it will make him stand out. He thinks it will make him glamorous. "I get it. It is like Superman's cape. It has magical powers. It brings you luck. And it brings you girls!"

Luke squats down beside him, absently picks up a can of beets, reads the label. "And how are you today, Basir?"

"The old woman upstairs?" says Basir, "Have you found her?"

"The apartment is empty."

"She used to sit by the window, watching. She saw everything. She got me in trouble many times. If you could only find her."

"I have tried, Basir," says Luke. "I have tried. But it's as if she's disappeared."

And even if Luke could find her, what more could she tell him? It is an event, a rather common event in this borough that has receded into the past, a part of the past nobody really cares about, not even the police. Everybody, it seems, has moved on except him. He is in a perpetual state of retrograde, seeking portals to a barred past.

He walks around the store again, pensively looking out the window. He finishes his coffee and asks Abdal for a refill. Abdal says, "Why do you like the things you do not like?"

Luke cannot answer that, but he wonders about the old lady, her sudden disappearance after Crissy's murder, and decides to look at her apartment again. He climbs a set of creaky, wooden stairs to the top floor and stands in front of apartment 6A. Making sure that he is alone, he picks the locks on the door and enters the empty, dark interior.

It is musty with a lingering smell of cooking odors, stale air, cat litter, and perhaps the old woman herself. The linoleum on the floor is peeling. Dust motes fall in the fragments of remaining light. He walks to the spot that was her small world from which she viewed the larger world and sees what she would see if she was here now. There is a plain view of Uncle Paulie's store, but only the exterior, nothing else. She could not have seen much even if she was watching the store the night Crissy was killed.

Or maybe not.

This is, after all, a different angle, and he believes in the law of angles even if it yields vacant spaces and no clues, for he has not come here for clues, at least not expressly. He did not visit the deli and ask the same questions and look out the same windows expecting a revelation or some new knowledge that would help him in his quest.

He came out of a compulsion, an inner need, an instinct that the vacant spaces are like spokes on a wheel, that all action revolves around them, and by placing himself in its center he will no longer be an outsider, the lost stranger, the damaged interloper arrived from a foreign landscape. He will be one of them, whether they like it or not, a part of their world, and by extension, a greater part of Crissy's world, the fatal world he never knew.

In the emptiness of the apartment, a small piece of paper catches the fading light. It is like a message sent from above. He picks it up. It is a receipt for Downtown Storage. He puts it in his pocket not because it means something to him, but because it means nothing to him and he finds that stirring. The clueless clue. Those are the best kind.

He looks out the window again. Traffic is heavy now, rush-hour traffic. Cars and cabs clog Nostrand Avenue, belching fumes, exhaust, grease. Horns honk. Buses rumble, and there seems no end to the hurrying pedestrians who emerge from the subway, all of whom are safe at this very minute, removed yet so close to the mortal dangers of this world.

CHAPTER SEVENTEEN

At the bottom of the landing Luke is accosted by Santiago, the owner of the building, who brandishes a baseball bat. Santiago is not pleased and makes the mistake of putting his hand on Luke.

"Please remove your hand," asks Luke. "I don't like to be touched by strangers."

"What the fuck were you doing up there?" says Santiago, pushing Luke, another mistake. "Did you break in? Who the fuck are you?"

Luke twists his hand one way, then the other, while simultaneously kicking his feet out from under him. Santiago, suddenly looking up at the ceiling, is more confused than hurt, the change in perspective unexpected and perplexing.

Luke puts his knee in his chest, grabs the baseball bat out of his hands, and presses it against Santiago's throat with just enough pressure to cause him moderate but not severe breathing difficulties.

"Okay," says Luke, "I'll give you one more chance to ask me politely."

Santiago does not capitulate. He is not afraid. He flails, knees Luke in the back, and swings at him, landing a solid punch to his head—more precisely to his ear, which rings. Luke falters and Santiago bucks him into the wall. Luke drops the bat. Santiago picks it up and lands a series of well-placed blows. Luke smiles. Finally, a gutsy man who knows how to fight.

Luke jabs, ducks, bobs, and weaves, and is amused at Santiago's spunk. But Santiago is no major league hitter. Luke moves into Santiago's range of motion, disarms him, and strikes a blow to the back of Santiago's knee with the bat. Santiago sinks a little and growls in pain, but stubbornly remains on his feet.

Santiago, though hobbled, is still in a fighting mood. He spits at Luke.

"Do you want me to crack your skull open?"

"This is my property," says Santiago. "I will kill you."

"I doubt you'll even be killing time."

"What do you want?"

"I was just looking for an apartment to rent and I heard that one was vacant."

"So you break in?"

"Tell me about the old lady who lived there. Where is she?"

"She's on a cruise in the Mediterranean. How the fuck would I know where she is? She still owes me one month's back rent. Moved out in the middle of the night. Are you with them?"

"With whom?" asks Luke.

"Never mind. I ain't talking."

"You just did."

"Get the fuck out of here."

"Such bad manners." Luke whacks him with the baseball bat. "Baseball's not my sport, but I do believe I hit that one out of the park."

"I know you. You work at the locksmith shop across the street owned by that Guinea bastard. You just walked into more trouble than you think. Ever since that robbery, the greaseballs are telling me to keep my mouth shut. As if I care what happens to them. Why are all of you so interested in that apartment?"

"Listen, scumbag, what happened over there concerns *me*. They killed my wife in that holdup, and if you know anything about it, you better tell me because I will beat you to death with your own Louisville Slugger."

"Fuck you and fuck your dead wife. I know shit."

Enraged, Luke lands a right cross that stuns Santiago, but he can take a punch. Luke admires that, makes note of it. He bounds down the stairs, about to hit him again, but he relents, backs off, thinks for a moment, and the thoughts that enter his mind are like blows themselves. What if they are all telling him the truth, that the robbery was nothing more than two punks high on crack, amateurs who were busted on some other crime, and are now doing jail time or maybe got their tickets punched, killed in gangland violence. What if the opportunity for cathartic revenge doesn't exist? He looks down at his hands and they are trembling.

But he cannot accept this. He needs them alive so that *he* can live with purpose. He mentally struggles to keep this notion real, fights harder than he's ever fought. Somebody must pay.

Luke staggers to the door, his head pounding with a savage migraine. He throws the baseball bat at Santiago's feet. Stars dance before his eyes. He is dizzy, nauseated, and his heart races.

"If you decide to rent it," says Luke, "you know where to find me."

"Yeah. I know where to find you. And I will find you."

"Try a golf club next time. I think you're strictly bush league."

"We'll see about that."

CHAPTER EIGHTEEN

It is dark now and Luke walks across the street to check on Laura. She smiles when she sees him. She notices his broad shoulders, his athletic physique, and the confident way he moves in his body-tracing suit that looks none the worse for wear. It is as durable as he is, though she does not fully comprehend that he is a wounded warrior who is marred on the inside, not on the outside.

Although his attire is formal in a world of flip-flops and cargo pants, he does not look out of place. It gives him an authority, a compelling mystique, and she must stop herself from staring.

"Oh, here he comes," she says sarcastically. "The Suited Hero."

"At your service."

I'm getting ready to close," she says.

"I've got some work to do. I'll close. Why don't you go?"

"I've got to wait for Christopher."

"Mr. Punctuality?"

"That's him. So what has The Suited Hero been up to lately?" she asks again. She still hasn't fully forgiven him for shooting the Russian.

Luke takes a vial out of his pocket and tips two 100-mg tablets of Imitrex into his hand. Then he tosses them into his mouth, jerks his head backward, and swallows them without water.

Laura watches and flinches. "You okay?"

"Just a migraine."

"So what have you been up to?" she asks again.

It's a seemingly casual question, but Luke is suspicious and this bothers him because he fears the return of the paranoia that preceded his mental breakdown. He tries to align his thoughts, clear his head, and think clearly. Lately Laura's been taking an interest in his activities. He is too much of a realist to think that her interest is completely romantic, though he does have feelings for her, which he pushes away, suppresses. Yet again he regards her as if she might be something more than what she seems. And there's only one way to find out. Get closer to her.

"I really think that you should let me give you some basic self-defense lessons. You can't rely on that boyfriend of yours."

"He's not my boyfriend."

"Come to think of it, you can't rely on anybody in this world except yourself."

"Is that what you really believe?"

"Pretty much."

"Sounds cynical."

"We all have our truth."

"Here's my ride."

"There's a dinner and a movie in our future," he says.

"That's so cliché."

He watches her exit, admiring her lithesome stride. He likes the way she walks, a mixture of enticing wiggle and purpose. He particularly likes the way she swings her handbag over her shoulder. There is a touch of dash about it, almost an athletic skill, even a vague sense of a wielded weapon. It fascinates him, and he watches her until she disappears into the crowds and darkness outside.

Then he sits alone in another vacant space, the space that Crissy once occupied, and feels a further connection to her chain of being. He waits for the silence to become articulate, but there is no voice, just a cold, empty silence; he patiently listens, and for the first time in a very long time feels an overwhelming depression, the kind of paralyzing, suffocating, lethal depression that broke him. He weeps.

CHAPTER NINETEEN

Luke climbs the gate of the Downtown Storage facility and enters a maze of singular storage units with corrugated aluminum doors. He looks at the receipt he found on the floor of the old lady's apartment on which is written "Unit F8–102."

The place is deserted and he walks the warren of dark alleys and corridors with a flashlight until he finds it. He smashes the lock with the heel of his boot and rolls up the gate. Inside there are tight stacks of furniture, quilts, carpeting, lamps, a sofa, photo albums, old paperback books, magazine racks, and other junk.

A sickening odor causes him to gag, step back outside into the fresh, evening air. It is a smell he has smelled before. And he knows its cause before he finds its source. He pulls out chairs, lamps, and the sofa, causing the mountain of stacked furniture to collapse at his feet. He digs deeper, covering his mouth with the front of his shirt.

First he sees a wiry gray mass, then as he peels away the layers of quilts and comforters it is clear that it is hair, human hair, the hair of a corpse, a putrefying corpse, half flesh, half skeleton, and he knows it is the remains of the old lady who lived in Santiago's apartment.

The wheels inside of his head spin. This will lead somewhere. He knows it will. Death always does. He smiles. He is elated, no longer aware of the stench of decayed flesh.

•   •   •

The next day he returns to Downtown Storage. He is there early, before the office is open. He waits but no one appears until fifteen minutes later. A short, fat man in cargo shorts, a greasy t-shirt, and a baseball cap worn ass backward drives up in an old pickup truck. He breathes heavily as he walks to the front door of the office. He does not acknowledge the man in the fine suit.

The fat man weighs at least 250 pounds, a lot of weight for his heart to cart around. He does not hold the door for Luke. Luke follows him inside. The fat man glances at the stack of papers on his desk and turns on his computer.

"Can I help you?" he asks, dialing the phone.

"Yeah. I'd like to know who is paying the bill for storage unit F8–102."

"We don't give out that information," says the fat man curtly.

"Don't make this difficult."

"Difficult?" scoffs the fat man, holding the phone to his ear. His stained t-shirt rises above his waist, revealing a pink patch of porcine flesh. "Yeah, I'd like to order scrambled eggs on a toasted English muffin with bacon and pepper jack cheese. I'd also like—" Luke abruptly grabs the phone out of his hand and wraps the cord tightly around his neck. He leaps over the desk and pins the fat man against the wall. The fat man struggles, and Luke hits him with the blunt edge of the telephone receiver until he is bloody and nearly unconscious.

"Cancel that order," says Luke into the phone. "He's decided to go on a diet."

The fat man plows into his waist, revealing impressive upper-body strength, but it is the wrong move. Luke knees him in the face more than once before he releases his grip.

Although clearly out of shape and gasping for breath, he still has enough feistiness to throw a few punches, but they are off the mark, and Luke cuts him with his MetroCard as a kind of warning before holding it up against his nose, giving him time to think what it would be like to go through the rest of his life with a maimed face, not that he seems to give a damn about his personal appearance.

Now," says Luke, "I want the name, address, and phone number of the person who is paying for storage unit F8–102. Don't make me ask again."

The fat man finally complies, tapping the computer keyboard. The printer engages and spits out a piece of paper that neatly lists all the requested information.

Luke says, "Thank you. Now that wasn't so hard, was it?"

CHAPTER TWENTY

A Crown Victoria makes a sharp turn grazing Luke as he crosses the street holding a brown paper bag that contains coffee and sandwiches for him and Laura. He hears laughter emanating from the car.

Pissed off, he stops and turns in the middle of the crosswalk to watch the car pull into a parking space on the corner. "Asshole!" He is prepared to rip the driver's head off, but then recognizes the two passengers, Detectives Heman and Fallon. They emerge in rumpled suits, giggling like schoolgirls, and walk toward him, hands on their guns. They seem tweaked, stoned, altered by some substance they filched from a drug dealer they busted.

"We've got to arrest you," says Fallon with a playful grin, almost as if this is some kind of game.

"On what charge?"

"Lots. We've got you on breaking and entering—twice: once at Downtown Storage and once at Santiago's apartment building. Nice guy, that Santiago. He's quite a baseball fan."

Heman adds, "And don't forget the assault charges."

"Oh, yeah, and we've also got you on assaulting a fat man at Downtown Storage and Santiago took quite a beating too. Ring any bells?"

"That's all you got? Any parking tickets? Those are bullshit charges and you know it."

"No, not really. What's in the bag? We just searched it and

found two rocks of heroin. And there's the matter of the corpse in the storage unit. Let's talk this over in the car, shall we? Get in. And don't try any of that Kung Fu crap or we'll add resisting arrest. Or a bullet. Don't matter to us."

"Okay," says Luke. "I'm a cooperative kind of guy."

"We're taking you to the station. Unless of course you pay up," says Fallon, his grin widening. "Paulie tells us you're doing high-level assignments for him now and you're making big money. We'd like a chunk of it. To make all of this go away, of course. Paperwork is a bitch, you know. We're doing it as a favor to your uncle."

"A favor to my uncle? He's paying you off. Isn't that enough?"

"Yeah, but we're close to retirement and every penny counts. These are inflationary times."

"I'm not doing any high-level work for him. And I'm not making any money except what he's paying me at the locksmith shop, which isn't much. He's rich but a cheap bastard, you know that. In fact, I can give you a cut of my first paycheck. My uncle pays me in cash. How's twelve bucks?" Luke facetiously fumbles for some crumpled bills in his pocket.

"Listen, Luke. We're not fucking around."

"Neither am I." Luke's glare makes them uneasy, forces them to take an added precaution. After all, Luke is a former Special Forces soldier, a trained covert killer with skills that are quick and deadly. He's also a loose cannon.

"So, tough guy, you gonna behave?" asks Fallon.

But before Luke can hear the last part of the sentence, he is knocked unconscious by a blow struck by Heman with the butt of a Smith & Wesson .38 Special. A few hours later, Luke wakes up in a jail cell at the Sixty-third Precinct with a throbbing headache.

The next day Laura bails him out and Luke is surprised to see her. It's another muggy morning and she's wearing a spaghetti-strap turquoise blouse, a short white skirt, and strappy sandals. He hugs her, filling his nostrils with the scent of her newly washed hair, the lotions on her skin, her perfume, and does not want to let go, for it is an antidote to the smell of the piss-stained rat cage he has just left.

He is surprised by the sudden depth of feeling he has for her. He is also unnerved and confused by it because it seems to expose a weakness, a vulnerability that he thinks he has avoided.

He wants to push her away, but instead he takes her hand and squeezes it as they walk to her car.

"You're not looking so good," she says with maternal concern. "Why don't you see a doctor, start cancer treatment? It's not too late. Why kill yourself?"

"How'd you know about the cancer?"

"Paulie. Everybody knows. They just don't understand why you're not getting treatment."

"I just don't care, that's why," he says crossly.

"I know, but I just can't stand by and watch you die. Please, get treatment."

"Maybe when this is all over. Maybe. If I can find a reason," he says, looking into her eyes for the depth of feeling that would lend meaning to his life and he finds it. The feelings that well inside him almost make him want to live. Yes, maybe treatment.

This is the first time he has even considered treatment. It is a kind of turning point, a shift toward the light, but he has spent so much time in the dark place of his past that this new landscape is disorienting. Laura's influence is forceful, and he resents as well as craves it.

"Paulie wants to see you. He's at the Saint's Lounge. He told me to get you," she says. Luke is disappointed; he thought she came to get him at her own behest.

"Uncle Paulie? Oh," says Luke disappointedly but tries not to show it. "I thought it was your idea to come and get me."

"Paulie posted bail."

"Fuck him."

"Luke, you really better see him."

Laura's words are tender yet tough, and they have a peculiar resonance, as if she is talking not just as a minor employee, but also authoritatively. Something in her tone convinces him to do what she says. This too rattles him. He is losing his grip. He is getting soft. He is falling in love.

"What a mess," he says, getting into her old Honda. "Don't you ever clean it?" His tone is much harsher and more critical than it needs to be. He notices a slight hurt in her eyes that is quickly retracted and he immediately regrets the comment, yet at the same time it puts a comfortable distance between them. Although he rebukes his own caddishness, it fosters a measure of safety that allows him to feel at ease.

She drops him off, and Uncle Paulie is waiting for him.

"Not exactly the Ritz, was it?" says Uncle Paulie, puffing smugly on a fat Cuban cigar, acting every inch The Big Man, and gloating as if he now has the upper hand. And perhaps he does.

"I've been in worse places."

They sit in the same booth in the back room where they engage in another chat. A busty woman in a glittery low-cut blouse who looks more like a stripper than a waitress brings Uncle Paulie his scotch and Luke a pint of Guinness. Almost on cue, Uncle Paulie's bodyguards take their same positions: some new guy by the door, Billy Dee at a table by the window.

"You've racked up some serious charges," says Uncle Paulie. "You're in deep shit."

"My suit is soiled. Know a good dry cleaner? Someone who doesn't use that Perk crap but can sponge clean and press it?"

"You got bigger problems than finding a good dry cleaner. I posted bail for you. And Detectives Heman and Fallon will make the charges go away. For a price. Which I've already taken care of."

Luke fusses with his suit, realigns his pocket handkerchief, ignores his uncle, infuriating him.

"Didn't you hear me? Aren't you grateful?"

Luke smiles, nods his head. But it is not enough to satisfy Uncle Paulie.

"You know, kid, you're aggravating me. You're aggravating my sciatica. You fuck with the wrong people in this city and you'll end up a corpse floating in the Gowanus Canal. There's a line, you know, and I won't always be able to save your ass. I know you can handle yourself, but you need friends here. You can't go it alone. You won't survive. Now I called in a lot of favors to save your ass and I want something in return."

"Mark Fister, the chemist," says Luke, "right?"

"Glad you pay attention."

"Why me?"

"Not to swell your head, but you're the best man for the job. He's outsmarted, killed, or maimed my best guys. They just don't have the training."

"I'm flattered," says Luke, his remark laced with sarcasm. "But you're afraid he'll come after you. That's it, isn't it?"

"I'll keep you out of jail, and after you take care of Fister, I promise you we'll get you answers to Crissy's death. Personally, I don't think there's anything there, or whatever there is won't mean much, but if it satisfies your bloodlust, well, I'll do it. Do we have a deal?"

Luke thinks for a second, sips his beer, gazes absently out the window. Uncle Paulie will tell him what he thinks he wants to hear just to convince him to do this one assignment.

"How much?"

"One hundred and fifty grand."

"That's on the cheap side and I don't work cheap. I can work for the CIA and make more than that. Plus, benefits of course—health, dental, and a pension plan. Tickets to the opera too."

"Three hundred grand and another hundred when the job is finished."

An amount this large would allow him to do exactly what Uncle Paulie does not want him to do—intensify his search for Crissy's killers, get his son back, and then disappear, maybe to Borrego Springs with his spook friends, and make a fresh start.

"Okay, Uncle Paulie. I'll do it. You win." Luke, unable to resist, quotes back Uncle Paulie's line, savoring the layered irony: "For family, of course, like you said."

"And the cash."

"And the cash. Again, like you said, everybody likes money."

Uncle Paulie slides a folder across the table. Luke picks it up, but Uncle Paulie stops him from opening it. "Not here," he says. "Burn it when you're done. Then we'll talk."

Luke gets up to leave.

"Oh, one more thing," says Uncle Paulie. "No more trouble, no more breaking down doors and kicking ass trying to find Crissy's killer until this assignment is done. I don't need the heat. Deal?"

Luke drains the last of his Guinness, wipes his mouth, and walks out the door. He hasn't lost one iota of his swagger, and Paulie takes note of it, extinguishing his cigar in an ashtray. "Punk," he says under his breath. "A soon-to-be-dead punk."

CHAPTER TWENTY-ONE

Luke walks two miles to where his car is parked, gets in, and drives straight to the address he extorted from the fat man at Downtown Storage.

But the address is fictitious, not a residence at all, but a Roll-N-Roaster, a chain restaurant, on Emmons Avenue in Sheepshead Bay, a hangout in his teenager years after a night of barhopping. The phone number is also useless, disconnected, and the name on the receipt is probably a fake too. He's hit another dead end. Looks like he has no choice but to take the assignment Uncle Paulie has offered him.

Hello, Mark Fister. Here I come. Wherever you are.

CHAPTER TWENTY-TWO

He revisits the Canarsie Diner, another hangout from his youth, where he orders coffee and scrambled eggs, light fare because he doesn't have much of an appetite, and reads the Mark Fister file. Fister has quite a résumé. A graduate degree from the California Institute of Technology, a four-year-stint at Mylan Pharmaceuticals, another four years at Procter & Gamble, and then ten years at Pfizer where he was laid off.

He then landed a much lower-level job as a pharmacist, but only for a little more than a year. Then he fell out of the job market. And for good reason. Arrested twice for trafficking in illegal prescription drugs, he managed to get both cases thrown out on procedural technicalities. Must have had a good lawyer.

Then he disappeared, learned to fly under the radar, quietly building an illegal international prescription drug business on-line that allowed him to amass enormous wealth.

Not hard to read between the lines. That's the kind of thing that would make Uncle Paulie salivate and want to muscle in on. Paulie's got his own lucrative illegal online prescription drug business and must want the competition eliminated. Unbridled greed. Some things never change.

Personal information about Fister includes a divorce, three children, a stint in rehab, and restraining orders from two girl-friends. Fister likes to bounce around: sixteen addresses in almost as many states and countries, five pages of phone numbers—he must change cell phones every other day, not wanting to be tracked by GPS—but there's nothing recent, a long lapse of five, six years.

There are a few handwritten marginal notes, but nothing that stands out except that he spends a lot of time in private jets and has a passion for rare books.

Rare books. You've got to be kidding.

Not much to go on, but it'll do. He closes the folder.

CHAPTER TWENTY-THREE

Luke sips his coffee, looks around the diner, which has been re-modeled. The red booths are gone. So is the shiny interior. It's more subdued now. Gone are the mirrors and chrome. The booths are mocha colored and the interior is sectional: some walls are white and cream, others polished wood paneling. Spacious, low-key, middle-class comfort. Big portions, bad food. Just the way they like it.

Still, it is like walking into the past, when he was a youth, a street kid, hanging out with Tony and Sal, the sons of small-time mobsters. Tony and Sal wore wifebeater t-shirts, tanned themselves to a rotisserie brown, and spent their time either in the gym building muscle—a kind of armature to compensate for a lack of physical courage—or committing petty crimes, like ditching cars in the Paerdegat Basin for fifty bucks so that the owners could collect the insurance money.

That was when they were seventeen. A short time later they graduated to more lucrative jobs. Local loan sharks hired them to beat up broken-down gamblers behind on their payments. His other friends all had nicknames like Four Fingers Frank who earned the moniker by losing his index finger for mouthing off to a psycho wiseguy who had no sense of humor.

And there was Football Head whose real name was Jack DelGado. At least his nickname made sense; Jack had a weirdly shaped skull, the result of a doctor's botched delivery and clumsy use of forceps.

Luke idly wonders where they are now but doesn't really care. Probably city councilmen, drug dealers, Mafia bosses, dead, in jail, or running a chain of fitness clubs.

After barhopping in Bay Ridge, they spent many nights here eating enormous plates of just about everything on the menu from macaroni and cheese to meatloaf to pastrami sandwiches and giant hamburgers washed down with Coca-Cola or coffee or both, and they never gained a pound.

They were regulars; even had their own table, the very table at which he is seated now. They liked it because it had a view of the parking lot, of the coming and goings of friends and females.

But Luke never really fit in. Never much liked them. They were a blustery bunch, braggarts, bullies, flexing their muscles, always on the prowl for some new piece of easy pussy, and there was a lot of easy pussy in those days. Big fish in a small pond.

Luke never had much to say, for he was thinking about the next step, entertaining bigger ambitions, yearning to move on, things that never occurred to them, so he was quiet, a loner, thoughtful, and for that they never trusted him.

But it was Luke who was the first of the group to whack a guy. Ten thousand dollars was a lot of money to a teenager, but he didn't do it just for the cash. He did it to test himself. After his mother died of an overdose of pain meds and vodka and his abusive father started using him as a punching bag, he spent most of his time at The Santoro Social Club, which was owned by the father of a girl his friend was dating. He worked as a factotum, running numbers, getting rid of bloodstained clothes, following cheating girlfriends or wives, fetching Italian pastries from Aliotta, the best bakery back then.

Mr. Santoro and his cohorts were racketeers and inveterate baseball fans. Bookies too. Luke enjoyed the adult view of sports; they talked more about the money the players made than their athletic skill. The arguments were heated, passionate, often leading to fisticuffs but in a sort of halfhearted, playful way. Luke liked the atmosphere, the adult jokes, the pretty women that came and went, the free blow jobs. Sometimes he even slept there. He felt safer with gangsters than he did at home with his own crazy father.

But he was also bored with Brooklyn. Boredom always got him into trouble. A good kind of trouble, as it later turned out. At least he thought so. The night Joe Santoro's oldest daughter was nearly raped by Jimmy Wilson, a postal worker, who must've been the dumbest jerk on the planet not to know that Santoro was mobbed up, Luke said he'd do the hit for half the going rate even though he didn't even know the going rate.

"This ain't Crazy Eddie," he remembers Santoro saying, referring to a retail store known for its deep discounts. Santoro told him to "get lost, you're still a kid, and you don't know what you're doing." That was true, except that he wasn't a kid. He was eighteen. He didn't know the ropes, but that never stopped him. He'd figure it out.

It was the challenge, the gamble, the risk, the curiosity, and the itchy desire to learn if he had the balls as well as the smarts to do a hit and get away with it—the same feelings that motivated him to join the Navy SEALs not much later. It was also the perfect antidote to his ennui.

He didn't know why, but Santoro eventually gave him the okay. "Just don't get caught, but if you do, don't talk or else *you'll* be the dead man. Got it?"

Luke got it.

"And one more thing. Make him suffer. Bring me back a trophy, too, an ear or something."

Luke could not tell if he was joking.

He researched and planned the hit carefully. The postal worker, Jimmy Wilson, was a failed football player, a star, a big deal in the neighborhood, well liked and popular. Played for

Rutgers as a wide receiver and would have been an NFL draft pick had an injury not brought his career to a premature end. How this transformed him into a rapist, Luke did not know. What he knew was that he lived in one of the small clapboard houses in Gerritsen Beach that was more like a cottage than the usual two-family sturdy brick houses in the Flatbush section of Brooklyn, the kind that he'd grown up in, and that Wilson left his house at precisely 7:30 a.m. every morning and returned at 5 p.m. unless it was Friday when he would stop at Pat's Bar and drink with his friends until he was walleyed blotto.

On the weekends he took great delight in home repairs, so one night Luke climbed up to the roof and loosened a few shingles above the sturdy white picket fence.

Then he sharpened the points on the pickets and painted them over to conceal the adjustment. One balmy Friday evening, he waited on the roof for Wilson to come home drunk. He arrived on cue. Wilson staggered, fumbled for his keys, and that's when Luke dropped a shingle on his head. Wilson looked up, and though intoxicated, was clearly miffed that the house seemed to be falling apart, so he fetched a ladder from the garage and climbed up to the roof to investigate.

Wilson comically struggled with the ladder as if there was a gale-force wind at his back, but he finally got it in place, clambered up the steps, and reached the roof. A bright moon made it easy for him to spot the vacant holes where the shingles had been loosened.

Luke, lying in wait, had removed his boot so as not to leave any marks on Wilson's back when he kicked him. All it took was a little shove with his shoeless foot and Wilson plunged forward, vainly grasping for support, and plummeted through the darkness, landing on the sharpened pickets below, impaled like a kabob.

One picket went straight through his heart, killing him almost instantly. He might not have suffered as much as Mr. Santoro wished, but at least he was dead.

The police ruled it a drunken accident, and Luke was in the clear, except for one thing. He forgot to bring Mr. Santoro a trophy. "You did good, kid," said Santoro. "That was clean, but I still want my trophy. No one messes with my family."

Guess he wasn't kidding about the trophy after all.

What was Luke supposed to do? Go to the morgue and cut off an ear? He thought about it, but no way that would happen, so he went to a sporting goods store, bought a real trophy, and had it inscribed: "Joe Santoro. The World's Greatest Yankees Fan."

Fortunately, Mr. Santoro had a sense of humor. He laughed and said, "You're all right. I might have some more work for you."

But then he met Crissy and all that changed. She never knew about the hit, but she encouraged him toward a different life, away from the tribal pettiness and dead-end violence of Brooklyn. She confirmed his belief that he was better than his peers, that he could do more, be more, accomplish more, that he needed to get out of Brooklyn, as far away as possible. He agreed. They got engaged and planned to start a new life together. With ten grand in cash they could go anywhere they liked, start new, so they packed up the car and hit the road with no destination in mind. They only had one criterion: it must be sunny most of the year. He'd never felt a greater sense of freedom and happiness. For the first time, he was in love.

The obvious first choice was Florida, but that was quickly nixed. They both agreed that it was full of the New Yorkers, the very people they wanted to escape, a kind of distant suburb of the city, only with more bugs. They planned to tour the East Coast, finding a quaint town maybe in Maryland or Pennsylvania, raise a family, but a snowstorm hit and they decided to drive cross-country to Southern California, to endless sunshine, palm trees, and sandy beaches. It sounded like a good idea and more of an adventure.

The charm of Coronado, a sun-splashed peninsula off the coast of San Diego and home to the Pacific Fleet, captivated them. There was something about the quality of light there—serene, magical, a kind of ablution—and they both felt it. They were happy, unable to believe their good fortune, and even more amazed when things got even better. Soon Crissy was pregnant with Jack.

Luke watched the Navy SEALs running on the beach and became fascinated with their grueling training, discipline, and, after a little research, the kind of work they did. They were, in essence, hit men sanctioned by the government. He could not ask for a more suitable line of employment. After talking it over with Crissy, he joined the Navy and completed the SEAL initiation program, BUD/S—Basic Underwater Demolition/SEAL—with flying colors.

The only sourness in this blissful time in his life was when he'd told his father about his plans to leave Brooklyn, probably for good, and make something of himself. Instead of being pleased or proud or encouraging, his father backhanded him and drunkenly said, "You're leaving me? Just like your mother?"

His father swung at him, but Luke caught his fist in mid-air like a line drive and bent his arm back until his father dropped to his knees. Humiliated, his father looked up at him with tears in his eyes. Tears for what Luke did not know and did not care. Something changed in Luke at that moment. It was almost like a biochemical restructuring. Right then and there he vowed never to take shit from anybody, not even his old man.

CHAPTER TWENTY-FOUR

Joining the Navy SEALS was the best decision he'd ever made. He was a natural. Mentally tough and athletic, he excelled at survival training and his violent urges found an ideal outlet.

He traveled the world, mostly on covert missions. He was an adrenaline junkie before he'd even heard the term. He was the first to volunteer for even the most suicidal missions. Parachuting into jungles wearing nothing more than a pair of shorts and gripping a knife between his teeth was his idea of recreation. The enveloping darkness, the unknown, never frightened him; it was more like a solitary refuge, a world within a world but one in which he could always find his bearings. The sounds, the smells, brought him in touch with something primordial, something more essential that he could not explain. All he knew was that he found himself in his element. How he adapted to an environment so antithetical to the streets of Brooklyn he did not know, but he liked the mystery of it and the fact that he could not explain himself to himself added something to the existential thrill of it all.

Capturing or killing high-value enemy personnel or terrorists around the world was his specialty. There was no one better. "The Only Easy Day was Yesterday," is a SEAL motto, but he never felt that way. In fact, he felt the opposite. As his skills improved, the work got easier, and he rose through the ranks quickly, often to his own surprise, looking forward to the next challenge, the next day. So what if he was considered something of an oddball? The only approval he sought was his own; the contest was with himself. "Loner Luke," they used to call him. Fuck 'em. And fuck all that camaraderie bullshit too. And the Medal of Honor.

Still, there was a drawback. He missed Crissy and Jack, but he was mature enough to realize that you couldn't have everything.

And now, sitting in the Canarsie Diner, he thought how ironic it was that he'd ended up in the very same place he tried to escape—and it was Crissy's doing, the very person who gave him the courage to change his ways, to leave the ties of the old neighborhood to pursue a better life. And it was Crissy's doing that forced his return.

As a SEAL he was deployed for long stretches, for six months at a time, often longer, and they were required to relocate to different bases around the world. She got tired of moving, setting up house in strange cities in foreign countries, enrolling Jack in new schools where he'd make new friends only to leave them a short time later. Even when they returned to Coronado, it was not the same; the sunshine that once seemed so glorious now seemed relentless. She missed the seasons, the autumn leaves, the eastern thunderstorms and snowfalls. She was homesick, depressed. He couldn't blame her. She'd make friends in some new outpost, usually moms with kids Jack's age, but it just wasn't the same. She'd commiserate with other military wives, but they were new friends, nice people, but different. They weren't the close friends she'd had back east, friends who shared an irreplaceable bond.

She particularly missed her mother and father and she wanted them to see Jack grow up. She was lonely, especially when he was gone for long deployments, so they moved back to Brooklyn where she could be close to her family while Luke traveled. She was happier and so was Jack. He loved his grand-parents and they adored him.

But, ultimately, it was a big mistake. Sometimes the best decisions are undermined by fate. The nice middle-class neighborhood Crissy and Jack lived in had gone downhill and the crime rate had gone up. But Crissy didn't scare easily; this is where she felt she belonged. This was her turf. She still thought like a Brooklyn girl. A short time later, her parents had moved out of the city, to a pastoral suburb and they wanted her to follow, but she had had enough of quaint suburbs and stayed put.

He rarely worried about her. Friends and family looked after her, and she was street-smart, wise, careful, tough. So her murder was unexpected and it unhinged him, for what good is it if you can defend your country with honor but can't protect your own wife?

"More coffee?" asks the waitress, but her voice registers dimly as Luke broods. "More coffee?" she asks again and he nods. "Didn't you like your eggs?"

"Those were eggs?"

The darkness outside seems like a projection of his inner state. Anger, simmering rage wells up inside of him like a chemical poison, and he realizes that, yes, he is filled with a murderous fury, but he also realizes that he is mad at Crissy too. How could she leave him? Now he knows how his father felt, and a strange sadness for all the things in this world overtakes him.

He is able to suppress these festering feelings, but he believes they manifest themselves as a literal cancer, Hodgkin's lymphoma, and it seems somehow fitting in his mind, a punishment he deserves for not taking care of her, for not being there when she needed him most.

Luke returns to the Mark Fister file to distract himself from these masochistic reminiscences and it seems like a giant puzzle.

He is certain about only one piece of this puzzle. He can't do it alone. He needs assistance. Or maybe he's just tired of going it alone. And there's only one person on this planet he trusts: Suggs.

Suggs will know how to proceed—if he can find him, and find him sober, find him alive.

But first he must make a slight detour.

CHAPTER TWENTY-FIVE

Luke drives the Porsche at full tilt to Downtown Storage and squeals into the parking lot. The noise alerts the fat man in the office who can see his arrival from the window. Chomping on a pastrami sandwich with great delight, he sees Luke emerge from the car and his face drains of color.

Before he is able to pick up the phone, Luke storms in and kicks over the flimsy aluminum desk, knocking him off his chair and the pastrami sandwich out of his puffy hands. Luke picks him up by the shirt collar and shoves him against the filing cabinets.

"Okay," Luke says, "let's go over this again. I need a name. You got a name for me? F8–102? Remember?"

"They'll kill me."

"What's your name?"

"Jerry."

"Jerry, what do you think I'm going to do? I want a name. Who pays the fucking bill?"

Jerry hesitates until Luke squeezes his neck and lifts him off his feet. He sputters, chokes. Luke loosens his grip. "Talk!"

"Okay, okay. Bobby Guerro. He's mobbed up. He paid me in cash for an entire year."

"Got an address, a phone number?"

"Nothing. That's all I know. Saw him once and then recognized him on the news when they hauled in a bunch of mob guys on a drug bust. Prescription drugs, not the usual stuff. That's why I remembered it. I guess that's the new thing."

"Thanks for the friendly chat. It was a friendly chat, wasn't it?"

"Yeah, yeah. I won't report it."

Yeah, right.

Luke slides into the Porsche and revs up the engine. In the rearview mirror he sees what he expects to see: Jerry on the phone. Calling the cops? No. Calling Guerro most likely. Big surprise. Luke peels out.

Next stop is Santiago's office.

Santiago is about as glad to see him as fat Jerry was, but Santiago is far less intimidated. In fact, he's not intimidated at all.

"What are you here for? More trouble?"

"Business."

"Business?"

"I want to rent that apartment."

"It's a dump. Hasn't been fixed up yet. In fact, I've got contractors scheduled to come in next week."

"I'll take it as is and pay you six months' rent in advance."

Santiago twitches his mustache. He likes the idea. He likes the idea a lot, but he says no.

"No?" says Luke. "Why the fuck not?"

"You Wops. Nothing but trouble."

"I ain't no Wop, not all of me at least, not the good part. What's the grudge?"

"Where do I begin?"

"Well, we're on the same side."

"Oh, yeah?" Santiago looks at him suspiciously. "Nice suit. You certainly don't dress like those greaseballs."

"I'd consider it a favor, a favor I'd gladly repay."

"How?"

"Need anybody killed?"

"My mother-in-law to start with, don't much care for my mechanic either or my dry cleaner, and then there's—well, it's a long list."

"You're a genuinely ballsy guy, Santiago. I like you for some reason."

"I can't honestly say the feeling's mutual."

"I grow on people. Is there somewhere we can talk?"

"As you know, there's an empty apartment upstairs. Follow me."

They walk the creaky flight of stairs, and Santiago fumbles with an enormous key chain.

"I can just break in again if that's easier."

Santiago smiles, opens the door.

"Okay, what's on your mind?"

"First, I want to rent this apartment. And—"

"Look, your uncle's been trying to steal this building out from under me for years, among other things. I don't need your kind under my roof."

"It's not like that. You got no worries as far as that goes. I'll pay you double, six months' rent in advance too. Cash."

"Still no deal. I've got it rented."

"Unrent it."

"You fucking Wops. You think you can walk in anywhere and bully your way into what you want. Ain't happening here."

"That's big money." Luke looks at him condescendingly. "I'm sure you can use it. Doesn't look like you're setting the world on fire."

"Everybody needs money," says Santiago with a smirk. It's as if he's been spending time with Uncle Paulie. Has he, Luke wonders?

"Seems I hear that a lot."

"Truer words. I'm listening."

"I want your help. I know you know something about the holdup. The guys who shot my wife. I want them. Information, a rumor, anything."

Santiago scratches his beard, hesitates. "I don't know. Don't see what's in it for me."

"Your life. And you won't be bothered by those greaseballs. Ever. And a chunk of cash."

"That'd be nice. But what's kept me alive is a simple thing called keeping my mouth shut. Unlike the old lady. She saw everything. And look what happened to her."

"What did she see?"

"Enough to get her killed. Two druggies from the Sheepshead Bay projects walked in, shot your wife, and then more or less as an afterthought, grabbed some cash and split. Didn't know it was owned by a mobster, of course. Dumb fucks. I doubt if you'll find them, though."

"Why?"

"Day after the holdup they were found floating under the Marine Parkway Bridge; two bullets in the back of their heads. Dead as Jimmy Hoffa."

"Sounds like a hit. Not a robbery."

"You think? Somebody wanted your wife dead. The holdup was just a cover. But listen, that's just the word on the street. All rumor. That's what you wanted, right? Hand over some cash."

"Some cover. Anybody with a brain can see that. Somebody hires two punks from the projects, drug dealers with a record, to off my wife and make it look like a robbery gone bad? Then they insure silence by offing the dumb fucks and dumping their bodies. Nobody cares about two dead drug dealers."

"Happens all the time."

"Who was behind it?"

"Beats me. Paulie's got a lot of enemies. Crissy got caught in the middle. Pretty simple. I don't see the point of looking at this like it's some big conspiracy. I'd leave it alone if I were you, pal. These fuckers stop at nothing."

"And neither do I."

Luke moves toward the door, stops, asks, "One more thing. Name Robert Guerro mean anything to you?"

"Bobby Guerro? Yeah. Rings a bell," says Santiago, scratching his face, feigning a ruminative expression as if he can't remember details. "Might be one of your uncle's lackeys. A punk with a mean temper. I'll look into it."

Luke pulls out a wad of hundred dollar bills and hands them to Santiago.

"Could you get this place furnished? Nothing fancy. A bed, a table, lighting, pots and pans, the basics? Internet, of course."

Santiago counts the cash, smiles widely. "Royal family coming to town for a visit? I think I can manage it. When are you moving in?"

"Soon."

Soon as I can find him.

"And the, ahem, extra fee?"

"We'll negotiate that."

Luke walks out, stops, and listens by the door. He can hear Santiago on the phone. "Paulie, he bought it," says Santiago. "Hook, line, and sinker. But he's trouble. You've got to get rid of this guy."

CHAPTER TWENTY-SIX

Luke leaves the apartment and when he gets into the Porsche he sees Billy Dee leaving the locksmith shop. He decides to look for Suggs later and follow Billy Dee.

Billy Dee drives to Sheepshead Bay. Luke parks nearby and watches unnoticed. Billy Dee walks into a restaurant and sits at a shadowy rear table. He orders a drink. Luke can see him through the restaurant window, but just barely.

A short time later, Laura arrives and removes a sheaf of documents from a briefcase and hands them to him. Billy Dee studies them carefully, nods, and makes a few notes. They talk. Then they order a light supper. Laura leaves first, gets in her car, and drives away. Billy Dee delays his departure, clearly wanting to minimize the chances of them being seen together.

Time to take Laura to dinner and a movie. Clearly, she and Billy Dee are closer than she's let on. Clearly, there's something going on between them and it's not romance.

CHAPTER TWENTY-SEVEN

Luke, walking down the aisle of the locksmith store, seductively brushes by Laura. He wants to gauge her reaction. She glances at him, but when she meets his lusty look, she quickly averts her gaze, lest she reveal the emotion she does not want to show.

The look in her eyes is familiar, tender, a reminder of the feminine force he has missed, lost; it both pleases and pains him. He removes a box from the shelf, walks back up the aisle, but this time stops behind her and kisses the nape of her neck.

"Dinner and a movie?" he asks, softly touching her bare shoulder.

"I don't know."

"You can even bring Christopher if you like. Just make sure he shows up on time."

She laughs.

He puts his arms around her, looks into her eyes, his gaze unwavering. She seems suddenly shy, even awkward. He takes her hand and holds it, saying nothing, allowing the silence to resonate.

"Okay," she says, "dinner and a movie. Against my better judgment."

Luke, ever cautious, thinks this was a little too easy.

CHAPTER TWENTY-EIGHT

Luke enters the shelter and finds Suggs, but he's in pretty bad shape. He's bruised and battered and suffering from one hell of a hangover.

"Who did this to you?"

"Who do you think?" says Suggs, his words slurred because of a fat lower lip.

"Get your stuff. We're getting you out of here. I'm parked out back."

Suggs sluggishly obeys, limping, clearly in pain. They head for the rear exit off the kitchen but are stopped by Hitler, Stalin, and Lenin, the unholy triumvirate of lowlifes.

"Move aside and let me go my way," says Luke. "One warning is all you get."

They cackle and pull out knives—big knives, serrated and curved knives, stilettos.

"Okay," says Luke, "you've got knives and we've got pots and pans. Seems like a fair fight to me."

"Hey, amigo, you left without saying good-bye," says Hitler, the biggest one in the gang, a thug with tattoos covering most of his blubbery body and a face as rough as a russet potato. He touches the scar on his neck, the one made by Luke's Metro-Card, and snarls, "Time to get even."

"This won't take long," says Luke, taking off his suit jacket and hanging it on a hook. He tells Suggs to wait outside, but

Suggs, despite being hobbled and in pain, remains by his side.

Luke decides that talking to these parasites would be a waste of time and strikes first. He kicks Hitler in the groin, grabs him by the hair, and slams his face into the stove. Dazed, Hitler struggles to his feet, but Suggs grabs a metal skillet and wallops him on the head, very nearly rendering him unconscious.

Lenin hesitantly attacks, thrusting a carving knife at Luke, but it is halfhearted, and Luke easily parries it. Suggs swings wildly with the metal skillet, making contact with an All-Clad stainless steel covered soup pot from the upper ledge of a crowded utility shelf.

"Careful with that thing," says Luke. "You're not licensed."

Lenin makes a grazing swipe at Luke, nicking his arm but nothing serious; it hardly draws any blood. Luke grabs a meat thermometer and aims for his heart but jams it into his shoulder, causing him to drop his knife. A rather graceful arc of blood spews from the wound. Luke hits him with his elbow, then the back of his wrist before smashing his head into a pot on the stove that shatters his teeth like a porcelain tile.

Stalin brings up the rear, nearly slashing Luke's bicep before Suggs can whack him with the skillet.

Still they keep on coming. Knives flash. Luke grabs a colander and uses it as an effective shield, fending off knife thrusts. Sparks fly as if an electrical current has been exposed.

Hitler rallies and Luke finishes him off with a series of jabs and a right cross that knocks him into the metal shelves that are filled with dishes, platters, and other culinary paraphernalia.

There's more fight in Stalin too, but a sidekick and a well-placed roundhouse slam him hard into the meat locker. Suggs swings and connects with the skillet, but it's a glancing blow. Stalin rips down the shelves on top of Suggs. Luke wields a roundhouse kick that sends Stalin into an open storage cabinet.

Assorted sundries spill in all directions, including a ten-pound bag of baking flour that covers the swarthy Latino, transforming him into the Pillsbury Dough Boy.

Luke helps Suggs to his feet. They leave the fallen foes whimpering in various places in the kitchen. Luke slips on his suit jacket and he and Suggs head for the exit, but Hitler attempts one last attack that Luke sees coming in his peripheral vision—a Bowie knife raised high with the intent to split him in half. Luke turns just in time, blocks the blow by making a *V* with his forearms, and hits Hitler in the throat with the knuckles of his right hand, cracking his windpipe.

"Adios, amigos," says Luke, and now he and Suggs freely exit through the open kitchen door. Suggs is still carrying the metal skillet.

"You're pretty good with that thing, but I don't think you'll be needing it anymore," says Luke.

"Really?" says Suggs smiling. "I thought I'd make us some breakfast."

Luke opens the door to the Porsche and says, "Let's ride. This baby can *move*."

"My, my," says Suggs, admiring the leather interior and the cockpitlike console. "You've really come up in the world. Where to? A doctor to see to that cut?"

"Hell, no. I can patch it up myself."

"So, then, to a drugstore?"

"Yeah. And then my tailor. Bastards ruined a custom-made shirt."

CHAPTER TWENTY-NINE

Luke drives with no regard for the speed limit to Santiago's apartment, which is now fully furnished.

"It's all ours, pal," says Luke, opening the door. "Clean sheets and everything. A bunk for you, a bunk for me. Just like in the Navy. Snoring and all. Rest up. We've got work to do."

"No espresso machine?"

Luke collapses on the sofa, catches his breath, looks over the place. "Not bad," he says.

"Hey," says Suggs in jest, "you're bleeding all over our nice new sofa."

Luke gets up to leave. "And I said 'rest up,' not 'drink up.' I'll be back."

"I couldn't afford a bottle of Ripple."

"The fridge is fully stocked—with food and nonalcoholic beverages. Get your strength back. The medicine cabinet is stocked too. And knock yourself out with a Valium if you feel an uncontrollable urge to get plastered. You've got to clean up."

"I have a feeling this payback is going to be a bitch," says Suggs.

"You've no idea."

The next day Luke returns with three computers and two boxes full of equipment that include a Brocade BR-MLXE-32-MR-X-DC router, link and local balancers, unmanaged and managed switches, and everything else Suggs needs to create a nifty network, a kind of hacker's heaven.

"You got stock in Brocade?" asks Suggs, his eyes lighting up like a kid looking at gifts under a Christmas tree.

"Get busy, pal. I got a feeling time isn't on my side."

"Just tell me what to do," says Suggs, rubbing his hands in delight, eager to get started.

"Okay. First off, I need you to find an elusive fellow named Mark Fister. Here's his file. I can't find an address, a phone number, anything about him in the last five years. Next, I'd like you to find a scumbag by the name of Robert Guerro. Guerro was arrested for illegal prescription drug trafficking a few years ago. And Fister had two brushes with the law. Just get me something to go on, anything, starting, as I said, with Fister. Got it?"

"Got it."

CHAPTER THIRTY

Luke picks up Laura at her apartment. She invites him in.

"My Suited Hero has arrived," she says, but the moniker she has given him is no longer barbed with sarcasm. "Welcome."

It's a clean, well-lit but small one bedroom that has a fake hominess and lacks personal touches. No photos of her family, just some magazines fanned out on the coffee table, a standard painting of a seaside over the sofa, sparsely filled bookcases, a flat screen, and a DVD player, both new, and a table and chairs made of maple, very plain. The window treatments and table-cloth lack the feminine frills and patterns he'd expect.

No plants, no clutter in the kitchen. It almost has the feel of a model home, the kind they stage for empty condos and houses for sale so that potential buyers aren't looking at a sterile shell but an actual home they can imagine living in.

And there's only one picture of Jonathan. He looks to be the same age as Jack. But the frame standing upright on the end table is portable, like the ones you take on long business trips to prop up by your hotel bed to ward off loneliness. Crissy had photos of Jack everywhere. And his toys were scattered in the living room, though they tried to confine them to his bedroom, but there is a noticeable absence of kid clutter here, which makes Luke suspicious. The whole thing smacks of a temporary lodging. Or maybe Jonathan spends most of his time at his father's house.

"I'll be right out," says Laura from the small bedroom off the living room.

Luke sees a briefcase tucked between a magazine rack and the sofa, the one she carried with her when she met Billy Dee in the Sheepshead Bay restaurant, and he wonders why a woman working in a locksmith shop for little more than minimum wage would need such an official-looking briefcase.

"Hey, Laura," he calls to her, "you taking night classes or something?"

"Been thinking about it. Why do you ask?"

"No particular reason. You just seem like a smart girl."

Luke also notices documents next to a coffee cup on a stand in the kitchen. Curious, he walks toward them and reads atop the page, "FS–2501." It's a government affiliation, perhaps the State Department, but he's not sure. He'll have to research it. Before he can read anymore Laura appears and says, "Okay. I'm ready."

They leave for Il Fornetto, a restaurant in Sheepshead Bay, and sit at a table outside with a view of the water. A skiff, a ketch, a few deep-sea fishing boats cruise by. It's a warm night with cool breezes and an orangey sunset. The breeze tussles Laura's long, blond hair. She wears a blouse that bares her shoulders and Luke again thinks that she has lovely shoulders. There are always unexpected parts of a woman that touch him deeply and he does not know why. With Crissy it was her hands—the long elegant fingers, the soft smooth skin, and the unadorned nails that were never colored, always natural.

After dinner they stroll along the quay, holding hands. Luke keeps the conversation light to create a mood that is relaxed, the sense of being together easy, natural. They fall into an embrace with their arms wrapped around each other's waist. He kisses her and she responds ardently. She's gentle and warm and seems almost somnolent. This is the moment he's orchestrated.

"I saw you and Billy Dee together."

Laura, as expected, is surprised and stiffens as if jolted by static electricity.

She pushes him away.

"So?"

"I thought you keep your work life separate, that's all."

"If I kept my work life separate, I wouldn't be out with you. Which seems to have been a mistake."

"You're very defensive."

"No, I think you're using me. Why bring him up at a moment like this?" Laura is annoyed, hurt. "Take me home."

"I'm sorry."

They ride to Laura's house in silence. But when Luke walks her to the door, she does not protest when he follows her inside.

"Coffee?" she asks with an edge still in her voice.

"Thank you."

"I want to know. Have you been following me?"

"I've been following Billy Dee."

"Why?"

"You know why. Crissy."

"You think he's involved? You think he knows something?"

"Dunno. That's what I've been trying to find out."

"I met with him because Paulie told me to."

"Really?"

"Really."

"What's with the exchange of documents?"

"You really were spying on us. The documents were just rental applications. I'm trying to find a bigger apartment and Billy Dee said he'd take care of it."

"How nice of him."

Luke takes one last sip of his coffee and heads for the door. Laura protests, says, "Don't leave. I— " She seems about to confess something, but then thinks better of it.

CHAPTER THIRTY-ONE

When Luke returns to the apartment, he finds Suggs asleep in bed with his arm wrapped around a pretty black girl, her purple lipstick smeared across his unshaven cheek. An empty bottle of tequila lies tipped over on the nightstand. The place reeks of flowery perfume and sweat. Luke shakes Suggs awake and tells the girl to get lost. Defiant, she slowly rises naked from the bed and gives him the middle finger. He slaps her on the butt and repeats, "I said, 'get lost.'"

Unchastened, she slips into her clothes, a tight pair of jeans, an even tighter tube top, and glittery high heels, very high heels. She does this with impressive alacrity, as if she's practiced it a hundred times. Then she counts a wad of bills she's pulled from her rear pocket as if making sure what was there before is still there. Satisfied, she stuffs them back into her pocket and swings her purse over her shoulder, nearly hitting Luke with it, but Luke doesn't flinch.

Suggs sleepily opens his bloodshot eyes, rubs his hairy belly, and looks at Luke, but Suggs is so hungover he squints as if having trouble recognizing him. Then he regards the girl and evinces the same puzzled look.

"Out," says Luke to the girl and swats her shapely butt again. She makes an abrupt stop, turns, and smacks Luke across the face, hard. The blow stings, and Luke rubs his cheek stamped with a red mark.

"You didn't pay for it," she says. "So keep your dirty hands off me."

"She's got game," says Luke admiringly. "Maybe we can use her."

"Oh, I plan to," says Suggs.

She slams the door on her way out.

"Spunky little thing," says Suggs.

"I thought you didn't have money for a bottle of Ripple?" asks Luke.

"I still retain the skills learned as an Intelligence Officer in the Special Forces. They come in handy just when you need them."

"I told you to stay off the booze. I need you, pal."

Luke sits at the desk behind a computer and types FS-2501, the letters and numbers he saw on Laura's papers, in the Google search bar. The results on Wikipedia confirm his suspicions that she might not be all she pretends to be.

He reads:

Within the U.S. government, the title of Special Agent is used to specifically describe any federal criminal investigator in the GS-1811 or Diplomatic Security Service FS-2501 job series as so titled according to the Office of Personnel Management (OPM) handbook . . . Special Agents are typically armed and have the power to arrest and conduct investigations into the violation of federal laws.

"She's a damn Fed!" yells Luke, and immediately realizes he's just jumped to a possibly spurious conclusion. He thinks it over, changes his mind. "Or she might be," he says. "Maybe she's studying for a law-enforcement job. Or maybe it was her ex-husband's paperwork. He's ex-military. That's a logical career path for a guy like that."

He needs further confirmation, but where can he get it?

"Who's a Fed?" asks Suggs, padding across the floor in his bare feet to make coffee.

"Laura. Not sure, though," says Luke, "the meek blond who took Crissy's place at the locksmith shop. But maybe she's not so meek."

"What are you going to do about it? Confront her?"

"Nope. I'm not going to do anything yet. We've got bigger fish to fry right now. Did you get anywhere with my requests?"

"Not to worry. Mission accomplished, sir!" says Suggs with an exaggerated salute.

"Okay, then, let's see what you got."

Suggs pulls on his pants and excitedly hurries to the computer, eager to show Luke what he's unearthed.

"Actually, it was pretty simple. I found Fister's court case. Court cases, rather. He's got a hotshot attorney named Barry Goldberg. Lives in a brownstone in Cobble Hill, Brooklyn. Which he owns. In fact, he owns quite a few and—"

"Suggs, skip the financials. Get to the point."

"I am, I am. If anybody knows where Fister is, it should be him, right?"

Luke smiles. "Nice work. Be ready at ten tonight. We're going to pay him a visit."

"Great. I could use a little fresh air."

"What about Guerro?"

"I'm still working on him."

"See you later."

But when Luke returns, he finds Suggs asleep on the coach, another empty tequila bottle on the nightstand and three empty bottles of Colt 45 malt liquor on the coffee table.

"Suggs!"

Startled, Suggs bolts upright. "Sir! Yes, sir! I'm not drunk, sir! No, sir! Just napping! Let the mission commence."

Luke regards him suspiciously and concludes that he's sober enough. The man can hold his liquor. Even drunk, he'd rather have Suggs riding shotgun than just about any other man. He fills him in on what they jokingly call the "scare the shit out of Goldberg" mission. Luke slips on a military jumpsuit over his formal suit, a protective measure, but he'll toss it in the car after the task is completed.

"You're always on my case about my drinking," says Suggs. "But what about you?"

"What about me?"

"Your cancer. Hodgkin's. You going for treatment?"

"How'd you know I had Hodgkin's?"

"I'm not as dumb as I look. And it's not exactly a secret."

"I'm going for treatment."

"Liar."

"This is not the time to argue, Suggs."

"Just tell me."

"I told you."

"I know you're lying. I just want to be sure you're up to this."

"You got no worries."

"I'm killing myself with booze and you're killing yourself with a curable cancer you refuse to cure. We're a perfect pair."

Cobble Hill is a tree-lined neighborhood in the northwest part of the borough, near the East River. Brooklynites call it "quaint and charming." It used to be a working-class neighborhood, mostly Italian, but it now has all the hallmarks of gentrification—trendy restaurants and bars, specialty cheese shops, and upscale hair salons. Renovated brick-and-stone houses and Italianate brownstones line the main streets, Court and Clinton.

It's really more Manhattan than it is Brooklyn. Or rather it's as if a piece of Manhattan drifted across the East River and clung to its shores.

The residents are a diverse lot: doctors and attorneys, hedge fund managers and plenty of artsy types—editors, famous writers and actors, and even a pop singer or two.

Luke and Suggs park on leafy Sackett Street. There's a yellowish light on in the top floor of Goldberg's brownstone. Luke has already scoped out the place.

"He's in his study," says Luke, "no doubt still working on freeing some scumbag criminal. We're going in through the skylight. Follow me."

Luke removes a snub-nosed Smith & Wesson J-frame .22-caliber from the trunk of the Porsche and puts it in the waistband of his pants. Although it is capable of firing loads with more stopping power like the .22 Magnum, .38 Special, and the even more powerful .357 Magnum, he loads the gun with .22 LR, the perfect caliber for what he has in mind. He wants to wound, not kill. Unless it's absolutely necessary.

"What about me?" asks Suggs. "I'm unarmed. And why the peashooter?"

"Suggs, until you sober up, all you get to carry is a metal skillet. And even that makes me nervous."

They enter an alley lined with trash bins that leads to the back of the brownstone. Luke scampers up the fire escape, but Suggs, out of shape, lags behind, puffing, drawing breath, his heart racing. Luke expects this and patiently waits for him and extends a helping hand. Suggs declines.

"I can do it," he says. "I'm a drunk, you know, not a cripple."

They reach the roof. Luke has already removed the hardware from the skylight so it opens easily. Then he extracts rappeling equipment from a small satchel—carabiners and connectors, descenders and belay devices, two harnesses, and ropes and webbing. He suits up quickly, then assists Suggs.

"Okay," says Luke, "when we drop down, please don't land with a thud. I want to make this easy. Got it?"

"Got it."

But, of course, Suggs lands clumsily and with a thud. Luke lands smoothly, soundlessly, and helps him to his feet.

"Why didn't we just ring the bell and enter through the front door?" asks Suggs.

"We need the practice."

Luke hears footsteps. A stout, bespectacled man appears in the doorway. His girth strains his vest and causes one button to pop open. His wrinkled shirt sleeves are rolled up to the elbows, his wild Einstein-like hair is shot through with gray and so are the whiskers on his face. He looks like an overfed housecat.

Luke draws the Smith & Wesson, points it directly at him, says, "Get into the kitchen."

"I have no cash on the premises."

"Right. But we're not looking for cash. Suggs, bring him into the kitchen."

"Please don't hurt my family. I'll give you whatever you want. I've got a safe."

"Good for you. Now. To the kitchen."

Suggs's job is to rouse the rest of the family—Goldberg's wife and teenage daughter—and bring them into the kitchen.

When Luke and Goldberg reach the kitchen, he tells Goldberg to sit on the floor and be still. Goldberg is compliant. Luke turns on the electric stove, all four burners. Goldberg's eyes widen in fright.

"What are you going to do?"

A commotion is heard in the rear of the house. Suggs enters the kitchen with Goldberg's wife and their sweet-faced daughter. He has warned them not to scream. They, too, are scared, trembling, but obedient.

The wife suddenly becomes hysterical when she sees Luke near the stove, pointing the gun at her husband. Tears stream down her face, but the daughter is more defiant until he gives the gun to Suggs and grabs her by the arm. She resists, kicking and pulling, but Luke locks up her arms so that he can move her about at will. He positions her in front of the stove and forces her face down, just inches away from the glowing red burners.

"I want you to tell me where Mark Fister is," says Luke to Goldberg.

"I don't know," says Goldberg.

"I will not ask you again. If you don't tell me exactly where he is, your daughter will have burns all over her pretty face."

"Tell him, please. Tell him for Christ's sake!" bellows Mrs. Goldberg.

"That's privileged information. I could be disbarred or worse. Fister will kill me."

"What do you think I'm gonna do?" says Luke, firing one round into Mrs. Goldberg's arm. "That should shut her up."

Although it is only a small-caliber flesh wound, she howls in pain and Luke has made his point, but Goldberg still refuses to cooperate, so Luke pushes their daughter against the stove and stands behind her so that they are unable to see what is really going on. He spills water onto the stove so that it makes a sizzling sound—the same sound flesh would make on a hot burner.

"*Nooo!*" screams Mrs. Goldberg. "*Please!*"

"It's up to you," says Luke, "how far I'll go. I'll barbecue her like a steak—like a steak well done, charred."

"All right, all right," says Goldberg. "He's in Mexico, a small town south of the San Diego border. I can't remember the town."

"Remember," demands Luke, pushing Goldberg's daughter's face closer to the top of the hot stove. Strands of her hair fall onto the hot coils, singeing them. The acrid smell fills the room.

"Tell him, dammit," says Mrs. Goldberg, "*tell him!* Oh, my poor baby—"

"Heroica Matamoros!" blurts out Goldberg. "That's where he is. That's where he was last."

Luke turns their daughter around so that they can see that she is unharmed except for a few burnt strands of hair. They sigh in relief.

"If you're lying or call the police, we'll come back here and do the job good and proper. And then some."

They exit through the front door and reach the Porsche. Suggs says, "Can you believe that guy? He would have let you barbecue his own daughter just to save his own skin."

"He's a lawyer. What did you expect?"

"Mexico," says Luke. "I hate Mexico. But that's where I'm going."

CHAPTER THIRTY-TWO

"So you found him," says Uncle Paulie. "Knew you would. Where?" Uncle Paulie looks at Billy Dee who is sitting by the window. Billy Dee is, as usual, expressionless but attentive, all ears in this case.

"My business," says Luke. "Can we talk in private?"

"*Our* business," counters Uncle Paulie. "And anything you got to say, you can say in front of Billy Dee."

"Did you wire the money into my account?" asks Luke.

"I did."

"Must check on that."

"Don't trust me?"

"We're family, right?"

"So where is he? I'm not paying you all this money to play games."

Luke hesitates, decides to keep the information to himself for as long as he can. Maybe Uncle Paulie will get tired of asking.

"Why do you want to know?" asks Luke.

"Just in case."

"In case of what?"

"In case you need help."

Luke does not like the tone of the word "help." In fact, it is uttered ominously, subverting its true meaning.

This should not be important to Uncle Paulie, but it clearly is and Luke wants to know why, and the only way to find out is to take the risk and tell him.

"Mexico," he says.

Uncle Paulie nods. Doesn't seem too surprised. It's as if he already knows. "It's hot down there," he says. "Bring plenty of sunscreen."

"Oh, I won't be there long."

Uncle Paulie seems skeptical. "Hotshot. When do you leave?"

Luke takes the last sip of his drink and says, "Now."

CHAPTER THIRTY-THREE

The plane touches down smoothly at Lindbergh Field in coastal San Diego. He knows it well. Nothing but blue skies and sunshine. He retrieves his duffel bag from the luggage carousel and rents a Chevy Tahoe at Hertz and drives south and then west across the graceful blue span of the Coronado Bay Bridge that connects San Diego with Coronado, home to the Pacific Fleet.

Suddenly he is flooded with memories, overwhelmingly so. This is where it all began, where Crissy found their first apartment, a small one-bedroom on D Avenue with a creaky wooden gate and a cramped patio where they kept their bicycles and a second-hand Hibachi charcoal grill that was given to them by a Navy family that shipped out to Guam, and where he first saw Navy SEALs training on the beach and realized that he had found his calling. And, of course, the place of Jack's birth, the Naval Hospital on the mainland.

Palm trees, night-blooming jasmine, fragrant jacaranda, ocean breezes, stately homes, clean streets, peace and quiet, friendly neighbors—it was everything Brooklyn wasn't and they thrived. They took long walks on the beach, barbecued steaks in the early evenings under a cerulean sky that was bluer than any sky they'd ever seen, and made plans, lots of plans, the way that couples do when they are in love.

Coronado is one of the most expensive places to live in the country, a resort as well as a Navy town, most known for the sprawling old Victorian Hotel Del Coronado located on the seaside of the peninsula and North Island Naval Air Station to the north.

The residential community is small, but affluent, with a population of less than twenty-five thousand, so they were lucky to find an affordable garden apartment from a realtor who took a liking to Crissy. Everybody liked Crissy. She made friends easily.

He remembers how happy she was: her beaming smile, her hair flecked with sunlight, her face aglow after a swim in the ocean. She was tan and it made her look healthier and more vibrant, qualities that only added to her beauty. She was never more beautiful than when she was bathed in the sunlight peculiar to Coronado, except for maybe when she was pregnant with Jack.

Luke tries to dismiss these images, but they are fixed, forever imperishable in his mind.

As he passes through the tollbooth—the tollbooth he had passed through hundreds of times during the six years they were based in Coronado—and drives down Orange Avenue, he is tempted to pass their old apartment, but he knows he will be scalded by the emotions it will create. The memories will be bittersweet, more bitter than sweet, for they underscore an idyllic past that he cannot savor without the pain of loss, a past that is impossible to recapture.

They will remind him of how far he has come, only to lose everything he has ever cherished. He tries to stifle the upwelling of rage, his own inability to accept his fate, a particularly cruel fate that seems to mock him by circumstantially forcing his return.

But he tells himself he must not think about any of that now; it will weaken his resolve, break him. He must concentrate on the present, on the singular goal for which he is here, his reason for being, his purpose, an event in a series of events that will eventually lead to his salvation: killing Mark Fister.

The five-hour-plus flight has given him plenty of time to read about the illegal prescription drug market in everything from the Los Angeles Times to medical journals. And it surprised him. He knew that there was big money in the sale and distribution of crack, heroin, cocaine, and all the so-called recreational street drugs, but the global black market for illegal prescription drugs is booming and might easily surpass it in profitability.

In fact, prescription drugs are now the preferred "high" for many, especially teenagers. Drugs like OxyContin, Vicodin, Xanax, and Fentanyl are among the most commonly abused.

He should know. His mother overdosed on prescription drugs and cheap vodka when he was thirteen, but back then it wasn't common. Now, though, things have clearly changed.

One article claimed that more Americans die each year from prescription drug overdoses than from cocaine, heroin, and other illegal substances. These drugs do not come from the jungles of Columbia, from poppy fields in foreign countries. They are not typically bought from corner drug dealers in bad neighborhoods or in crack houses or sold under sickly elm trees in sketchy public parks.

Painkillers and antianxiety drugs are manufactured by Pfizer, Roche, Johnson & Johnson, Merck, and other publicly held firms, legitimate companies that pay dividends and whose shares are openly traded on the New York Stock Exchange. Their products are sold at the corner drugstore—CVS, Walgreens, DUANEreade, and Rite Aid, among others—with a doctor's prescription.

But prescriptions are becoming harder to come by. Doctors are scrutinized by the DEA, state control boards, and the health care systems that employ them, limiting the number of opioid prescriptions they can write.

This has created a burgeoning black market, a huge money-making payday for opportunists like Mark Fister who are happy to sell to a growing population so desperately addicted to prescription drugs that they are willing to pay five, six times the pharmacy prices—upward of eighty dollars a pill to get their fix, according to one source.

Fister has reaped enormous wealth from his involvement in the illicit prescription drug business, but he is no street-corner drug dealer selling painkillers for eighty dollars a pop. At least not when he was in Brooklyn. He had bigger ambitions. His involvement was strictly at the top levels—an angle boy making deals with big-name drug companies that often involved fraud, illegal sales activities, price setting, bribery, extortion, and methodologies as brutal as any of the Columbian drug cartels.

And, if there was potential for enormous wealth, it didn't take a genius to figure out that Uncle Paulie would want a piece of it. Luke didn't know what Uncle Paulie's beef was with Fister, but it was easy to guess. They had been partners who, as a result of greed, Uncle Paulie's greed most likely, had a falling out, then became rivals, and then bitter enemies. That kind of big-time money can do that to partners, even best friends. He saw that a lot growing up. The blood feuds, the vendettas, the bloodlust, the irrational rage that pitted friends against friends and divided families into rival factions.

So Fister moved his operation to Mexico where he found doing business more congenial in a culture of corruption. Smart move. You can bribe anyone in Mexico. Get whatever you want for a price, control the police, government officials, politicians, DEA agents, border guards—everybody—and Fister had plenty of money to make his life and his business trouble free.

But it was now Luke's job to eliminate Fister so that Uncle Paulie, the control freak among control freaks, could access a bigger slice of the illegal prescription drug pie.

Or dominate it completely.

Or avenge some wrong, real or imagined. Something like

that. Just speculation. Luke didn't know all the details. It didn't really matter. And he didn't really care. All he cared about was the quid pro quo of the assignment. In exchange for Fister's demise, Luke would receive information from Uncle Paulie that would allow him to avenge Crissy's mysterious murder and find his son.

And, finally, get on with his life, what was left of it anyway.

CHAPTER THIRTY-FOUR

Luke checks into a suite with an ocean view at the luxe Hotel Del. He's flush now and can spend freely, but he still occasionally lapses into his frugal ways, like buying a bottle of Johnnie Walker Red from the corner liquor store instead of drinking at the pricey hotel bar.

He travels light, with just a backpack and a duffel bag from which he withdraws the bottle of scotch, and opens all the windows. The room is freshened by the briny breezes that waft in from the Pacific Ocean. He pours himself a drink, no ice, and drains it in one swallow, then pours himself another.

He enters the screened-in porch and sits in a white wicker chair. The sun is setting and the horizon is streaked with multicolored lights casting a diminishing sparkle on the water.

He takes off his suit and calls the hotel dry cleaning service, giving them specific instructions—spot cleaned and sponge pressed; no chemicals. Then he sits on the bed, pours himself another drink, and stares out the window. The night is clear and calm, but he feels anything but calm and is not at all touched by the scenic beauty.

Memories force themselves on him again. They are arbitrary, fragmented, and form no coherent narrative. He remembers the time during BUD/S when the class was taken to San Clemente Island, "where no one can hear you scream," for a night swim. The instructor barked, "San Clemente Island, you dirt bags should know, is home to one of the largest breeding grounds for great white sharks in the world." The instructor paused, letting the fact sink in, then said, "Okay, hit it," and they dove in.

Soundless images rise up in his consciousness too, also arbitrary, disconnected. The vague outline of a Black Hawk helicopter banking portside in a misty sky, sounding like a cross between a leaf blower and a car wash. Claymore mines. Light antiarmor rockets and antitank weapons. Smells and sounds follow. The peculiar odor of a sweaty rifle stock, the high-pitched whine of a Chinook, the hot gritty sand of the desert, the ear-splitting blasts of an AK-47. Tastes too, one in particular: the taste of green face camouflage.

He keeps drinking until all the images and sounds and smells and tastes are extinguished and he drifts off into a fitful sleep.

The next morning he looks over the maps and coordinates and checks the plans that he and Suggs carefully created before he left with the help of Broyles and Bishop, two Navy buddies still living in San Diego. A knock on the door interrupts his train of thought. It's a hotel staffer with his suit draped in plastic.

"Hang on a second," says Luke before the staffer can leave, and inspects the suit carefully.

"Nice job," he says, and tips generously. Then he puts the suit on and immediately feels better, as if he has been reunited with some essential part of himself. It makes him feel better than the scotch, better than the serene sunset over the Pacific, better than the plush comfort of this five-star hotel.

Broyles and Bishop, the Navy buddies whose help he enlisted, are already waiting for him at McP's, an Irish pub in Coronado that is a well-known Navy SEAL hangout.

They sit outside on the patio and order frothy pints of Guinness, just like in the old days. He's forgotten how bright the sunshine is here and squints. Nothing seems to have changed; yet everything has.

He has sat in this very spot many times with Crissy, with his SEAL buddies, with friends visiting from the East Coast. His son, Jack, took his first steps on this patio as Crissy watched, beaming with pride. Once again, he is assaulted by memories, tender memories that he must squelch because the time has come for serious concentration and the mental discipline needed to focus singly on killing Mark Fister, which is very nearly a suicide mission, and Bishop bluntly tells him so.

"You got a death wish?"

"Something like that."

"You're not making sense. We know you went off the deep end a few years ago. Hell, we've all had our dark moments. And we are, of course, sorry about Crissy. And understand your motivations. You disappeared and it's nice to have you back. But do us a favor and stick around. Revenge isn't worth it."

"Sometimes," says Luke, "you have to disappear to figure out your life."

"But what you're about to do," says Bishop, shaking his head. "That's psycho stuff. You're one man invading a country. You're good, but not that good, and with all due respect, not the man you once were. Worse, you're going after Mark Fister. You're playing with fire. He's in collusion with the Columbian drug cartels. Eventually, they'll turn against each other, and you don't want to be around when that happens. And trust me. It'll happen. And soon."

"That's why I need you gents."

"Still."

The doubts about his ability raise his ire, but he hides it, smiles pleasantly. Although they have not seen him in years, they have kept tabs on him. Or at least tried to. Their friendship has not suffered. In fact, it is stronger than ever. They can tell each other anything, so they pull no punches. They tell him exactly what they think.

"Don't do it."

He does not take their advice lightly, but dismisses it.

"And the cancer?" asks Bishop. "Hodgkin's, right? How are the treatments going?"

"Fine. Never felt better. Caught it in its early stages." He lies, of course. No sense giving them further reasons to doubt his capability.

"You're going to need every bit of strength you got."

Luke knows it better than they do, but he also knows that he's combat tested, that force of will trumps medical doctoring, maybe not forever, but for as long as he needs it and he does not need it for very long.

Bishop is a commander now, a career Navy man, still stationed at North Island. His uniform is impeccable, crisp and fitted. His hair is cropped short and slightly grayer than the last time Luke saw it, and although his face has aged with visible lines, he is in top shape, still a regular runner and weight lifter, and it shows; his biceps bulge when he picks up his beer and his uniform strains at the chest.

He's risen up the ranks through an unusual mixture of combat heroics and shrewd political instincts. And, moreover, by lessening risk through an obsessive-compulsive need for preparation and calculation. He'll make fleet admiral one day, the highest rank. He was the first man Luke thought of when he needed help planning the Mark Fister hit.

Broyles, just as capable, left the Navy years ago. He was more of a risk taker and in some ways that made him a better soldier than Bishop, but it was a major drawback that didn't sit well with the top brass and his career stalled. Not that he cared.

He was confident, independent, and when he left the service, he started his own successful flight-instruction business.

Both are well off financially, family men, and devoted to the military. They are even more devoted to the men with whom they served.

"I think you can do it," says Broyles. "Nothing much different than the missions we were on. It's a takedown, a VBSS." Luke recalls the Navy's fondness for acronyms. This one is indelibly impressed on his mind. He'd been on so many. VBSS stands for Visit, Board, Search, and Seize, a standard SEAL mission that usually involves commandeering a rogue vessel claiming to transport harmless cargo, like cement, when in reality it is stocked with Scud missiles or chemicals used to create nuclear weapons.

"But you're just one guy," says Broyles, "so luck will have to be on your side. And, of course, we'll do our part."

Luke can tell Broyles has missed the action. He's gained weight and has that slightly bored look men have who have settled down to a comfortable life after a career in the Special Forces.

"And what's with the suit?" Broyles asks. "You come from a job interview or something?"

"Traded in my Navy uniform for this one. Like it? Or did you expect me to show up in camos?"

"Sharp," says Bishop admiringly. If anybody can understand sartorial empowerment it's Bishop.

"All right," says Broyles, unfolding a map and spreading it across the table. "Let's get down to business."

The plan is simple in concept. According to Bishop's intelligence work, Fister is aboard his yacht that is docked in the Marina District of the Cabo region of Mexico, just over the San Diego-Tijuana border. Luke will hitch a ride during SAR (Search and Rescue) ops on a Navy helicopter, most likely a MH-60R Seahawk, that routinely flies over Baja California on training missions and often recons the area to collect data on the movements of drug cartels to share with other government agencies.

Luke, as he has done many times before in many different countries, will jump out of the helicopter, swim to shore, and find his target—Fister's yacht, aptly and rather boldly named *Hookup*, slang for drug dealer.

Then he will stealthily board the vessel. Gear will be minimal to improve mobility—a wet suit and a waterproof backpack that will contain a luminous compass, a GPS device, a fillet knife, explosives, and, of course, his trusty MetroCard. Light and lean. He will sneak up on Fister, cover his mouth, and drive the blade of the fillet knife into the flesh beneath his collarbone, puncturing the heart, an easy and efficient kill, one he has done many times before.

Naturally, security thugs will surround Fister, but they will not be expecting a one-man invasion from the gentle waters of a marina filled with recreational sea vessels. He is sure he can evade them. And if he cannot, well, every mission has its collateral damage.

Then he'll dive back into the water and swim out to sea where Bishop will be hovering in the Seahawk. They will drop a line and he will climb up and board, then they'll return to North Island. The entire mission will take two hours and forty-five minutes, tops.

As a precaution, they will drop a satchel filled with survival supplies, a 9mm and an AK-47 at predetermined coordinates. Luke doubts he will need it, but Bishop and Broyles convince him otherwise.

Broyles jokes, "It'll be under the third mango tree from the bus station on Avenida Revolución."

"If you get in the shit," says Bishop, "you don't want to be caught with just your dick in your hand."

"My best weapon."

But the timing must be perfect. Fister could move at any minute. He might already be on the move, but that is a chance Luke will have to take.

"Okay, then," says Bishop, as he slides a document-filled envelope toward Luke. He will need the documents to get on base, but more importantly, they will cover Bishop's ass should things go awry.

"We go tonight at twenty-one hundred," says Bishop.

"Oh, and here," says Broyles. "Take this. A newer, more sophisticated GPS device so I can track your ass."

CHAPTER THIRTY-FIVE

Luke is about to leave for the base when his cell phone rings. It's Laura. She sounds upset and is very brief. "Don't go through with it," she says. "Can't say anything more."

Then she abruptly hangs up. It leaves him stunned and frazzled. How does she know? She could have overheard one of Uncle Paulie's conversations. Or as a federal agent she could be monitoring Uncle Paulie. A warning from Bishop and Broyles is one thing, but a warning from her carries even greater weight. And she must have put herself out on a limb to make the call, dangerously exposing herself for his sake.

But there's no way he'll cancel his plans now. He's come too far to back down now, and his own safety is not a concern. If assassinating Fister is what he must do to find Crissy's killers and get his son back, well, he'll do whatever it takes.

He calls Suggs to ask if anything has changed, if there is anything out of the ordinary going on back there, but Suggs says, "Nothing. Whiskey is still whiskey and I can't afford much."

He asks him to keep an eye on Laura, snoop around, make sure she's safe. She knows something she shouldn't know.

Suggs says, "Sure. Nothing I like better than looking at Laura. She is one fine specimen of a woman."

This is one task that Luke must do without his charmed suit and he feels like Samson stripped of his locks, without which he was powerless, but Luke puts on his SEAL gear—a wet suit underneath his old Navy khakis—and feels potent again, for they are both similar, at least in his mind, they are essential equipment for practical and psychological empowerment.

Still, Luke leaves the hotel with an uneasy feeling that he can't shake. He stops at the North Island gate and is waved through. It's a strange feeling, this homecoming, but again he resists going down memory lane and concentrates on the task ahead.

He's right on schedule. He finds Bishop and his crew in a hangar already briefed and climbing aboard a helicopter, a Seahawk. As they run through the preflight checklist, Luke takes a seat on the port side. Nobody says a word to him. Nobody looks at him. As far as they're concerned, he doesn't exist.

They wait for clearance and then take off. The whirling of the helicopter blades and the grind of the engine are sounds he has not heard in a long time, sounds he thought he would never hear again, sounds that are literally music to his ears.

Life seems to be a circle, he thinks, overlapping circles that continually bring him back to the past so that he can move forward. All of his self-doubts disappear, even his uneasiness about Laura. He is now completely focused on Mark Fister.

The helicopter glides through the night sky—and it is a beautiful night sky, clear, warm, and starry. They reach the U.S./Mexico border in less than fifteen minutes. Then they veer toward shore and begin a quick descent. Luke looks out the portal at the ocean below. It is as calm as the sky. There is still just the whir of the helicopter blades, the engine purring. No one talks. When the hatch slides open, one of the crew members drops a rope, and Luke latches onto it.

"Good luck," says Bishop. "You'll need it. If you're not back at this coordinate at 23:45, we're outta here."

He hits the water and the rope is pulled back up into the helicopter. In a few short minutes he is alone, profoundly alone, in the darkness, swimming in the placid waters, heading toward the lighted shore, heading toward his target, heading toward *Hookup*, heading toward Mark Fister.

It's less than a two-mile swim and he is surprised by his own stamina. But he slows down to conserve energy, to lessen the adrenaline pumping in his veins. He spots a panga, a small, open craft that is often used by Mexican smugglers to run drugs and migrants. He dives and resurfaces, finds his coordinates, and is soon in sight of the shore. Palm trees and mango trees sway in the breeze. He also sees the marina.

And there it is, still docked, the *Hookup*. It is easy to identify, for it is the biggest and most ostentatious yacht in the marina. He feels a tremendous sense of relief.

But a squall followed by a dense fog obscures his visibility, forcing him slightly off course. He finally makes landfall, but a long stretch of rock blocks his entrance into the marina. He can swim around it, but there is no time for that. And he is also tired, so he climbs over the rocks and traverses a small section of littoral where he can access an inlet into which he will dive and find *Hookup*.

But suddenly floodlights illuminate the darkness that concealed him and five Federales armed with Glock pistols and Heckler & Koch HK21s, German 7.62mm general-purpose machine guns, surround him.

Clearly, they've been tipped off. He's not surprised. Laura knew and tried to warn him. And if Laura knew, then that means that she somehow heard about it from the only other person who knew about his plan except for Suggs. The person who assigned it: Uncle Paulie.

Uncle Paulie has set him up. At least now he knows where he stands.

There is enormous satisfaction in finally discovering the truth of what he has suspected all along, that Uncle Paulie, for some unknown reason, was behind Crissy's death and knew that when Luke found out about it, he would come after him with a merciless vengeance. So Uncle Paulie figured out a way to get rid of him. And this was it. Death at the hands of the Federales.

But the Federales greet him with greasy smiles and laughter as if they've just caught a big but harmless fish.

"Welcome, Americano. We've been waiting for you. What took you so long?"

He drops the GPS device and kicks sand over it. He also manages to insert his MetroCard between his ass cheeks.

One of the Federales, the biggest of the lot, a jowly Mexican with jet-black hair and a sadistic smile, orders him to put up his hands, and when he does, he hits him in the stomach with his rifle butt. Luke falls to the ground, the wind knocked out of him, and pretends to be hurt worse than he is. He writhes in the sand, a ruse to buy time so that he can formulate a plan of escape.

Or a plan of attack.

They frisk him and are puzzled by what they find in his back-pack—a fillet knife? They expected to find a more lethal weapon.

"Hey, amigo. You going to cook us a seafood dinner?"

Then they shove him into a rusty Jeep that looks like it served in World War II and transport him along a dusty road lined with palm and mango trees to a Tijuana jail. Luke thinks this a curious course of action. Why don't they just shoot him and dump his body? It would make more sense. Surely that's what Paulie has paid them to do. What reason could they have for taking him prisoner?

The jail is a cinderblock hovel, hardly a high-security prison. Apparently, the sadistic Federale has more important things to do and drives away with three of his men, leaving Luke guarded by only two of the five who pay him little mind. They converse in Spanish, laugh and chuckle.

They lull easily, Luke notes, and plans to take full advantage of it. Two overfed Federales, he thinks, against one decorated

Navy Seal. Yeah, that's a fair fight. He's been up against worse, a lot worse.

A Federale grabs him by his arm while the other one keeps a pistol trained on him. They escort him down a filthy corridor, past a Federale dozing in a swivel chair. His paunchy partner watches television with his feet up on an office desk, his hands clasped comfortably over an enormous stomach. A rusty ceiling fan clanks noisily overhead.

Luke takes in as many details as he can, for details will be the key to busting out of here. He notes everything from the location of the fire extinguisher to the pole that holds a limp flag of Mexico.

Hapless faces stare at him from behind bars. Some yell in Spanish. One prisoner spits at him, but misses. Luke kicks his fingers that are wrapped around the jail bars and the man squeals like a dog whose tail has been stepped on. The other prisoners laugh, curse, cackle, and make obscene gestures. One guy even drops his pants to display a pimply ass.

His captors push him into an empty jail cell, but before they can slam the door shut, Luke jams his hand between the door and the latch so that it can't close. In fact, it springs open into the faces of the Federales. Luke's hand hurts like hell and a bone or two might've been broken or fractured, but he is so full of adrenaline he feels no pain.

He head butts one Federale, slices his neck with his Metro-Card, and grabs his machine gun. He spins him around so that the Federale is now a human shield. The other guard takes aim, but holds his fire, not wanting to shoot one of his own. Or maybe he'll risk it. He does. Misses.

Luke knocks his machine gun aside with the stock of the weapon he has just confiscated. The guard stumbles and reflexively pulls the trigger. Bullets ricochet off the jailhouse bars and cement walls. Although prisoners howl, curse, and duck, they enjoy the show and cheer him on.

Two Federales appear from a side room. The corridor is narrow, but Luke wields his MetroCard in economical strokes, following the lines of the body, and cuts ribbons of flesh out of his jailers. Then he opens fire and empties a clip into their bodies that twitch and bounce as if they've been shocked by an electric current.

He tosses the machine gun aside and moves down the corridor to the office where he encounters the two Federales he has seen on his way in. They rush him, clumsily reaching for their holstered handguns, but Luke grabs the flagpole, wielding it like a Kenpo staff, and jabs it into the ceiling fan, unhinging it so that it is like a loose propeller, wildly twirling like a pinwheel. It nearly decapitates the fat Federale. Luke hits his partner across the face with the flagpole and jabs the one who was nearly decapitated in the groin before he can fire his pistol.

But more Federales keep on coming. They get off a shot and Luke rips the fire extinguisher from its wall mount and ramrods them into the wall. One guard wields a baton, the other aims a pistol and fires. Luke drop kicks the Federale with the baton, spins, and hits the other with a sidekick, knocking him over a cluttered desk.

But they are not down for long. Luke spins again and delivers the coup de grâce: a strike to each of their noses with the palm of his hand, pushing a shaft of cartilage into their brains, a quick, efficient, and lethal blow.

He hurries toward the exit but stops for his backpack. Thirsty, he sees bottled water on a shelf. Although he must beat it out of there quickly, he must avoid dehydration. It's a long swim back to the coordinates where Broyles will hopefully be waiting and he can't afford muscle cramps or fatigue.

So he quickly gulps down two bottles, and walks out the front door.

And that's when he is met with another surprise. The sadistic Federale has returned, smiling and leaning up against what appears to be an armored limousine.

"You really are as good as we've heard," he says, and opens the rear door of the princely limo that looks out of place in these environs. "Please," he says cordially, directing him with the upturned palm of his hand, "there is someone who is eager to meet you."

CHAPTER THIRTY-SIX

That person is Mark Fister.

He leans back into the plush leather seat of the limo, one leg elegantly crossed over the other. He is deeply tanned, rail thin, with long shoulder-length dark hair, and dressed in a crisp blue linen suit. His white shirt is loosened at the collar and his Charvet tie is a riot of tropical color.

He is maybe in his early forties and bears the smug smile of a man who does what he pleases and somehow gets away with it. He is also wearing sunglasses, but he takes them off to regard Luke. His gaze is intense, penetrating, and his eyes glint with a malicious intelligence, a well-earned arrogance.

"So," says Fister matter-of-factly, "you are here to kill me."

Luke remains silent, looks out the window, tries to get his bearings, and wonders how he can get out of here alive.

Fister runs his hands through his hair, pushing it away from his eyes. His hair is lustrous and well kempt and the gesture has an aura of vanity about it. Fister politely asks him if he would like a drink from the fully stocked bar.

"Just water."

"I meant a real drink."

"Water's fine."

Fister hands him a glass, one pinky extended. Fister is mannered, almost genteel, an Ivy Leaguer, and strangely calm. Not exactly your run-of-the-mill drug lord.

Luke has the MetroCard palmed in his hand and thinks that

he could easily cut his throat but where would that get him? Stranded? Or more likely killed.

"Who ratted me out?" asks Luke.

"Who do you think?"

"No idea." But, of course, he does.

"Well, if you haven't figured it out by now, I'll tell you. The Feds got onto Paulie's prescription drug business—illegal prescription drug business, the one I set up for him. Big money, even bigger now. Crissy was implicated and was looking at serious jail time."

"Crissy was dealing prescription drugs?"

"She was unknowingly involved, an innocent bystander, really, just a low-level bookkeeper. Unfortunately, the Feds didn't see it that way. Or maybe they did. They forced her to cut a deal to avoid prosecution, to hand over evidence, and, eventually, a promise to testify. She had everything documented on two CDs —compounding pharmacies, names of pharmaceutical contacts, manufacturers and distributors in foreign countries, bribes, rogue pharmacists, websites, money-laundering channels, chemical formulas, lots of names, even spreadsheets.

"Paulie found out about it and had her killed. Set it up to look like a robbery. He thought you were out of the picture, locked up in some psycho ward, harmless, a nervous wreck, zoned out on meds, but when you came around, he was scared, scared to death you'd find out the truth, so he sent you down here, far away from home, where people disappear all the time and nobody talks."

"How do you know all this?"

"Do you know a well-dressed black man name of Billy Dee? He's on my payroll."

"Billy Dee. Yeah. That makes sense. Quiet, beady-eyed fellow. Has a certain sartorial style. Followed me for a while. I've always wondered about him. Playing both sides."

"Dangerous but lucrative. Anyway, Paulie thought he could kill two birds with one stone, so to speak: you and me. You were supposed to kill me and then a hit squad was supposed to take care of you." Fister laughs. "A hit squad. They're as easy to hire here as plumbers are in Brooklyn. Didn't quite turn out like that, now did it?"

"Never trusted the bastard. I just woke up from my psychotic stupor one day and knew, I just knew that I had to find out the truth, and knew in my gut he was key."

"So here's what I want you to do. I want you to turn around and go back to New York and kill *him*. I'll pay you well. Five hundred grand."

"Hell, I'll kill him for free."

"I know that. But there's more. I want you to blow up the warehouse in downtown Brooklyn. I'll send you the floor plans."

"What warehouse?"

"It's a front, a telemarketing firm, for Paulie's illegal prescription drug racket. It was ours. Then he took it. I don't want it back. I've got my own operation now, bigger and better, but I want his shut down, destroyed."

"That'll cost you."

"How much?"

"Another five hundred grand."

"A bargain," says Fister.

"Paulie's only got one disk, the one confiscated from Crissy. Guess where the other one is?"

"I have no idea."

"Crissy gave a copy to her parents. Smart gal. Paulie wants it bad. He's a paranoid little fuck. He'll do anything to get his hands on it, but he doesn't know where they are and he's looking for them."

"Why don't they just turn it over to the Feds and help Paulie go away for a long time?"

"They made a deal. Paulie leaves them and your son alone, and they keep the disk—and all they know—a secret."

"So why would he want to hurt them?"

"Paulie trusts nobody. Crissy told her parents everything, but they haven't cooperated with the Feds. But they might. They could. And that makes Paulie crazy. After all, they know he had her killed. They want revenge too. But they also want to be left alone. They want Jack safe. But as you know, revenge is a very strong and very unpredictable emotion. It can, as you see, get you killed."

Fister pours himself a drink, looks out the window, observes the activity of his security staff and the Federales who are no doubt on his payroll too.

"Ah," he says, "something's about to go down. But no matter. Where were we? Oh, yes, your son and in-laws. So here's the deal. You work for me now. You whack that thieving uncle of yours who stole millions from me, and I will tell you where your son and in-laws are. Hopefully you can get to them before Paulie does."

"I've got to take a piss. Can you let me out?"

"Not at the moment."

"Why?"

"Wait for it. One, two, three—"

The roar of machine gun fire and small explosions suddenly shatter the quiet. Bullets skid off the window of the limousine, riddle the side of the car, and ping off the wheel rims. The sound, though, is harmless, like rain on a tin roof. This is more tank than limo, seemingly built to withstand a nuclear attack.

Fister is unfazed, even a little bored, and leans toward the bar to refill his glass.

Gunfire is returned. Smoke wafts past the windows.

"What is this?" asks Luke. "The Wild, Wild West?"

"A lot worse, but nothing to worry about," he says, his eyes widening with that arrogant glint that first impressed Luke. "Hit squads. Like I said, they are a dime a dozen. Happens a lot. In my line of work, you have a lot of enemies, but I am well protected and always, and I mean always, one step ahead of everybody. Including you, my friend."

The sound of gunfire dissipates.

"All clear?" asks Luke. "Can I get out and take a piss before my bladder bursts?"

"Can we do business?"

"I think so."

Fister presses a button on the armrest and the door locks unbolt. "As if you ever had a choice."

CHAPTER THIRTY-SEVEN

"It's noisy and ugly here," says Fister with no sense of under-statement. "And will probably get noisier if we stick around. Would you like to see my yacht? After all, you came all this way."

"No, thanks. I've got a flight to catch."

"There are a few gaps in your knowledge that should be filled."

"Like what?"

"Bobby Guerro."

"Now you've got my attention."

They drive along another rural road bordered by palm and mango trees. Mountains loom dusky and jagged to the east, the ocean murmurs to the west, both seem somnolent, like sleeping animals. Luke watches the shadowy figures on horseback that move cautiously along the ridgeline.

The limo doglegs onto another path, a road that is roughly hewn in the cliffs. It rises and falls, twisting around canyons and gulches before it wends its way toward the sea again, past grim villages comprised merely of shacks festooned with laundry and long stretches of questionably arable land.

Farmers and banditos stop and watch the motorcade with rapt fascination. Some bob and weave, others duck, hide, scatter. They are all mere silhouettes, vague shapes in the darkness, but even at a distance he can see their eyes and the curiosity or fear or hatred that makes them glow.

A truck mounted with machine guns leads the way. Another one takes up the rear. The Federales also accompany them, but they mysteriously vanish and resurface. The sound of gunfire intrudes on what is basically a peaceful and rather scenic drive.

They reach a fork and take the low road, but before they descend, Luke glimpses a suspicious movement of vehicles in the distance. He's sure they're being shadowed. He says nothing to Fister. After all, Fister is "one step ahead of everybody," or so he believes, so Luke just watches, alert, while Fister sips his tequila.

Finally, they reach the shoreline and Luke sees the faint outline of a caravan in the distance. He has always possessed keen eyesight, has always been able to find more significance in that which is covered by darkness than exposed by light.

Although he cannot identify exactly what or who they are, his instincts tell him that they are perhaps if not a military caravan, then one that is well armed and that they might represent more trouble than Fister has ever encountered before. If Luke is right, he'll be in the middle of it. "In the shit," as Navy SEALs say about being in combat.

Fister, though, is his usual complacent self, waxing eloquent about the beauty of coastal Mexico, the ambrosial delights of his expensive tequila, and his love of bespoke suits and shoes, something they have in common.

He almost seems boyish, a precocious kid giddy with a lot of toys, acting but never quite convincingly playing an adult.

"Join me," says Fister. "Best tequila you will ever have."

Just to be agreeable, Luke says, "Why not? You only die once, right?"

Finally, they reach the marina and Fister expansively alights from the limo—stretching his arms, taking a deep satisfied breath, surveying his little army, and admiring the view.

A real Master of the Universe, Luke thinks, and regards him

with critical disdain. Fister's confidence seems boundless, but Luke has seen the pitfalls of bravura, complacency, and arrogance, and Fister fits the bill to a T.

"There she is," he says proudly. "*The Hookup*. Three hundred seventy feet of pure beauty. It was made in the UK by Stuart Hughes of Liverpool and took over two years to build. Worth the wait. Powered by two kick-ass thirty-six hundred horsepower Wärtsilä engines, it has an onboard seventy-four-foot sailboat, a ten-man submarine, an indoor pool with a glass roof, a wine cellar, and a movie theater. And my personal favorite, a hydraulic platform covered in sand that can be lowered to the waterline, where beautiful girls can suntan, swim, get drunk, blow me, and enjoy what amounts to an onboard beach party. Nifty, eh?"

"Might be a stupid question," says Luke, "but why not just go to a real beach?"

"Ah, where's the fun in doing what everybody else can do? And it is safe, but never safe enough. I am constantly losing bodyguards." The word "losing" has a menacing ring to it. "They betray me, but I find out. I always find out. I am always careful, some say paranoid, but you can never be too careful in this business. Or," he adds with a chuckle, "too paranoid."

They are escorted along a series of ramps that lead to the yacht. Fister, beaming with pride, continues to describe the vessel in what seems to Luke endless and tedious detail.

"Oh, and check this out. I just installed a laser shield that can scan for nearby cameras and direct a beam of light at a spying photographer's lens to ruin the photos. Pisses off the DEA. It's illegal too," says Fister as if this pleases him more than the gadget's capabilities. "Don't you just love technology? The master bedroom is lavish. It's decorated in twenty-four-carat gold, an actual bone from a Tyrannosaurus rex, and rocks from a meteorite. Can't get that at the Ritz."

The bodyguards suddenly break ranks and veer off in different directions. Luke's training has taught him that this is a lapse in protocol and regards it as suspicious, a red flag.

"May I borrow your cell phone?" asks Luke.

"Sure."

It is long past the hour he was scheduled to meet Bishop. The little detour in the Mexican jail was not on the itinerary and cost him precious time. He must think of an alternate plan. And he does. Broyles. Luke texts the coordinates to him and requests a pickup in one hour, in the same spot where Bishop dropped him, about two miles offshore in what appears to be a calm surf barely illuminated by a waning moon.

"Come on," says Fister. "I'll give you the grand tour."

"I'd much prefer a swim," says Luke. A swim that will take me the hell out of here and back to the U.S.

Luke spies a hulking shape on a hill and the outlines of what looks like small artillery. The air becomes oddly still, quiet, ominous. Even Fister is silent.

Luke recognizes the piercing sound, a kind of low, ambient whistle, for he has heard it many times. It is the noise that an antitank missile makes when it is incoming, probably, from the sound and what he can see in the shadows, an FGM-148 Javelin, a portable antitank missile, the kind used in the 2003 invasion of Iraq. Still works just fine, he'd bet. Illegal arms. Now there's a lucrative business.

The sky suddenly lights up in bright orange and red bursts. A zigzagging vapor trail is also visible in the distance. The bodyguards run for cover. Fister, oddly unafraid, looks admiringly up at the sky as if he's viewing a fireworks display. Luke throws his arms around him in a kind of lover's embrace, and they both plunge into the marina just as a missile strikes the main deck of the yacht.

The water is warm, murky, the visibility poor. Miraculously

unhurt, they both rise from a modest depth to the surface. Fister flicks the hair out of his eyes and says, "You were really serious about wanting a swim, weren't you?" His sense of humor remains odd and oddly unaffected.

The yacht takes another direct hit and the pier and ramps are soon engulfed in flames. A shower of splintered debris sullies the air, but they are out of harm's way.

Fister's laugh is more of a cackle than a guffaw, a sound that emanates not from his belly but high in his throat, a raspy irregular bleat. It is, Luke thinks, the brazen cackle of some delusional wanna-be deity. Fister is not fazed by the attack or that he nearly lost his life. In fact, he seems entertained and amused by it. He floats on his back as if he's on a Florida vacation. His laughter grows louder, deeper, as if he's just witnessed the funniest show on earth.

"Hit squads," he says. "Hah! I told you! I told you! They are a dime a dozen."

"I hate to restate the obvious, but we almost got blown to fucking hell," says Luke.

"But you saved me."

"I saved my five hundred grand."

"You see," says Fister, "it's not my time, not my destiny to die now. Still, I am always one step ahead of my enemies and two steps ahead of my friends, but I am also—" Now he is laughing so hard he can hardly get the words out. "—very, very lucky."

Fister glides across the water in a leisurely backstroke, bobbing like a cork floating in the surf, his laugher softer, a kind of demonic giggle. He gazes up at the moon, a broad smile across his lean face. He really is bonkers, thinks Luke. Fister playfully spits water in a perfect arc. If there were a beach ball around, he'd probably want to play catch, the crazy fucker.

"Everybody," says Fister, "wants to take from me what isn't mine. Hah!"

They swim away from the yacht, parts of which are now a conflagration that can probably be seen from Jupiter. But well-armored and apparently well-built, the yacht stays afloat and fire hoses are already trained on the damaged areas.

Luke observes the movements of Fister's bodyguards. They return fire, but halfheartedly, perfunctorily. More bodyguards appear as if they have been dropped from the sky. Armed with man-portable missiles that are launched from the shoulder, they fire randomly, emblazoning the hillside until it is a blackened hole of fire, smoldering ash, and thick smoke. Not exactly tactical geniuses, Luke thinks.

"I thought you loved that yacht?" asks Luke.

"I love the idea of it. I'll just repair or rebuild it or buy or build another one."

They swim to the beachhead and rest at the long stretch of rocks that jut out into the sea. It offers them protection and seclusion, at least for the moment.

"Do not worry," says Fister. "This is just a skirmish. My men will pick me up." He removes a GPS device and a cell phone and looks approvingly at them, for they work just fine, not the least bit affected by having been submerged in salt water.

"Sorry not to keep you company, but I got to hit it," says Luke, "so can we cut to the chase?"

"Sure, sure. I know, I know. Bobby Guerro. He killed your wife. Sorry to be so blunt. Paulie's orders of course, but he did the deed. The drug dealers were just some dumb stooges. And he retrieved the disk. One of them anyway."

Fister watches Luke closely, observing his simmering rage. It seems to delight him.

"Where can I find Guerro?" asks Luke.

"There was a hit on you before your little excursion down here, but no doubt when you show back up in New York surprisingly alive, it'll be reinstated. So you won't have to find him. He'll find you. Just don't get yourself killed. I need you to get to Paulie."

"With pleasure," says Luke as he strides purposefully into the surf.

"Oh," says Fister, "before you go: one more thing. You'll love this. I saved the best for last. Laura. She's an undercover FBI agent."

This is the confirmation he wanted. His suspicions that she was pretending to be somebody she wasn't were indeed well founded. Her faked incompetence on the firing range, her meeting with Billy Dee, the apartment that never looked convincingly lived in, just a place to stay until her assignment was completed, working in a job for which she was obviously overqualified— all a cover.

"She's after the same thing you are: evidence of Paulie's drug racket. And, of course, the information on that disk," says Fister as Luke strides farther out into the surf. "The Feds want to nail Paulie & Company as much as you do. It'll be interesting to see who gets there first."

"You taking odds?"

"I'm betting on you, my friend."

A stray ordnance lands and detonates about fifty yards from Fister, but he remains undaunted, as if he barely heard it. He doesn't even jump, just turns, and glances over his shoulder as if a pretty girl might be walking by.

Although the water is warm, Luke feels a slight chill. Fatigued, he wades farther out into the briny waters and dives into the murmuring waves, hoping Broyles will not let him down.

Bishop, he knows, will not take any risks that might harm

his ever-ascending naval career, so Broyles is his only chance to get back to the United States in one piece.

Soon he is invisible from the shoreline where Fister remains, a shadowy figure sitting in the sand with his arms around his knees, rocking back and forth, but Luke can still clearly hear the humming of the madman who has told him everything he needs to know.

CHAPTER THIRTY-EIGHT

Bullets skim the surface of the water, about twenty feet behind Luke who is swimming as fast as he can, but his strength is waning. He does not know who or why he is being targeted. It's certainly not Fister's men. Fister wants him alive, not dead, and on his side, an ally not a foe, an employee and not a corpse.

He just chalks it up to, as Fister would say, "Hit squads. Dime-a-dozen hit squads."

The air is too misty to see clearly, but he can hear the roar of an outboard engine—maybe two or three. Maybe they're all mounted on one vessel; maybe they're a fighting flotilla. One vessel shines a light in his direction but they must have night-vision goggles too, so he evades them by diving below the surface and swimming away from them.

He can hold his breath for long periods of time, but this detour will put him off the coordinates he sent to Broyles and he can't miss this rendezvous, the last hope he has of being flown the hell out of here. He must reverse course, take a more aggressive tactic.

It's risky, but he swims toward the sound of the engines pursuing him and when he is in sight of one of the pangas—which is indeed fitted with an outboard motor; three in fact for extra speed—he floats on his stomach and plays possum as if he's been shot.

He judges the distance wisely—close enough for them to see him, but far enough away so that he will not be an easy target should they take another shot at him. If they do and miss, he'll have at least a chance to submerge and evade them again.

A hulled boat with mounted M240 machine guns is the first to approach the area. He hears the men onboard talking in Spanish, which he assumes is a debate over his life. Finally, the talking stops; they have settled on a plan. They use a long pole with a hook to drag him onto the boat. If there was a hit out on him, they'd need definitive proof that the job was done right. No better evidence than a fresh corpse.

And they are armed with AK-47s slung over their shoulders. But that is fortuitous. They'll come in handy when he takes them away from them.

He makes himself deadweight and they are cautious but not overly so. They have hooked a seemingly lifeless and harmless catch, but as soon as Luke gets a foothold onboard, he grabs the pole away from his captor and swings it like a Kenpo staff, knocking two of the captors overboard and hooking a third whose AK-47 he confiscates. He opens fire and is the last man standing, but there are more gunboats roaring his way, their outboards at full tilt, muzzles blazing.

He can outrun them into U.S. waters, he thinks, in this pumped-up panga. After all, it's not much different from an RHIB—a rigid hull inflatable boat—a cross between a rubber life raft and an open speedboat, usually about thirty-six feet long with two monster motors in the rear, and used for a variety of SEAL tasks.

RHIBs can rev upward of forty-five knots on a calm sea, but this panga has not been tricked out and maintained with the same exacting standards of the U.S. military, but what other choice does he have?

Then a strange thing happens that makes it a moot point. It's as if God in heaven has suddenly decided to join the firefight. And God is on his side. Bullets rain down on his would-be captors, who take several direct hits, and then turn tail and head in the opposite direction.

Luke looks up and there in the sky is the outline of a stealth helicopter. He waves and he can see the pilot waving back. The side panel opens and a rope is dropped. He clambers up it until he is safely onboard.

"You okay?" asks Broyles.

"Never been better, thanks to you."

"You were really in the shit. I was watching you every step of the way. Ready to roll?"

"Ten-four, Captain."

Luke is, of course, pleased to be on his way back across the border, but what pleases him even more is Broyles's smile—the smile of a man who is thrilled to be back in action again.

CHAPTER THIRTY-NINE

On the return flight to JFK, Luke does not feel well. He has a slight fever and fatigue causes him to drift in and out of a hallucinogenic sleep. He also can't shake the cold sweats. He's had them before. He knows what they are. They are symptoms of Hodgkin's lymphoma.

He wakes often with a start, not knowing where he is, and is beset by a momentary panic, a fear that is alien to him. But there is still a clear place in his mind where plans for Uncle Paulie's demise form effortlessly. Bobby Guerro too. The drive to avenge Crissy's death has never been stronger.

Laura meets him at the airport and is shocked by the change in his appearance, the ashen pallor, the slow gait, the weakened demeanor. She takes him straight to her apartment where she feeds him and puts him to bed, but his fever worsens. This time he falls into a deep slumber but wakes again with night sweats. He remains in bed at Laura's behest for ten, eleven hours, but still feels exhausted, practically immobilized by an unshakable fatigue.

Getting dressed is an effort, but after he puts on his suit the color comes back into his cheeks, as if it has a nourishing effect, like a shot of vitamin B12.

Laura looks him up and down. "My Suited Hero," she says affectionately, stroking the side of his face.

She puts on a robe and makes coffee. They sit at the kitchen table. She puts her hand on his.

"Get treatment," she pleads. "Before it's too late."

He looks in her eyes and sees real tenderness, caring, love. Although he is touched, he can't help feeling that he has been betrayed by her secrecy, her undercover status.

"I know you're an FBI agent," he says.

She doesn't seem surprised. "I knew you'd figure it out sooner or later. And I'm glad. I did want to tell you. We're on the same side now. And you can help us. But you can't take the law into your own hands."

"I found out more in the last forty-eight hours than you've found out since you've been working for my Uncle Paulie for how long? Months?"

"I found out where you were, what you were going to do, and tried to warn you, didn't I?"

"How'd you know? Wiretapping?"

"Billy Dee. He's on our payroll."

"Jeezus! That guy's on everybody's payroll!"

"He's working for us."

"You mean *he's* an agent too? Figures. There was something in his eyes, a kind of intelligence that made him stand out, not at all like the typical mooks who work for my uncle."

"No, not an agent, an informer."

"Then I don't trust him."

"You have no idea how big this thing is. It's global. We're talking millions in illegal prescription drug sales, distribution, and manufacture. And it gets bigger and more lucrative every day."

"Like I give a shit."

"We'll get Crissy's killers. I know that's all you care about."

"How? And you don't even know who Crissy's killer is. But I do. And I don't have to contend with a bureaucracy, a flawed justice system, a career path, and organizational corruption."

"You must tell me what you know. We can do this together."

"Not a chance."

"I know where Crissy's parents and Jack are."

"Where?"

"They're safe. In the witness protection program."

"*Where?*" demands Luke hotly. Everybody, including a drug-dealing lunatic, seems to know where his son is except him.

"I can't tell you that. Not now."

"You know if Paulie finds out, you'll be in serious trouble. He's not above torture, to get what he wants."

"I can handle myself," says Laura. "But I want a promise from you that you'll let us take it from here. When we take down Paulie, then I'll be able to tell you where Jack and Crissy's parents are."

"You're blackmailing me?"

"I'm not blackmailing you. I'm trying to help you. We've been working on this case for a long time. I've got superiors to answer to. We're almost there. And I don't want you to get hurt. We've got to play this one smart, by the books. He's eluded us before."

"By killing Crissy."

Luke gets up to go, falters, and uses the chair to support himself.

"You're ill, Luke. Don't go. Stay. Don't you trust me?"

"I *don't* trust you. I think I love you. And I don't know which is more dangerous."

CHAPTER FORTY

They hesitantly embrace, then kiss. It is a long, lingering kiss, a curative kiss. Luke feels a sudden surge of desire, strength, and leads her into the bedroom where he kisses her neck, something he has often thought about, and then strips off her robe, turns her around, and lifts up her hair where he lightly kisses the area just below her hairline.

She relaxes, moans softly, and reaches for him as he runs his tongue down her spine to the rise of her two shapely mounds. He touches her. She is wet, very wet, and he turns her over again. Her eyes seem different in this light. Bright as emeralds, more green than hazel. She fumbles with his belt, then his pants, but he removes her hands and straddles her. She watches raptly as he takes off his shirt and pants.

He enters her gently, his mouth kissing her shoulders, the nape of her neck, her lips. He increases the power of his thrusts. Moisture forms on their skin, releasing a musky scent. He can feel her nails on his back, her pelvis thrusting to meet his. She yells, "Harder, harder," until her head rears back in a limb-shaking orgasm.

They make love again, but this time even more passionately. He lets the full force of his weight bear down on her and she draws him closer as if he is still far away. They look into each other's eyes and she can see in his a feral desire, a pent-up passion. This alone makes her come again. Her entire body quivers and she seems momentarily unable to catch her breath.

He lets her rest and wipes her brow with a soft touch. Then he wraps his arms around her, squeezes her tight, and grasps the back of her thighs so that he can pull her onto him and guide her, twist her, align her, and enter her from slightly varying angles, nuanced angles, until he hits her spot perfectly.

Now his thrusts are almost brutish and she is writhing in pleasure, in a multiorgasmic gyration, her legs like scissors crossed over his back, tightening and then tightening some more. "I don't want to ever let you go," she says, "and I want more, more."

Luke draws power from her clear expressions of desire. He feels an inexhaustible strength as if she has both cured and brought him back to life, and renewed his desire to live and love, all in an unplanned but inevitable moment.

Finally, when they are spent, she rolls over and rests her head on his shoulder. He wraps his arm around her, pulls her closer.

"I lost a child," she says, "before Jonathan," and Luke can feel the tears pool up in the declivity of his collarbone. Now he understands the loss that connects them.

CHAPTER FORTY-ONE

Luke sits in the Porsche, revs up the engine, and takes a moment to think. Time to take care of business. This is the moment he's been waiting for, but he can't reach Suggs. No response from the two urgent voice mail messages he left. He calls him again. No answer. He must get to the apartment. Either Suggs is drunk or fallen into the hands of Uncle Paulie or both.

He floors the Porsche, shifts into high gear, and the engine growls—a cross between a blowtorch and a meat grinder. It might need an oil change and a tune-up, but it'll do. He weaves through traffic, disregarding the speed limit and flouting every traffic law.

Then he calls Uncle Paulie.

"So you're back," says Uncle Paulie. "How'd it go?"

"You know how it went."

"Yes, I do."

"I know everything now," says Luke.

"You mean you *think* you know everything."

"You had Crissy killed because the Feds wanted information and testimony from her. You were afraid she'd provide evidence that would put you away for a long time, possibly the rest of your life."

"And who told you this fairy story? Mark Fister?"

"That's right."

"And you believe a wacked-out drug dealer?"

"Somehow I do. And the Feds."

"The Feds? Well, then, that's a big mistake, kid. You've just dug your own grave. But we can make a deal."

"No deals. I'm coming after you."

Uncle Paulie laughs. "Oh, really? You think you can get to me before I get to you?"

"That's right."

"I hate to inform you, but I've already gotten to you."

"We'll see about that."

"You always thought you were a hotshot. Big football star. Military hero. But never had a dime to your name. Just like your loser father, my brother the saint, always walked the straight and narrow and look where that got him."

"That's what you had against him. He was a good man."

"You know what they say about nice guys."

"When I gut you like a fish, it's going to be slow and painful and before you die you'll watch as I wrap your intestines around your neck. This is a long time coming. This is long overdue. I know what you did to my parents. You were always quick with the cash, eager to play the hero, but it was always with dirty money and low intentions."

"Your father certainly didn't mind the loans I gave him."

"You were supposed to look out for us. But instead you fucked your own brother."

"And I fucked your *mother* too."

"I know you did. And it destroyed my father, that betrayal. He's a wreck now and my mother's dead, all because of you."

"And guess what, kid? When I get hold of you, I'm gonna fuck *you* up the ass before I cut off your head."

"The time for talking is over. I just wish I could kill you a hundred times."

"You'll die trying."

"And a happy death it will be."

CHAPTER FORTY-TWO

Luke glances in the rearview mirror. He's being followed again. Fucking Russians. They're right on his tail. But this time he'll outrun them. Shouldn't be too hard in a Porsche, even an old one, but another glance in the rearview mirror instills doubts. The Russian fleet has been upgraded. A black BMW 135i coupe, a blue Corvette ZR1 that can easily top 200 mph, and a Chevy Camaro SS, have no trouble keeping up with him.

These cars were chosen for speed as well as flash. The Beamer boasts a 3.0-liter turbocharged 300-horsepower inline-6 engine and can possibly outpace this old rattletrap of a Porsche, if only by seconds, but seconds could be crucial in this situation. The Camaro SS is the real worry. Equipped with a 6.2-liter V-8 and paired with a six-speed automatic transmission it can easily hit a 400-horsepower gallop.

Still, it's the driver's skill that counts, and he plans to put theirs to the test.

A beeline down Nostrand Avenue is the fastest way to get to his apartment, but he makes an abrupt turn on Avenue U and pulls into Marine Park, a lively 798-acre recreational area, especially on a summer afternoon. It has three athletic fields, a bicycle and jogging track, basketball and tennis courts, and a nature center. It also has a junior high school on its northern end.

But Luke has his eye on the five hundred-plus acres of grassland that he plans to tear up like an old carpet.

He knows every inch of the grounds because he spent his youth here playing just about every game with a ball—football, baseball, tennis, and handball.

Or just hanging out with friends at the hot dog stand watching what seemed then to be an exotic game played by dark-skinned men in white suits—cricket.

At night it was a different story, a lover's rendezvous, a haven for drunks sleeping off a night of boozing, and a meeting place for drug dealers under the elms and other sketchy characters. Every once in a while a dead body would turn up on third base or in the outfield, a Mafia hit or drug deal gone wrong, or just your run-of-the-mill senseless crime.

He pulls into the parking lot and, disregarding the directional arrows on the ground, nearly runs head-on into an oncoming Nissan. He veers around a neat row of idle cars and checks the rearview mirror. Sure enough, the Russians are right behind him, logjammed into what amounts to an automotive maze. He guns it, jumps the curb, and lands with a slight jolt onto the grassy field where just ahead there are two baseball diamonds, one with a baseball game in play.

The pitcher winds up, throws a fastball over the plate. The batter connects and pops it up deep into center field. The center fielder has a bead on it, and it looks like an easy out until he hears the roar of cars traversing the field. He can't believe his eyes. "What the fuck?" he shouts. He takes his eye off the ball and it drops with a thud a few feet away. Then he runs for cover.

The rest of the players scatter too. They yell, curse, shout. One player even wings a bat in Luke's direction, but it's way off the mark.

The Russians are still fairly close behind. They have taken the bait. Luke weaves a figure eight in the infield that raises a gritty dust cloud, obscuring their vision, at least momentarily. He uses the opportunity to elude them and speeds to the east end of the park, weaving in and out of the neat rows of trees—oaks, dogwoods, and poplars—that line the parallel walking and bicycle paths.

Cyclists run into joggers, joggers run into strolling pedestrians, pedestrians trip, fall, and stumble into each other. The peaceful park has been turned into a chaotic dust bowl, a speedway for flashy cars.

The playground at the junior high is abuzz with activity. Looks like summer classes have just let out. Though old, the Porsche is light and limber and handles well, and he thinks he'll try it—scare the hell out of a few school yard bullies. You can always spot them.

He points the Porsche directly at the basketball courts and spies a big kid spitting Gatorade at smaller kids. The tall kid's expression widens in delight when he sees that a drag race is taking place in the park and saunters closer to get a better look, but when he realizes that he might very well become roadkill, his expression turns to alarm and he flees.

But he need not worry. Luke spins out at a safe distance in front of the basketball courts and contemplates his next elusive maneuver.

It's a little more difficult tearing up the handball courts and he must, by dint of necessity, take a few rusty chain-link fences with him to enter and exit conveniently. The Russians, however, create a lot more damage. The Camaro collides with a hot dog stand and a park bench, sending them both into the air.

Now the picnickers and even the vendors scatter, their idyll disturbed by the gassy exhaust clouds that spoil the azalea-scented summer air.

The Beamer seems to have run aground in a mud flat or salt marsh, but the Corvette is like a shark navigating familiar waters and roars up on his tail until Luke spins out again, raising more dust, and pops the clutch, the front end bucking like a bronco.

He heads to the north parking lot, veers around a more densely packed row of vehicles, and hits the gas pedal hard so that when he rams the curb it sends the Porsche flying across the sidewalk and into busy Avenue R.

Cars jam on their brakes, skid, screech, fishtail, and crash into each other, making a rhythmical metallic sound as they skid off parked vehicles like a pebble skimming the water of a lake.

He drives at a sensible speed on Gerritsen Avenue for a few blocks before making a hard left onto Kings Highway, a broad thoroughfare with buzzing traffic. George Washington, recalls Luke from his school days—he always liked history, especially local history—rode on horseback down this road with the beleaguered Continental army during the Revolutionary War. My, my, he thinks, things haven't changed all that much.

For a second or two he thinks he's lost them, but the Corvette skids along his passenger's side, just having made a daring or possibly suicidal move, depending how you look at it, across three lanes of traffic. The Camaro skids out of a cloud of exhaust and appears on his driver's side—close enough to brush each other's side view mirrors.

They try to box him in, squeeze him, and steer him over the median and into oncoming traffic, but he grips the leather-trimmed steering wheel tightly and jams on the brakes. A Lexus SUV is coming straight at him, so he whips the nimble Porsche around and turns down leafy Bedford Avenue. The Beamer suddenly appears, banged up with a carpet of lilacs on its hood, but still operational, and sticks to his tail.

They've got driving skills, concludes Luke, that's for sure.

CHAPTER FORTY-THREE

Traffic is heavy and when he comes to a red light he can't blow through it without getting T-boned, but the Corvette and the Camaro are coming straight at him from the opposite direction and at full speed—red traffic lights be damned.

When the light turns green, he drives straight at them in a game of chicken. It'll be one hell of a crack up if they're not fainthearted because Luke has no plans to turn tail.

But the Camaro is the first to flinch. Luke can see the driver's eyes. He is that close to him. His eyes are as white and as wide as coffee cup lids. He loses his nerve and evasively veers left, but his skills fail him because the adjustment is too precipitous and he runs up onto the sidewalk, taking out a fire hydrant and nearly mowing down a half dozen pedestrians who have no doubt wet their pants.

One car down and two to go. Or so it seems.

Luke heads for Prospect Park, a 585-acre oasis he knows almost as well as Marine Park. It's an even better locale than Marine Park because it has steeper hills, Brooklyn's only forest, broad meadows, bridges and tunnels, a lake, a ravine, a gorge, a carousel for the kiddies, and hilly terrain that will make it a hazardous race course for his pursuers—and a true test of his and their automotive skills.

Prospect Park is equally festive with urbanites enjoying a summer afternoon in a pastoral setting. Until, of course, the

Porsche enters the Willink entrance on Flatbush Avenue and off roads it, blazing onto the Nethermead, a rolling meadow filled with picnickers, kite flyers, sunbathers, dogs, slackers, and bird watchers.

The Park attracts about ten million visitors a year, and judging by the crowds, they all seem to have shown up today.

George Washington and his weary army also strode through here. They decamped in the forest for several nights when they were getting their asses kicked by the British in what is oddly called The Battle of Long Island, even though it took place right here in Brooklyn.

The area is filled with monuments—war heroes, civic leaders and, of, course rich philanthropists. At the south end of the traffic roundabout at Grand Army Plaza is the Soldiers and Sailors Arch that features a sculpted tribute to the fighting men of the Civil War.

A couple of hotshot skateboarders use makeshift ramps to launch themselves into the air and land on the cement walkway, scaring new mothers pushing baby strollers. Luke makes a friendly advance toward the skaters, keeping a safe distance. They turn and are not sure what to make of him. A Porsche in the park? Isn't that illegal?

Two skateboarders cut in front of him, defiantly blocking his way, as if to say, "This is our turf," but Luke stops, revs the engine, and shifts into gear, bolting forward, causing them to come to their senses. They run like hares flushed from the brush.

Finally, the Russians arrive. Luke wonders what took them so long. Probably a complete lack of familiarity with the area, so he takes them on a little joyride, leading the Camaro and the Beamer into the Ravine district that has the Park's most rugged terrain.

He also knows this section from his youth when he and his

friends would ride sleds down the snowy slopes and skid across the frozen lake, occasionally cracking its surface and nearly drowning or freezing to death. Those were the days.

Unless he's mistaken or it's been restored, a precipice lies hidden just beyond a copse of trees and if you don't know it's there, which the Russians surely do not, they'll take off like a 747 and plummet into a rocky ravine that should just about finish them for the day. Then he will only have to worry about the Vette, his feistiest four-wheeled foe.

Luke lets the Camaro and the Beamer catch up, but this proves to be a mistake. Apparently, in the time that has elapsed since he's last seen them, they've acquired weapons and are firing at him. He can only hope that they are worse marksmen than they are drivers.

Not so.

Luke sees the driver of the Camaro lean out the window and aim at him with a 9mm. Luke swerves in an effort to evade him, but a loud crash blows out his rear window. Time to take things to the next level. He races toward the precipice, narrowly avoiding clumps of trees and brush and hopes he can stop before he himself reaches the forested edge.

The Russians are emboldened now by what looks like a sitting duck in their sights, so they increase their speed. They are alongside of him now and again take aim. Luke hopes the aging Porsche can keep up with them because if it doesn't, they'll slow down and try some other maneuver, but he wants them at full throttle for a little longer.

Another shot rings out. They've suddenly acquired a modicum of intelligence because instead of shooting at him, they're aiming at his tires. And they come close. Bullets ping off his wheel rim. Just another hundred yards is all he needs to be free of them.

He floors it and pulls ahead. They overreact, playing into his hands, because when they finally see the precipice it is too late. They are already airborne, flying off the hillside, the Camaro listing to one side and the Beamer twirling in the air like a thrown dart. For a moment they seem to stand still, almost as if they've been embraced by the ether, but it's an illusion, and they fall fast, making an explosive landing that sends two fireballs high into the sky.

Luke backs away from the precipice and takes a breath of relief. Another few feet and he would have gone over the edge with them. He rumbles down the hillside and veers onto the Long Meadow, where there is no sign of the Corvette, and makes his exit, again startling pedestrians, on the Grand Army Plaza side, and drives down Flatbush Avenue, heading toward the apartment he shares with Suggs. Suddenly, the Corvette appears in his rearview mirror.

"Fuck."

CHAPTER FORTY-FOUR

The driver's lumpy shaved head gleams in the sunlight. Looks like his old nemesis Alexei, but all these Russians look alike—sallow, thick-necked, ugly tattoos, vaguely Cro-Magnon. The Russian extends a tattooed arm alongside the driver's side window, pistol in hand. He fires once, twice, missing both times. He's not as good a shot as his comrades.

Police sirens wail. Again, he wonders what took them so long. Now he's got the Russian Mafia, the police, the Italian Mafia, and who knows who else after him.

He calls Suggs again. Still no answer.

Stuck in traffic, Luke swerves into the oncoming lane, a risky maneuver, the Corvette right behind him, and makes an abrupt turn down Church Avenue, which is clear of traffic, at least for the moment. He floors the Porsche and purposely plows into a fire hydrant in front of a Caribbean restaurant, gashing open his forehead on the steering wheel.

The patrons, familiar with this sort of thing, look out the window of the restaurant and are more entertained than they are concerned. It's not exactly an upscale neighborhood. In fact, it's infested with crime, one of the worst in the borough. This kind of thing happens often here. Nobody makes a move to do anything, not to dial 911. They have learned to mind their own business.

The driver's side door is mangled. Luke pushes it with his shoulder, trying to spring it open. The door won't open, so he slithers out the rear window and clambers under the car. He hears the brakes screech on the Corvette and the door open. He lies quietly on the ground, bleeding, and watching the Russian's slow, cautious approach.

By this time crowds have gathered. They want a closer view of the action.

Brandishing a handgun, the Russian tells them to back off, fires a warning shot that riles them. Not the best way to make friends. Luke recognizes the voice. It is indeed his old nemesis, Alexei.

He can hear Alexei's shoes on the pavement, the click of his heels coming closer, until he's so close his legs are in front of the driver's side of the Porsche, easily within Luke's grasp.

Alexei, gun drawn, leans into the window expecting to find Luke dead or unconscious, but he is surprised to find that the interior of the wrecked car is empty, that Luke has escaped.

And that he has walked right into the trap Luke has set for him.

Luke grabs his ankles and pulls. Alexei lands on his back and hits his head on the pavement. Luke scampers out from under the car, blood from his wound now a mere trickle, and kicks Alexei in the groin.

Alexei lets out a pained bellow and grabs his crotch, then woozily points his gun at Luke and fires. He misses, hitting the window of the Caribbean restaurant, shattering it, not a popular move. A patron pulls out a gun of his own and points it at Alexei.

"Uh-uh," says Luke. "He's mine."

"You need a Band-Aid, sir."

Luke plants a dropkick in the center of Alexei's chest, knocking the wind out of him. Then he steps on Alexei's hand until he lets go of the gun.

"A Glock," says Luke, picking it up and cradling it in his

hand. "Nice balance. Better than that secondhand piece of shit Ruger you had last time. Somebody's supplying you with good gear. Not that I give a shit. But I do want to know who hired you. Paulie?"

"Fuck you. You American pussy."

"Wrong answer."

Luke wipes the blood that has dripped into his eyes, aims and fires, hitting Alexei between the eyebrows. Alexei's eyes flutter delicately like a butterfly and his last gasp of breath is audible. He's dead before his blood flows onto the curb and into the street.

The assembled crowd gasps; some applaud. Guess they don't like Russians around here.

CHAPTER FORTY-FIVE

Luke climbs into Alexei's Vette. The keys are still in the ignition. And better yet: the passenger seat is filled with handguns and clips and other useful paraphernalia. Luke reloads and sticks the Glock in his belt.

The police arrive just as Luke is leaving the scene. He can see in his rearview mirror the look on the cop's face. The cop is startled because apparently nobody has seen anything. The crowd disperses, and the police return to their squad car to fill out the usual paperwork and call in an ambulance and a tow truck. Luke is delighted because they will find that the Porsche is registered to none other than Uncle Paulie.

The Vette is a sweet ride and he can see the enviable looks from people on the street as he cruises down Flatbush Avenue, but it's a momentary distraction. His mind is on Suggs.

When he reaches the Junction, he veers onto Nostrand Avenue and passes by the apartment and Uncle Paulie's locksmith store. He recognizes the Crown Vic parked on the corner, the one that belongs to Detectives Heman and Fallon.

The locksmith store is open for business, and he wonders if Laura is inside. She should be. She's scheduled to work today, but he has a bad feeling about what he might find in the apartment, so he drives into a street leading to the Brooklyn College quad.

He tucks the Glock into his waistband and puts a fresh clip

in his back pocket. Then he walks to the apartment and climbs into Santiago's office through an open window.

Santiago is on the phone, and Luke sneaks up behind him, waiting for him to finish his call, but Santiago hears his approach and whips around.

"How the—what the fuck—?"

"Where's Suggs?"

"How the fuck should I know? I'm not his brother."

"What's going on in the apartment upstairs?"

"Oh, all kinds of wicked things," says Santiago slyly reaching into his desk drawer for a handgun, his back turned to Luke. "They're playing cards, watching *Sesame Street*, baking cookies, that sort of thing."

"Let's go upstairs and see."

"You're not going anywhere," says Santiago, spinning around in his chair and pointing a very big gun, a Magnum, at Luke.

"I thought we were friends."

"Don't make a move or I'll blow your greaseball head off, though I'd hate the mess, but don't think I won't. You're worth a lot of money, dead, alive, or anywhere in between."

"Paulie, eh? Well, my friend, you've chosen the wrong side."

"Oh, yeah. Let's go. Out the door. And put your hands up where I can see them."

They walk into the hall where Heman and Fallon are guarding the doorway, making sure no one enters or exits the building. They have been expecting him.

"Hey, look who it is," says Fallon, his trademark grin even wider than usual. "Heard you've taken up drag racing."

"What kept you?" asks Heman. "We've been waiting. And waiting. And we don't like to wait."

"For what?" asks Luke. "Another pay off, bribe, contribution to the pension fund you'll never live to collect?"

"Whoa!" exclaims Fallon. "Brave words."

"Everybody's a tough guy," says Luke.

"Not tough enough," says Heman. "You're coming with us." There is a pregnant pause. "Well, sort of."

Heman and Fallon go for their guns. They're not the quickest draws in East Flatbush. Luke has enough time to reverse positions with Santiago. Santiago is now in front of Luke and Luke has him in a choke hold with one arm and grasping his gun hand with the other.

Fallon fires first and wings Santiago in the shoulder. Luke, making sure that his trigger finger is placed over Santiago's so that the only fingerprints on the gun will be those of Santiago, fires and hits Fallon in the throat.

Before Heman can get off a shot, Luke—or rather Luke's puppet, Santiago—shoots and hits Heman in the chest. Heman, seriously wounded, staggers, but gets off another shot that doesn't hit its target, for Luke has shifted Santiago to take the bullet. It hits Santiago in the eye, an instant kill.

But now Santiago is deadweight. Luke must hold him up by tightening the choke hold he has on him so they can move in tandem to get within point-blank range of Heman and Fallon, both sprawled on the floor.

Must make sure they're dead, thinks Luke. These guys are nothing but trouble. Luke squeezes Santiago's finger and puts a bullet in each of their heads. When the bloody crime scene is examined, it'll be viewed as a shootout between two cops on the take and a corrupt landlord. There will be no evidence that Luke was ever there.

Now Luke must face what's waiting for him behind the apartment door. He takes his own gun from his waistband and climbs the stairs. Odd, he thinks, that who's in there has not come out after hearing a dozen gunshots. He knows what's waiting for him behind the door can't be good, but he has no choice. He's come this far and can't back down now. He is, he knows, finally, finally, finally about to come face-to-face with Crissy's killer.

CHAPTER FORTY-SIX

He kicks open the door and the first thing he sees is Suggs tied to a chair with a bull-faced man standing over him. Suggs is bloody and has been beaten.

"I didn't tell 'em nothing, Luke," says Suggs, "nothing."

"You want your buddy alive or dead?" asks the man standing behind Suggs who is holding a sawed-off double-barrel shotgun, an effective weapon in close quarters, thinks Luke. You don't even have to be a good shot to do major damage.

"Who the fuck are you?" asks Luke.

"I'm the guy who killed your wife, the bitch that was about to rat us all out."

"You're Robert Guerro."

"The one and the same." He takes a smug little bow. "But you can call me Bobby. All my friends do."

Luke can hardly contain his rage. He actually contemplates sacrificing Suggs to get to Guerro. It would be easy. Just blast away and let the bullets fly. A few would hit Suggs, but enough would make their way to Guerro too.

Luke, of course, cannot do it.

Guerro, though, is strangely cocky, almost ADD, for he hardly sees Luke as a threat. He seems more interested in looking out the window, the one that overlooks Paulie's locksmith shop, than he does in Luke.

"Yeah, the nosy old lady who sat in this very place saw the whole thing," he says. "Was just about to finger me. The world is filled with snitches, especially if there's money involved. Fister would have paid her well. So I had to off her. Sweet old bird, though. Never even put up a fight. I think she was bored with life, ready to meet her maker. I did her a favor."

Luke moves slightly to his left to avoid the sunshine in his eyes. This makes Guerro nervous, and he levels the shotgun at Luke. It also forces him to move slightly closer to the window.

"Don't even flinch," he says, smiling. "I got a call to make."

Guerro phones Uncle Paulie. "Hey, boss," he says. "I got 'em dead to rights. The guy in the smart suit who ain't so smart. No, haven't seen Heman or Fallon in the last few minutes. I think your boy got the drop on them. Heard gunfire in the hall downstairs, and Santiago ain't here either. I guess your boy is the last man standing."

Luke looks around the room, at the computers, at Suggs's unmade bed, just taking a general inventory, looking for a way out—or rather a way in, a weak spot, an opportunity to end this fucker's life.

"So," continues Guerro to Paulie, "you want me to off him? What? Okay? I'll put him on." Guerro hands the phone to Luke. "He wants to talk to you," he says, and then laughs. "Or rather say bye-bye."

"So, tough guy," says Uncle Paulie. "Still think you're hot shit now? I told you I'd get to you first."

Luke notices a beady red light on Guerro's torso. It is, he recognizes, a laser from the scope of a sniper's rifle.

"I can handle myself," says Luke. "But I don't know about the guys you hire. You sent the police, Russian mobsters, and a Mexican hit squad after me, and I'm still here. What's next? The Albanians? KGB? Israeli Special Forces? Or something more quaint, like a hit-and-run driver, a poisoner, the Boy Scouts?"

"I say the word and you're a dead man. Last chance. Want to make a deal? It'll make you rich."

"Fuck you."

Suddenly the window shatters into pieces, the result of a bullet that hits Guerro directly in the temple, blowing his head practically off his shoulders. A pulpy mess and brain fragments splatter the wall and moisten Suggs's shoulders, but Suggs is unfazed. A combat veteran, he's seen it all before. He even smiles.

"That one must've come from the Lord himself," says Suggs. "Out of nowhere. From heaven above. Thank you, Lord. Thank you."

Luke talks to Uncle Paulie who is listening on the cell phone.

"What was that?" asks Luke's panicky uncle. "What the fuck's going on there. Put Guerro on."

"Can't do that."

"Why the fuck not?"

"Because he just got his head blown off. And you're next."

Luke cautiously moves toward the window and sees Laura standing in the alcove of the locksmith store holding a freshly fired sniper's rifle.

CHAPTER FORTY-SEVEN

He gives Laura a thank-you salute from the window, but he really would have preferred to have done the job himself. In fact, he was counting on it. It was what he'd been living for.

But Guerro was just the triggerman, a hired hand, a lackey. It's really Uncle Paulie he wants.

He unties Suggs. "You okay?" he asks.

"They want you bad, Luke. Real bad. They were just about to start breaking my fingers. More out of boredom, I think. They expected you here a lot sooner."

"Sorry. Had to make a little detour."

"Let's get out of here."

"Where are the weapons I stashed? The backpacks?"

"In the closet."

"Get 'em. We're gonna need every last one of them."

Suggs opens a closet door and grabs a bulging duffel bag that is so full of weapons and ammo he nearly drops it on the floor. They strap on the equally heavy backpacks and walk down the stairs and over the bodies of Santiago and New York's Not-So-Finest. There's so much blood on the floor that when Suggs tries to step around it, he slips and falls.

"I told you to lay off the booze," jokes Luke.

"I see you haven't lost your touch," says Suggs, surveying the bloody carnage.

They dash across the street to Uncle Paulie's locksmith store, but when they enter, the greeting they receive surprises them: Laura aiming a rifle at them.

"Get on your knees. Both of you," she says. "Hands behind your heads."

"Thought you were on our side, Laura?" asks Luke.

"Yeah," says Suggs. "That was a nice shot."

"I am on your side," she says, "and that's why I can't let you do what you're planning to do. It's for your own good."

"And what is that?"

"Take the law into your own hands, killing Paulie, and who knows who else."

Laura stands behind the counter. Luke and Suggs have their backs to the door.

"Into the back room," says Laura with an authority he's never heard in her voice.

Suggs begins to move, but Luke says, "No way. You'll have to shoot us."

"Hey!" yells Suggs. "Speak for yourself." Suggs takes a step toward the rear of the store, but Luke gives him a look and Suggs stops.

"Now what are you going to do?" asks Luke.

"Wait until backup gets here," says Laura.

But then the door opens and a customer enters. Laura puts down the rifle behind the counter.

"We're closed," says Laura. "Sorry."

"It's the middle of the day," says the customer, a construction contractor dressed in dusty denim overalls.

"Inventory. Forgot to lock the door."

"Yeah. But I need a home alarm system for a customer. Nothing too fancy. Something easy to install. Can't you do me a solid? I'll pay cash."

"I'd like to help you," says Laura, "but we're right in the middle of things."

"I can help him," says Luke. He walks around the counter and grabs the rifle. "Alarm systems," he says with a friendly smile. "Okay. You've come to the right place. What's the size of the house, the square footage, and how much are you looking to spend?"

The contractor answers his questions, and Luke recommends the Frontpoint alarm system. "Rated number one," he says.

Meanwhile the rifle has been handed off to Suggs without the customer being the wiser, and Suggs carries it into the back room while Luke rings up the sale.

The satisfied customer exits and Luke and Suggs gently grab Laura and tie her to a chair.

"It's for your own good," says Luke mimicking her own words and gives her a gentle kiss on the mouth.

"You'll only end up in trouble," says Laura. "Or dead. Let us handle things."

"Are you really concerned about us?" asks Luke. "Or your career?"

This makes Laura livid and she twists and turns and stomps her feet trying to wiggle loose from the ropes that bind her.

"You bastard!" she says. "How could you even think that? *My career?* I just put my career on the line for you. Not to mention saving your life."

"I know, I know. But I've got to finish what I started, regardless of the consequences."

"Yeah, yeah," she scoffs. "A man's gotta do what a man's gotta do."

"Don't make me gag you."

Another customer walks in.

"Hey, pal," says Luke. "We're closed."

"Closed? I just locked myself out of my car and my kid's in the hospital and my cell phone died so I can't call my wife and—"

"I said, 'We're closed.' Piss off!" Luke utters these words with such force and an implied threat of violence that the guy exits without protest.

"Okay, Suggs. We're outta here."

He gives Laura a kiss good-bye and places the closed sign in the window. Then they pull the gates down and look at each other.

"So now what?" asks Suggs.

"We've got a building to blow up."

CHAPTER FORTY-EIGHT

But Luke takes a second look at Suggs and wonders if Suggs is up to it, if he would be more of a liability than an asset. Then he decides.

"On second thought, Suggs," says Luke, "I'm dropping you at the hospital. I don't think you're healthy enough for what amounts to a kind of *Mission Impossible*, especially after what you've just been through. Looks like they worked you over pretty good."

Suggs is insulted. "What do you mean? A broken rib, a few bruises, and one killer headache can't keep me down. You know that. But there's just one thing I need."

"Oh, yeah, what or who's that?"

"Jack."

"Jack who?"

"Jack Daniel's. My hands are shaking from withdrawal."

"I should've known."

Luke needs Suggs. What's ahead of him is something that will be well-nigh impossible to do alone. Moreover, if Luke doesn't make it, if he gets killed in the crossfire, he would like to know that maybe Suggs could finish what he started.

But Suggs needs medical care. He probably has a concussion. Luke will have to go it alone.

"I'm dropping you at Kings County Hospital."

"No way, Luke," says Suggs. "I could use the dough to start

over with too. You ain't the only one who hit bottom and is trying to climb out of a dark hole."

"Who said anything about money?"

"Knowing you, there's a payday. I'm sure you'd kill Crissy's killers for free and with extreme delight and pleasure, but my bet is that Mark Fister is paying you a pretty sum to whack Paulie, and if whiskey hasn't totally rotted my brain, I'll bet you got paid on the deuce—by Paulie to whack Fister and now by Fister to whack Paulie."

"Well," says Luke, "you sound clear headed enough to me. If you're game."

"Let's hit it. But what's my cut?"

"You'll be taken care of," says Luke, "but first let's get out of this alive and then money will be the least of our problems."

They walk to the Corvette through the throng exiting Brooklyn College. Suggs is a bit wobbly but seems to revive with every step in the breezy summer air.

Suggs feasts his eyes on the Corvette and exclaims, "Wow, Luke, where do you get these fine automobiles?"

"I borrow them. Get in," says Luke, slipping off his backpack and tossing the duffel bag into the space behind the two bucket seats. He sees trouble up the street. "Hurry."

But before Suggs can open the door, a bullet whizzes by his head, nearly cutting a second part in his nappy hair. Suggs ducks, hits the ground. His head on a swivel, he gauges the landscape, then dives into the Corvette through the open window. Luke is pleased to see that his reflexes are sharp and he can still move quickly despite his injuries.

"Ouch!" squeals Suggs, landing on the weapons pile.

"Are you hit?" asks Luke.

"Hell no. But give a guy a warning when you've got a cache of arms in your front seat. Almost got a silencer up my butt."

"Well, don't just sit there and complain," says Luke, starting the engine.

"Fire back!"

"At who?"

"Anybody who's shooting at us."

Luke springs a quick U-turn nearly causing a crash with another vehicle. It jostles Suggs, aggravating his injuries, but Suggs manages to select an assault rifle from the cache of weapons and loads it just in time to let fly a bee's nest of bullets at an approaching caravan of black cars—no doubt filled with Uncle Paulie's henchmen. A Hummer with six doors to a side and black-tinted windows leads the way. A Bronco and an Infiniti QX56 bring up the rear.

"This car," says Suggs, shaking his head, "has more bullet holes than the thirty-two Ford Bonnie and Clyde were killed in. And here comes a few more."

They both duck and what's left of the rear and front windshields shatter. Suggs picks the glass out of his hair and returns fire, but the bullets bounce off the Hummer like frozen peas.

"Bulletproof glass," says Suggs. "Bulletproof everything. You could have used some of that."

"Keep firing," says Luke. "I'm heading up Flatbush to Prospect Park where there should be quite a mess caused by yours truly. I'll lose them in it, and then we'll head to the warehouse."

"Hey, what about stopping off for my Jack Daniel's?"

"Are you serious? They'll drive by, mow us down, and then go out for cannoli and espresso."

"I've got an idea," says Suggs.

CHAPTER FORTY-NINE

"You've got an idea? I'm worried."

A blaze of gunfire knocks out the Corvette's taillights and ricochets off the bumper.

"Yeah. And it'll save our asses because this car won't hold up much longer."

"They're trying to shoot out the tires, and I can't lose them in this heavy traffic."

"We've got to get them out of those tanks and give chase to us on foot," says Suggs. "A liquor store would be the perfect place for it. And I know just the one. Drive, mother, drive. It's just up ahead."

"Why would a liquor store be the perfect place for it?"

"Erasmus Liquors has a secret room that connects to a dry cleaning store."

"A dry cleaning store?"

"You got something against dry cleaning?"

"No, nothing at all. Maybe I can get my suit sponge cleaned and pressed."

"I know the owner. He used to let me crash there sometimes. We duck in. Let them shoot up the place. They're probably smart enough to send someone around back, but we'll be in the dry cleaning store by that time and out another way before they blast us to hell. And you know what's even better?"

"What?"

"I can finally get that bottle of Jack. My nerves are as taut as guitar strings."

"Okay, Suggs. I got you into this, I'll get you out of it."

Suggs licks his lips and fires another enfilade at the caravan with a renewed sense of purpose and vigor. Luke observes this and notes that we all have our peculiar brand of motivation.

"Erasmus Liquors is just up ahead on the right-hand side. Big neon sign. Can't miss it."

"I see it," says Luke, cutting across three lanes of oncoming traffic and aiming the nose of the Corvette at the storefront. But before he can get there, a bullet blows out a rear tire and he loses command of the car. He struggles to regain control but sideswipes a passing vehicle and skids into the front end of a parked truck.

He shifts into reverse but the bumpers are locked like conjoined twins. He turns to the right and to the left, trying to jar the Corvette loose, but the bumpers do not release.

Shifting back and forth doesn't do much either to disengage the mangled metal but it does force the truck into a different position. It is now aligned diagonally to the curb, its rear end sticking out in traffic. Oncoming cars are unable to stop and a pile up ensues that forms a kind of fortuitous fortress of twisted steel and metal. The black caravan is immobilized half a block south.

Suggs grabs the duffel bag and opens it. Luke gathers the weapons scattered on the floor and adds them to the cache. Then they duck into Erasmus Liquors, bullets whizzing over their heads.

"I told you, Luke," says Suggs. "They want you bad."

"That isn't exactly breaking news."

Goro, the owner, a young Japanese with a nose piercing, thick Buddy Holly glasses, and a weirdly buzzed haircut that has a bluish tint, is standing outside the store smoking a thin cigarette and surveying the damage. He recognizes Suggs and giggles. "And they say Asians are bad drivers. Ha-ha-ha."

"Goro," says Suggs, "we need to use the secret room."

"Ah, secret room is not secret anymore."

Suggs grabs a bottle of Jack Daniel's from a shelf crowded with brands of bourbon, opens it, and drains about half of it in a few gulps. He smiles, smacks his lips, and suddenly his demeanor is brisk and confident as if he just drank a restorative elixir.

"I'm sorry to bring this on you," says Suggs, "but we've got no choice. Get behind the counter and stay there."

"I don't understand."

"You will in about five seconds."

He still doesn't get it until Suggs and Luke pick him up and dive behind the counter in time to avoid being cut in half by raking gunfire. As expected, Uncle Paulie's henchmen have abandoned their vehicles to chase them on foot. Machine gun fire rips through the store causing shelves filled with bottles of booze to burst like punctured water balloons. Goro whimpers and then, unable to hold back the tears, breaks out into hysterical sobs.

"Man up," says Suggs. "You got insurance."

This aligns Goro's perspective and his sobs are reduced to a low whimper.

Luke jumps up from behind the counter, takes aim with his 9mm, and drops the henchmen with one shot to the head.

"Let's go," says Suggs, "before the rest of the posse gets here."

He leads them down a corridor and turns right. They pass a utility shelf, a small bathroom, and arrive at a wall pasted with photos of nubile Japanese pop singers. Suggs is stunned.

"One problem," says Goro, lighting up another cigarette. "No more secret room. It was my father's gambling den but it got raided. Since it wasn't up to code, they made us seal it off."

"Oh, jeez," says Suggs. "Now we're really fucked."

"No we're not," says Luke.

CHAPTER FIFTY

Luke remains calm, contemplative. His training has taught him to make use of whatever materials are within reach.

Suggs is less optimistic. "Of all the gin joints—"

"And you, the man who knows every liquor store in the borough, had to pick this one."

"I really needed a drink," says Suggs, about to take a swig of Jack Daniel's, but Luke stops him. "You've had enough."

"We're sitting ducks," says Suggs.

Luke taps on the wall, listening to the sound it makes. "It's just cheap Sheetrock," he says. "Shouldn't be too hard to penetrate."

He inspects the utility shelf filled with a jumble of cleaning and aerosol products and finds what he needs—a can of WD-40 and rubber cement.

"Stand back," he says, and shoots a hole in the wall. He widens it by chipping out chunks with the end of a mop that was in the bathroom. Then he inserts the can of WD-40 and covers it with rubber cement. He can hear the crunching footsteps of Uncle Paulie's henchmen as they make their way across the floor filled with broken booze bottles.

One appears at the end of the corridor and Luke drops him with one shot. The others back off, at least for now, and then peer out from behind the doorjamb and resume taking potshots. Suggs fires and wings one, fires at the other, and scares them off, again for the time being.

"Goro," says Luke, "give me a match." Luke lights the rubber cement and the can of WD-40 goes up in flames. "Okay, everybody in the bathroom," says Luke. "This will get loud."

Suggs and Goro duck behind the sink. Luke stands in the doorway and takes aim. He fires and hits the can of WD-40 causing it to explode and expulse a mushroom cloud of gritty smoke and metal fragments.

Holding their shirts to their mouths, they slither through the hole, watching their backs. More henchmen arrive and fire at them, but they are safely behind the wall, a perfect redoubt to return fire.

Goro, meanwhile, looks around nostalgically, still smoking his cigarette.

"This was once a Prohibition speakeasy," he says. "Or so they tell us. But we made more money gambling here than we did selling booze. One time my father went up against this hotshot poker player and took him for not only fifteen grand but also the pink slip to his sixty-six Mustang. Cried like a baby. Funniest thing. You had to be there. And then another time—"

"Skip the history lesson, Goro," interrupts Luke, "and get us out of here."

Goro tries to open the door that separates the secret room from the dry cleaner next door, but it is locked tight, rusted shut, and corroded. He kicks it, but it doesn't budge. Luke inserts another clip into his Glock and blasts the lock until the door swings wide open.

He notices that Goro, who has gone from a nervous wreck to Buddhist calm, has wet his pants.

The store employees are in the midst of waiting on customers and look up in shocked surprise. Goro, Suggs, and Luke greet them with friendly smiles and shrug apologetically. Goro leads them to the rear exit that opens onto an alley. They move south. At the end of the alley is a street full of dumpsters and garbage containers. They turn right and are back on Flatbush Avenue, which is a mess of traffic congestion. They are behind the caravan, an ideal place for a sneak attack.

"I want that Hummer," says Luke. "Goro, you're free to go. No need your getting hurt. You've got nothing to do with this. But we'll need your cell phone. Hand it over. And cigarettes and lighter."

"Nope."

"What?"

"I'm not going anywhere until he pays me for the Jack Daniel's."

Somehow Suggs has managed to hang on to the duffel bag *and* the bottle of Jack.

"Only joking," says Goro with a laugh that tinkles. "Here's my cell and cigarettes. Bye-bye. I call insurance now. Get all new stuff."

Goro dashes down a side street, tripping on the laces of his vintage Keds High Tops. Suggs and Luke creep up on the Hummer. There is no sign of the other two cars. To their surprise the Hummer is occupied. Luke taps on the tinted glass. The driver rolls down the window and Luke knocks him practically clear across the cabin with one punch. Then he unlatches the door and they climb in—Suggs in the backseat, Luke in the front.

He's a big man, maybe six foot four, an olive-skinned Italian with a pasta paunch, a scarred lip, and follows a dress code right out of the book of mobster clichés—open shirt revealing a hairy chest and a gold chain, a chronometer 'don't-fuck-with-me' watch that must weigh more than a brick, and Ferragamo horsebit loafers.

"Drive, motherfucker," says Luke, pointing a gun at his head.

"In this mess?"

"It's a fucking Hummer, you pussy. Would you like me to blow your head off and do the driving myself?"

Something close to a demolition derby ensues. The Hummer bumps, grinds, flattens, rolls over, and bulldozes about a dozen cars in its path until it finds daylight. And just in time too. Police and fire department vehicles approach, sirens blaring.

"Step on it," says Luke.

"Where to?"

"Just drive, asshole."

CHAPTER FIFTY-ONE

They drive to DUMBO—Down Under the Manhattan Bridge Overpass—where they will blow up the warehouse, Uncle Paulie's warehouse. All part of the bargain Luke made with Mark Fister.

The waterfront warehouse is quite a slick operation. Fister has given him all the details as well as the floor plans. It houses Landslide Communications, a telemarketing company that is a front for Paulie's far more lucrative business. Staffed with cyber doctors and banks of computers, it functions as the nerve center of a worldwide illegal prescription drug distribution and manufacturing operation that has made him rich—so rich he can painlessly outspend the paltry sums allocated to the DEA to crack down on such enterprises and stay one or even ten steps ahead of them.

Federal law prohibits buying controlled substances such as narcotic pain relievers that include the wildly popular OxyContin and Vicodin, a long list of sedatives and antianxiety medications—Valium, Ativan, and Xanax—stimulants—phentermine, phendimetrazine, Adderall, Ritalin—and anabolic steroids—Winstrol, Equipoise—without a valid doctor's prescription. That's where Uncle Paulie comes in. No prescription, no problem. Just log onto one of his websites and order as much as you like. You don't even have to walk to your local drugstore. Orders are shipped promptly to anywhere in the world.

Of course, buying controlled substances in this manner is

illegal and punishable by imprisonment under federal law, but it is hardly a deterrent because hard-core addicts couldn't care a drift about the threat of doing time—very little time as it turns out. Sentences are light. Moreover, busts and successful prosecutions are extremely rare.

So there is very little risk for both parties. And getting the stuff isn't like smuggling in a boatload of heroin bricks. Although it is a felony to import drugs into the United States, supplies are readily available by mail not only from the United States, but also from Asia, Europe, the Caribbean, Costa Rica, New Delhi, Agra, and Bombay, among other places. The sources are endless. Paulie uses them all interchangeably to avoid a paper or cyber trail and changes websites, servers, and domains almost daily, a contribution made by Mark Fister. He also bribes pharmaceutical reps and executives for supplies and information.

But the real money is brokering illegal prescription drugs from places like Mexico to other cyber pharmacies and sources around the world, a part of Paulie's operation that augments his profits and puts him nearly on a par with some of the biggest Colombian drug cartels in the world.

Still, there is always the annoyance from prying authorities. Uncle Paulie's operation grew so big that it stood out from the smaller, less greedy rogue pharmacies and attracted the attention of not only the DEA but the IRS—for money laundering—and the FBI, one of whom discovered that Crissy was a treasure trove of evidence and a key witness, the event that led to her murder.

And now that murder will finally be avenged.

Luke's blood is up. He feels like blowing the driver's head off just because he's Uncle Paulie's lackey, but it's Uncle Paulie he wants to kill—and anybody who gets in his way—but he must be patient and calculating. Uncle Paulie's blood is up too, and he is a force to be reckoned with.

CHAPTER FIFTY-TWO

"What's your name?" asks Luke.

"Mother Goose," says the driver.

Luke backhands him, says, "Let's try this again."

"Lois Lane."

"Everybody's a tough guy." Luke takes out his MetroCard, waves it in front of his face.

"Want me to drop you at the nearest subway?"

Luke slashes an X into the skin on his hairy right forearm. "Next time, I go for your throat."

"Tony. My name's Tony."

"Like I'm gonna believe you. Take out your wallet." Tony takes out his wallet with defiant slowness. "Well, what do you know, your name really is Mother Goose, Anthony. Okay, listen up because this time I'm only going to ask you once. Tell me about the security at the warehouse—personnel, CCTVs, number of armed guards, that kind of thing."

"It's like Fort Knox. You'll never get through."

Luke flips the Glock over and grabs it by the stock. He smacks Tony's knuckles with the butt of the gun and says, "There are twenty-six bones in your hand. Next I start breaking them two at a time."

"You don't know who you're fucking with, do you?"

This sends Luke into a rage and he pistol-whips Tony so severely, Suggs must restrain him before they careen into a telephone pole.

Bloodied and bruised, Tony is a bit more submissive and begrudgingly describes the security detail at the warehouse.

"Piece of cake," says Luke. "You're going to drive us right in."

It's getting dark and up ahead are the red brake lights of cars that blink on and off like winking eyes. They reach an underpass where it is shadowy and cavernous and veer onto streets that are strewn with leaves and trash until they reach a building with a canopied limestone front that takes up almost the entire block and rises high above the on ramp to the Manhattan Bridge.

"So, Tony," says Luke, "what are the working hours here? Must be quitting time soon."

Tony sneers. "Quitting time. It's a twenty-four-seven operation, you dumb shit."

Luke threatens another lashing with the butt of the Glock, but Suggs holds his arm back.

"You didn't count on that, did you?" asks Tony snidely. "They're all civilian workers, not mobsters, except for a few."

"Doesn't matter," says Suggs. "Every war has collateral damage."

CHAPTER FIFTY-THREE

"This is how we're going to do this," says Luke, pressing the barrel to Tony's temple. "You're going to drive us into the garage, check in with security, wish them a nice night, and take us on a little tour of the place. We're your guests. You fuck up and you're dead. It's that simple. Got it?"

Tony doesn't answer. Luke cocks the gun. "Okay," says Luke, "we'll do it your way. I'll blow your brains out, and we'll go it alone."

"Yeah, yeah," says Tony, nodding his head in reluctant agreement.

"Now drive. Slow."

Tony drives the Hummer around the block and down a ramp to a security gate where a guard is on duty. The guard recognizes the Hummer, waves, and walks up to the driver's side window.

"How you doin'?" asks the guard who peers into the car and sees Luke and Suggs but doesn't seem the least bit curious about their presence. In fact, he greets them with a friendly nod. If they're friends of Tony's, then they're friends of his.

"All right," says Tony. "You?"

"Busy night as usual." He gives the signal and the gates open into a four-story garage with circular cement ramps. Two exiting trucks pass them. Nearly every space is filled. Tony parks in a reserved spot and they get out.

"Now hand over your piece," says Suggs, taking a swig from the bottle of Jack. Tony does as he is told and leads them into the building.

"Do you want the grand tour," asks Tony sarcastically, "or the discounted version?"

"We're going to have a little dance when this is over," says Luke, his face reddening with anger, his eyes alight with the threat of violence.

Tony, though, is unafraid. "Can't wait," he says hardly raising his voice.

Suggs takes the last sip from the bottle of Jack. "May I borrow that?" asks Luke with snide politeness. Suggs is puzzled but hands it over. Luke smashes the bottle over Tony's head.

"That's just for starters," says Luke.

But he's disappointed with the results. Tony must have a head like sedimentary rock because he seems hardly more than dazed, and only momentarily, and his glare at Luke remains resolutely sharp and venomous, a flinty "I can't wait for the chance to get a piece of you."

They walk down a corridor with clean floors and cinderblock walls painted a depressing green, the kind you see in public high schools.

"Take us to the mainframe," says Luke.

Tony opens a door and says, "After you, gentlemen."

"I know the floor plan," says Luke. "Take us there on the restricted-access elevator."

"Whatever you say," says Tony obligingly, leading them down another corridor, but this one is ill lit and shadowy with labeled boxes piled in neat stacks.

He tells Tony to wave at the CCTV cameras whenever they pass one to signal to the security guards watching that nothing is amiss, that these men he is with are friends, allies, business associates, customers, whatever, surely no one that means to do him or them any harm.

They board the restricted-access elevator that takes them to the subbasement. Panels of electrical boxes line the walls, a neat configuration of rectangles and squares that look fairly new, given the building itself was probably built almost a hundred years ago when it was used as a manufacturing plant to produce machinery, paper goods, and things like Brillo Pads.

Uncle Paulie must have renovated the entire building to his specifications—similar but on a much grander scale than the artists who, after the neighborhood's industrial heyday, infiltrated the area in the 1970s because of its cheap rents and spacious well-lit rooms and high ceilings, ideal for converting them into lofts, studios, and galleries.

"Suggs, open the duffel bag," says Luke, "and give me one of those limpet mines."

"Limpet mines?" says Suggs. "You've got limpet mines in here?"

"Among other explosives."

"Jeez! Had I known! We could've all been blown to hell."

The series of electrical boxes are locked, but easily pried open. The largest one holds the data processing system, otherwise known as a mainframe. It is used for bulk data, process control, compiling industry and consumer demographics and statistics, enterprise resource planning, and, most importantly, financial transactions. In other words, all the important stuff that makes this moneymaking operation tick like a Swiss watch.

Luke examines the network of workstations and servers, a proprietary operating system that is based on Linux. It's an extremely cost-effective tool for e-commerce hosting and development. He's impressed. Uncle Paulie—or the company he hired—spared no expense acquiring cutting-edge technology.

But all this doesn't really matter. It's just Luke ruminating, enjoying the mental stimulation, because he's going to blow it all to hell anyway. Such lovely hardware, so elegant in its construction and deployment. What a pity.

CHAPTER FIFTY-FOUR

Luke attaches the limpet mine to the mainframe and sets the timer. Then he moves to another electrical utility storage unit that houses the setup for the CCTVs and disconnects a series of wires, including BNC connectors, routers, and Cat5 cables, and, lastly, attaches another limpet mine to the side of the box.

One more to go. There's got to be a backup generator somewhere. He surveys the large room, and spots it in the corner. Another limpet mine is attached, its timer set, and then they move on to the shipping and receiving department upstairs where more boxes are stacked from floor to ceiling, their contents clearly labeled—OxyContin, Vicodin, Alprazolam, Adderall. An addict's wet dream. Luke is so stunned by the size and magnitude of the operation that he is filled with a kind of admiration for his uncle.

The scale of the interior reminds him of an airplane hangar. Forklifts move pallets with boxes and containers down long corridors to freight elevators where they are off-loaded and taken to another large room. Diligent workers sit behind computers entering data; others walk around in white lab coats with clipboards. Some are equipped with headsets and engage in multilingual conversations. The room has the bustle and buzz of a major-city newsroom on steroids.

"This place will go up like wildfire," says Luke, reaching into the duffel bag. He strategically places plastic explosives that are no larger than a paperback book in each corner of the room.

No one seems to notice, no one seems to mind. Tony's intimidating presence keeps their noses to the grindstone. They suddenly look busier, less casual, and far more diligent, even a little nervous. Obviously, they fear this man.

Rooms connected with this one form a kind of grid, but Luke is not interested in them. He is only interested in one room, an office on the top floor, the one that is occupied by Uncle Paulie's son, Paulie Jr., Luke's drug-addled ex-con cousin whom he has not seen in over a decade.

Luke is surprised, though, that Tony has not made a move yet, nothing at all to stop what will amount to a giant conflagration on the edge of the East River and the destruction of a multimillion-dollar enterprise. So he's wary, very wary of him.

Tony is at least four inches taller and must outweigh him by sixty pounds, but he also exudes a chilly confidence that bespeaks a man who is intelligent and cunning, qualities that are always more dangerous than brutish strength. Luke discreetly sticks the muzzle of the Glock in his back to remind him that he is one hair trigger away from getting his guts blown out.

"Let's go pay Paulie Jr. a visit," says Luke.

"Whatever you say," says Tony, who leads them to the elevator.

"No, not the elevator," says Luke. "The stairs."

They climb six flights, open a heavy, blue fire door, and step into a plush corridor. The premises are decidedly more luxurious here. Paintings line the walls. A lounge with club chairs and a liquor trolley occupy a softly lit area with a curtained booth. They walk down another corridor with a suite of offices, most of them with their doors open and unoccupied, until they come to a corner office outside of which stand two burly men in ill-fitting black suits holding walkie-talkies.

They greet Tony pleasantly and nod to Luke and Suggs.

"Here to see the boss?" asks the larger man whose long arms and simian distribution of weight tilts him forward.

"That's right," says Tony.

"Boss is, ahem, busy," says the guard with a wink.

"We need to see him," says Luke.

The guard does not like Luke's tone and looks at Tony for guidance.

Luke prods Tony with the Glock, as if to say, "You better follow my direction or else."

"Yeah," says Tony. "We need to see him. It's all right."

"Well, no, not really," says the guard delicately, trying not to sound insubordinate.

"Fuck it," says Luke who launches into fighting mode, hitting one guard with a right cross and then the other with a blow to the head using the butt of the Glock. He spins around and hits Tony with a sidekick that sends him reeling backward into the loving arms of Suggs who lets loose with a series of punches to his kidneys and then a kick behind his knee that collapses him like a card table.

"I've been wanting to hit this arrogant bastard since we met him," says Suggs. "Ever take an instant dislike to somebody?"

"Everybody stay where you are," says Luke, brandishing the Glock.

"Suggs, take over."

Suggs rummages through the duffel bag and pulls out an AR-15, a lightweight magazine-fed 5.56mm semiautomatic rifle, while Luke unceremoniously kicks open the door where they find a blond secretary with thin-rimmed black eyeglasses and full red lips bent over the desk, her plump breasts spilling out of her bra, her skirt flipped over her back as Paulie Jr. penetrates her from behind, his pants around his ankles, his shirttails flapping like laundry on a clothesline.

On the desk amidst a pile of paperwork is a bottle of Cristal, two glasses, both empty, and broken lines of coke on a mirror.

"Oh, fuck me," says the girl, "fuck me harder, *harder*."

Paulie obliges, grabbing a handful of her hair and pulling her deeper into his thrusting pelvis.

"What a big cock," she coos. "I love your big cock. Yeah, yeah. Pound me, baby, pound me."

They are so engaged in coitus that they don't seem to notice the intrusion.

"Hey, cousin," says Luke. "Sorry to interrupt."

"What the fuck?" says Paulie Jr., startled. He looks like a fatter version of his father and is as slovenly as his father is fussy about his appearance. He reflexively reaches for a gun in his desk drawer, but Luke fires a warning shot that shatters the bottle of Cristal. The girl screams and Paulie backs away from the desk drawer that secretes the gun.

"Is that you? *Luke?*"

"It's me," says Luke.

"You might knock next time or make an appointment."

"I'm through making appointments with you and your dirt-bag family."

"Do you know who—" Paulie starts to say before Luke interrupts him.

"Yeah, yeah," says Luke, "we know who we're fucking with. We're fucking with you, cousin. We're fucking with Tony here. We're fucking with your two worthless bodyguards and we're fucking with your father and we're going to burn down this whole fucking operation. Does that explain it?"

Paulie pats the girl on her naked butt and tells her to get lost. She hobbles to the door half undressed, one high heel on her foot, the other in her hand, and her strawberry Pop Tart lips in a pout.

"You really think you're going to get out of here alive?" asks

Paulie. He snickers, shakes his head. "You must be brain damaged, Soldier Boy."

Paulie Jr., while pulling up his pants, surreptitiously removes a knife from his sock.

"Just wait," says Luke looking at his watch.

A tense moment transpires before the first explosion rocks the building.

"What the fuck was that?" asks Paulie Jr.

"The beginning of the end," says Luke.

CHAPTER FIFTY-FIVE

Paulie Jr. throws the knife that he removed from his sock and nearly hits Luke in the neck. That's when Tony makes his move. He goes straight for Luke, hitting Luke's trigger finger with a well-placed slap kick that sends the Glock skidding across the floor. Luke knew it all along. Tony's got skills. Martial arts skills. But Luke's got martial skills and a suit, a suit with potent powers, a suit that does not inhibit but enhances his speed and efficiency, a suit whose texture becomes more, not less, durable with every militant encounter. It is a suit tailored for fighting, as reticulated as a snake's skin.

But Luke is pleased. Finally, a worthy opponent. They square off, throwing roundhouse kicks and twisting punches, most of them blocked, even fewer landing with any great force, proving that, at least so far, they are evenly matched.

Luke tries a sweep, but Tony, who appears to be something of a lummox, possesses a surprising amount of feline quickness and jumps up, avoiding the strike that would have taken the feet out from under him.

Luke is quick to launch another volley of straight punches culminating in a jump kick that hits Tony square in the chest, sending him reeling backward into the space between two bookshelves. Tony uses the shelves to lift himself up and propel himself forward with both feet extended so that they connect with Luke who stumbles and crashes into a glass coffee table, shattering it.

With facial cuts and scrapes, and a cracked rib, Luke clambers to his feet, once again a standing target for a series of snap kicks that Tony executes with impressive precision and agility. Luke is able to block them by lowering his elbow, but they keep on coming with simultaneous punches.

Luke dodges them, covers his head with his arms, but they are delivered with such strength and speed that a few of them land with damaging force. He responds, but not with enough deterrent blows to stop Tony's momentum. Luke must resort to a different style of fighting. He must get in close to diminish Tony's long reach, his clear advantage.

But is there time? Luke is keenly aware that the timers have been set on the explosives to detonate in sequence, each blast more powerful than the previous one. If he doesn't finish off Tony soon, they'll all be blown to hell.

Luke blocks one of Tony's punches and spins into him with a bent elbow that cracks Tony's nose as if it was hit with a crowbar. He follows up with a reverse punch and then a concatenation of straight leads, punches that are thrown with an extended arm in swift, direct movements that are similar to fencing thrusts.

Then he delivers what he thinks will be the coup de grâce — a series of tightly executed roundhouse punches thrown straight from the shoulder with the full force of his body behind them, a kinetic chain that has felled stronger opponents.

Tony is muddled, befogged, but not conclusively defeated. He can take a punch, more than a punch. He can take Luke's best traditional martial arts techniques. It is time, Luke decides, for a lethal strike, but he must lure him in closer.

He lets Tony flail away in an attempt to tire him, to destroy his rhythm, and it works. Tony resorts to swinging and hooking, a primitive, less precise mode of fighting. His form becomes sloppy, degenerating into robotic, mechanized attacks that Luke easily evades. Frustrated and angry, Tony's emotions rise to the surface. He has lost his calm, and in one-on-one combat, that could be fatal.

Luke, on the other hand, remains pliable, losing all self-consciousness. He becomes more mind than body, a serene presence in the center of the storm. With a symphony of movements that are all muscle memory, he creates a power chain, body and mind acting in harmony, and leaves his feet to deliver a corkscrew kick in midair that smashes Tony in the throat.

But a more imminent danger lurks in his peripheral vision—Paulie Jr. aiming a gun at him. Luke leaps forward, avoiding a bullet in the back, and delivers the blow that will, if not kill, then seriously disable Tony—a finger jab to his eye that penetrates deep into his skull to the brain mass that is as pulpy as a marshmallow Peep.

Gunfire roars outside and Suggs enters just in time to drop Paulie Jr. but Luke yells, "Don't! We need him!"

"Okay, but lose the gun," says Suggs.

"Fuck you. You heard what he said," says Paulie Jr., still defiantly pointing the gun at Luke. "You need me."

"Yeah, but we don't need you that much."

To prove his point Suggs rakes the office with gunfire, including the mahogany desk, which fills the air with shards of glass and wood. Paulie Jr. jumps, twitches, backs away. He lets go of the gun and it drops to the floor.

"That's a good boy," says Suggs.

Another explosion jars the floor beneath them. Two more follow in quick succession.

"You're going to get us out of here," says Luke.

"Like hell I will," says Paulie Jr.

Luke hits him with a right cross, bloodying his lip, and he falls over the desk chair. "I won't ask you again. I need you, yeah, because it'll make my life easier, but if you end up like your two dead bodyguards that Suggs just offed, I wouldn't give a fuck."

Paulie Jr. is suddenly more compliant, but when they move into the hall, stepping over the bullet-ridden bodyguards, they are greeted with clouds of acrid smoke surging up from the floors below.

"You fucked us both," says Paulie Jr. "Shouldn't you have blown up the place *after* we were out of here, dumb ass?"

Luke employs a curved blow to Paulie Jr.'s head and throws a high kick that hits him in the jaw. An instep kick collapses him, whereupon Luke rips down his pants. He removes a small tubular explosive from his backpack and inserts it in Paulie's anus like a suppository.

"How's that feel?" asks Luke. "Just like you were back in prison. Pull up your pants and do what I say."

"Hope he doesn't have too many hemorrhoids," quips Suggs. "That's gotta hurt."

"If we're not out of here in five minutes," says Luke, "you're gonna suffer a shitty death. Who's the dumb ass now?"

"All right, all right," says Paulie Jr., pulling up his pants. "This way."

CHAPTER FIFTY-SEVEN

They reach an emergency exit in less than thirty seconds.

"Amazing how cooperative some people are with an explosive stuck up their butt," observes Luke.

Four guards confront them, but Suggs, liking the efficiency of his AR-15, mows them down in short order and lets it rip with extra zeal as well as ammo. Suggs has risen to the occasion. He's like a new man—purposeful, alert, and sober as an eye surgeon. He's like the Suggs he knew, the one decorated for valor in Afghanistan, the Suggs before PTSD got the better of him, and his life fell apart in a way not much different from Luke's.

They are safely outside on the street as the last explosive is detonated, the most powerful of them all. Debris rains down like a hailstorm and fireballs shoot out of the top-floor windows like bursting Roman candles.

"My, my," says Suggs, "isn't that pretty?"

Paulie Jr. looks up in mystified horror. "You don't know what you've done," he says. "You think my father is the only one you've fucked. They'll hunt you down, both of you, and make you suffer."

"I'm shaking in my boots I'm so scared," says Luke, holding out his hand and pretending to tremble. "Now shut the fuck up and take us to your car."

"My car, shithead, is in the garage you just blew up."

"Oh, yeah," replies Luke, "I forgot about that. It was a very nice car, wasn't it? One your daddy bought you? Too, too bad.

Looks like we'll just have to find an alternative means of transportation. Suggs, see anything you fancy?"

Suggs surveys the line of parked cars that stretches around the block and focuses on a black Mercedes S500 coupe, a gunmetal gray SUV, and a Mazda CX9.

"I think something sporty yet luxurious," he says. "How about the Benz?"

But Luke overrules him. "I think I can get into that old Toyota and hot-wire it a lot easier than those fancy new cars with all the bells and whistles."

Luke, true to his word, is behind the wheel in ten seconds and tickling two wires that he dislodged from underneath the ignition. The car starts up with a less than impressive purr, but it has a full tank of gas and a messy but roomy backseat into which Suggs pushes Paulie Jr.

"Better get that bomb out of his ass," says Suggs, "or we're all likely to go up in smoke."

"Good idea," says Luke. "But tie his hands and shoot him if he resists or misbehaves in any way."

"Where we going?" asks Paulie Jr.

"We're going to pay your father a visit."

CHAPTER FIFTY-EIGHT

The streets in DUMBO are slick and wet, almost as if it has rained, but it hasn't. A thin film of grit and grease reflects the streetlights in circular pools that seem to bore into the ground.

The Toyota Camry wends its way through the potholed lanes on the Belt Parkway to the lower level of the Verrazano, a double-decked suspension bridge that connects Brooklyn to Staten Island, its necklace lighting fully aglow now that the sun has set.

Luke calls his uncle. "Did you hear?" he asks.

"Of course I heard!" roars Uncle Paulie, on the verge of apoplexy.

"I think there was a fire in your DUMBO warehouse," says Luke. "I hope it doesn't set your...your what is it? Oh, yeah, your telemarketing business too far behind."

"You son of a bitch. You'll pay for this. With your life."

"Really?"

"Really. No matter where you go, no matter where you hide, I'll find you."

"Well, you won't have to look too hard. I'm right here. On the Verrazano taking in the sights. Nice night. Great view. You can see everything. Manhattan all lit up, dingy Jersey City, the garbage scows in the harbor, Pier 17 at the Seaport—"

"You're gutsy, kid," says Paulie. "I'll give you that, but it won't save you, no, it won't, not by a long shot."

"I'm coming for you."

"Do you think I'm gonna let you walk right in the front door?"

"Indeed, I do," says Luke confidently, "especially with a little persuasion."

"Cut the bullshit. I've got a deal for you and this time you better listen."

"No, I've got a deal for *you*," snaps Luke. "So *you* better listen."

"Guess who's keeping me company?" asks Uncle Paulie.

"Mayor Bloomberg."

"Someone you care for," says Uncle Paulie, "someone you would not like to see harmed."

At first Luke thinks it might be his father, but Paulie and his father haven't spoken in years. They're not exactly close. In fact, he doesn't even know where his father is. No one else makes the list, but when he thinks about it a little longer he has a sinking feeling and hopes his gut is wrong.

"I'm stumped," he says.

"Laura," says Uncle Paulie in a kind of juicy whisper.

Luke is stunned. He certainly didn't see this coming. He feels wounded, a testament to how much he cares for Laura, which comes as a surprise, but he tries not to reveal it. He keeps his voice steady, unemotional, feigning disinterest.

"Did you hear me? I said, 'Laura.'"

Pitiful how many people are left in the world that he truly cares about, enough to count on one hand with plenty of fingers left over. It brings home to him the depths to which his life has deteriorated, but kidnapping a federal agent is just stupid. And to do her harm would be even more self-destructive. Uncle Paulie must be desperate to try a stunt like this. Although with the money he has, he can buy off just about anybody.

"Yeah, Laura," repeats Uncle Paulie, his tone now barbed

and aggressive. "Lovely Laura, your new true love. She's tied up and if you fuck with me or my family, I'll kill her just like we killed Crissy."

Furious, Luke takes it out on Paulie Jr., throttling him while driving the car. His control is dubious and they nearly veer into another motorist.

"Luke!" yells Suggs. "I'll do the beating. You do the driving. Deal?"

But Luke doesn't hear him. A thought occurs to him. Maybe his uncle doesn't know her real identity.

"She's a federal agent," says Luke. "Do you know that?"

"Of course I do," says Uncle Paulie. "Think I'm stupid?"

"I do."

"Not as stupid as you."

"So what's this deal you keep talking about?"

"It's changed a little," says his uncle with brash confidence; he obviously thinks he's in the driver's seat. "But here it is. You piss off and I'll let Laura go."

"What makes you think I care about a Fed?"

"I know about your little romance with her."

"She's a great piece of ass," says Luke, "but she's not going to get in my way." Luke is bluffing and Uncle Paulie knows it.

"You're full of shit, kid."

"Try me."

"I just might. In fact—"

Luke can hear background noises, the sound of Laura being slapped around, the sound of her muffled screams, whimpering, and sobs.

"Stop it!" It pains him more than he can bear. He's revealed his hand.

"Fuck you," says Uncle Paulie and continues to work Laura over.

"I said stop it or you'll hear a lot worse."

"What?"

"Yeah, you've got Laura and I've got, guess who? And it ain't Mayor Bloomberg. It's your beloved son, the oldest one, the only one who isn't dead or in jail, Paulie Jr., your namesake, and he's right here with me. Up until a few minutes ago he had a plastic explosive jammed up his ass to keep him quiet. Don't make me insert it again."

Luke tells Paulie Jr. to come closer; he wants to tell him something. When Paulie Jr. leans across the seat, Luke cuts him with the MetroCard, eliciting a yelp that travels across the cell lines and can be easily heard by his father.

"You harm one hair on his head and I'll—"

"You'll what? Smack Laura around? I told you I don't care. But the Feds do. You'll bring more heat on you than you've ever had before."

"So you want to make an exchange? Is that it?"

"Exchange? Fuck off. I told you. I don't give a damn about her. I want you. You had Crissy killed, and I'm going to get even—even if I have to come back from the dead to do it."

"You wouldn't—you wouldn't hurt him," says Uncle Paulie. "He's blood."

Luke laughs. "Blood? So was Crissy. That didn't stop *you*."

"She wasn't blood. And she was going to turn state's evidence. She was a rat."

"She was an innocent bystander who got caught up in your drug trafficking greed," says Luke. "And when the FBI and the DEA got onto you through her, she had to be eliminated. Or so you thought. No finesse. You never had any finesse. You could've gone a different way. She didn't have to die."

"Wrong place, wrong time."

"I'm going to kill you and kill you slowly. I'm going to enjoy making you suffer. Paulie Jr. too, among others. How's *your* wife?"

"Paulie Jr. had nothing to do with Crissy's death. You know that. You know that, don't you?"

Luke can hear the panic in Uncle Paulie's voice, the pathetic pleading, and knows that he's got him right where he wants him. Well, almost.

CHAPTER FIFTY-NINE

"See you soon," says Luke, snapping his cell phone shut.

Once past the tollbooth, Luke drives faster, but carefully, not wanting to attract the police. He stays more or less within the speed limit, though it takes an act of will, for he wants to get to Laura as fast as he can; the urge to floor it is almost irresistible. Uncle Paulie's brutality knows no bounds.

Gripping the steering wheel tighter, his knuckles turn white and his face glistens with blood and sweat like a wet canvas. He can't let Laura down.

That would be too much for his fragile psyche to bear—losing Crissy and then Laura. He could not live with the guilt, no, he must penetrate Uncle Paulie's compound and he knows just how to do it, though it won't be easy, not even with Paulie Jr. as bait.

He gets off at the Slosson Avenue Exit. Slosson Avenue becomes Todt Hill Road. He makes a left on Willow Pond Road and then another left onto Benedict Road that is lined with stately houses, verdant escarpments, flowing fountains surrounded by flower gardens, and mansions with circular driveways set back from tree-lined streets.

"Want to see John Gotti's old house? Or where they filmed the *Godfather*?"

"Skip the sightseeing," says Suggs. "And tell us how we're going to pull this off."

"I've got an idea. Look in the duffel bag," says Luke, "and see if we have any more limpet mines."

"Only one left."

"That's all we'll need."

Luke pulls over to the curb, a block away from Uncle Paulie's house, and parks in the darkest spot he can find.

"Okay," says Luke, "out of the car."

Paulie Jr. pushes the seat forward with his shoulder, about to climb out, but Luke hits him in the face with his elbow, jarring him back into submission.

"Not you," says Luke. "Lie down back there and don't make a sound. Suggs, tie him up and stuff a sock in his mouth. And, just for added insurance, insert that tubular explosive in his ass."

"I feel like a proctologist."

Paulie Jr. is too exhausted to protest. He groans but does not struggle as Suggs plugs his anus and ties him up. Meanwhile, Luke crawls under the car and attaches the limpet mine to the chassis. He sets the timer to go off in exactly one hour and ten minutes. Then he locks the door of the car with Paulie Jr. in it, and asks Suggs to hand him an assault rifle from the duffel bag.

"Let's go," says Luke. "Got extra ammo?"

"Extra ammo for what?"

"Just in case."

"Just in case of what?" asks Suggs nervously.

"In case they do something stupid."

"Wait a minute. We're walking straight up to the front gate?"

"Yeah. They won't fire on us. They know we have Paulie Jr. They'll let us walk right in."

"Armed with assault rifles? Like hell they will," says Suggs, stopping in his tracks. "You need to rethink this."

"Suggs, we've only got an hour before Paulie Jr.'s ass is blown into orbit, so don't waste my time, okay? I've got it figured out."

"Okay, you're the boss," says Suggs, shrugging his shoulders.

But as soon as they approach the security gate they are fired on—fired on with guns equipped with silencers. They're just warning shots fired over their heads. The bullets whizz by and the sound they make is no louder than a volley of tennis balls. No need to wake the neighborhood. And no need to alert the police.

"I feel like we're making Pickett's Charge," says Suggs. "This is suicide."

Taking no risks—what if one of these mooks is a bad shot?—they dive into the hedges in front of the house and then scramble for safety, ducking behind a row of trees.

Another shot is fired, this one zips by a little too close for comfort.

"What the fuck?" yells Luke, taking out his cell phone. "Is he nuts?"

"So much for Paulie Jr. as bait," says Suggs observantly. "What if there's no love lost between father and son?"

"You know the Italians and family. Bad blood, maybe, but it's still blood. Must've been a miss communication."

"Dumb Dago Wops," says Suggs, then looks at Luke. "Oh, sorry. Forgot. You're half Wop."

Luke phones Uncle Paulie. "What the fuck are you doing? I've got a gun to your kid's head. Even better, if you don't let Laura go, I've got a timed explosive in him."

"Let him go," says Uncle Paulie, "and I'll let Laura live and maybe you too."

"Fuck with me, you fuck with your life—and your son's," warns Luke.

"In that case, come right in."

Luke hesitates. Trying to get inside of his uncle's thought process is no easy task. Surely he must be setting a trap. It's not like him to give up ground that easily. But he has no choice. Or does he? Luke must give it a try.

Suddenly floodlights glaringly illuminate the darkness. The gates open slowly, ominously, like the gaping maw of death. Luke has a bad feeling. Uncle Paulie's henchmen are armed, rifles at the ready, red laser points darting in the darkness, trying to get a bead on him.

"What'll we do?" asks Suggs.

"Good question."

CHAPTER SIXTY

A black cat with white spots prowls the pebbled path and eyes them without concern as if they're just another feature of the densely wooded landscape. Luke watches it, admiring its stealth, its fearlessness, its ease and freedom. It doesn't know whether they are friend or foe, but it still inches closer, warily but closer, sniffing and purring, its whiskers wiggling.

"Cool little fellah," says Suggs. "But you better beat it before all hell breaks loose."

The gates remain open, but hardly welcoming. Luke changes his mind. He's not going in. At least not that way. He remembers the ridgeline behind the house, the cover provided by the tall trees, the dense woods, the swimming pool, and the two dumpsters used by the construction crew remodeling the posterior part of the house. It would be a perfect point of access, an entrance he could use unseen—if he can get by the sensors and webcams.

"Suggs," says Luke, "grab the cat and follow me."

"What for?"

"Just grab him."

Suggs tries to grab the cat, but it bolts.

"Get 'im!" says Luke. "Must I do everything?" He lunges at the stray, but it also eludes his grasp.

Suggs gives chase, then trips headlong into a bramble bush, kicking up dust and dirt, and nearly firing off a round of his AK-15.

"Jeez, Suggs!" bellows Luke. "You'll kill us before they do."

Suggs is as mad as he is embarrassed.

Determined to catch the damn critter, he runs in hot pursuit, ducking under low-hanging tree limbs, but for all of his good intentions, he is upended by a sprinkler and falls flatly, his arms and legs in the position of a snow angel.

"I've never had to work so hard for pussy."

Luke takes a less aggressive approach and kneels down under the leafy canopy of an oak tree and coos softly. Soon the cat is coaxed out of his hiding place, a line of shrubs with dense flora, and Luke grabs it. He pets it and says, "You're one cool cat, aren't you? You must have a good life up here because you don't seem afraid or aware of the dangerous types who are your neighbors."

Luke gives it a nickname. He simply calls the cat, "Cool."

"Okay," he says, holding the cat like a football, "follow me, Suggs."

They use the tall wrought iron gate to guide them to the cement retaining wall that protectively circles the property until they enter another dense area of woodlands in the rear of the house. Then they climb up to the ridgeline that allows them to look down on the sprawling house.

The cat—or Cool—has a consistent temperament. He doesn't try to scamper away, but rather enjoys the attention and hangs onto Luke as if he's found a new friend, purring contently, rubbing his snout affectionately against Luke's arm.

"I'm exhausted," says Luke, stroking the fur of his new comrade. Must be the Hodgkin's, he thinks, but he must not relent.

"And I'm thirsty," says Suggs. "What I wouldn't give for a Jack and Coke on ice."

"First thing we do if we survive this is get you into rehab. You've got to stop drinking."

"Don't knock my hobbies."

"We'll see. Now listen up. I set the timer on the Toyota for three a.m." explains Luke. "That should give us enough time to launch what will be our main offensive. In and out. Quick. Fingers crossed."

"Main offensive?" asks Suggs. "You're really in military mode."

"I've been planning this for a long time," says Luke, his tone somber and a bit wistful as if the day of reckoning that he has longed for has come too soon, ending a journey he would like to continue.

Luke reviews with Suggs the details of the property, the layout of the house, points of entry, and the security system, but Suggs is already fast asleep, spread eagled with his back against an elm tree.

Luke removes the AR-15 from his grasp and safely lays it down beside him. Then he sprawls out, using his backpack as a pillow, and follows Suggs into a deep slumber, but it doesn't last long.

They both awaken after what amounts to a five-minute catnap to the sound of voices, a patrol of security guards with attack dogs on leashes who are reconnoitering the rear of the house. Movements are detected by sensors that set off another brash blast of bright floodlights. The dogs bark, howl, and sniff the air.

Luke expects as much. He also knows that the closer to the house the more sophisticated—and possibly deadly—the security system will be. He remembers Uncle Paulie boastfully telling him about the special security features he installed in the rear of the house, a lethal surprise for anybody who gets past the first line of defense. With all the enemies Uncle Paulie has accumulated over the years, they are essential. He's had more attempts on his life than a South American dictator.

The state-of-the-art security systems, armed guards, attack dogs, and secluded nature of the property are, thinks Luke, paradoxically its greatest weakness. It will be easy to create private chaos that will enable him to sneak into the house undetected, wreak havoc, and rescue Laura before the police, if things get noisy, can even man their squad cars. But it's not a grave concern. Uncle Paulie has probably warned them off already. He's bribed every cop, especially the ones in the local Staten Island precincts, from here to south Jersey, to stay out of his way.

Or so Luke hopes.

"Suggs, here's the plan. Go around front and hide in the hedges until you hear the confusion I'm going to create. Most of the security guards will leave their posts when I attack from the rear. They don't know about you. When that happens, take out the guard in the gatehouse—and anybody else who gets in your way—and disable the webcams, motion sensors, and any other surveillance devices you can find. Then enter the house and rip apart the electrical box in the basement. That'll kill the lights and alarms. Then phone me. Got it?"

"Doesn't sound difficult. Just impossible."

"I'm counting on you, Suggs. Okay, hit it."

Suggs scurries with a limp to his post while Luke sets up in a supine position, his rifle pointed at the house, his eyes peering through the night-vision scope for webcams mounted on the fascia. He fires three shots in rapid succession and misses the webcams but hits their mounts, making a pinging sound. He adjusts the scope and has better luck firing the next round. He knocks out two cameras, and three sensors, but there must be more. He needs to light things up and that's where Cool comes in.

Luke slips on his backpack and carries the duffel bag to the bottom of the escarpment, concealed by the tall trees and pitch-black darkness. He approaches the box frame fence at the perimeter of the rear driveway and climbs to the top of it where there is a small ledge. He straddles it and calls for Cool. Cool obediently follows.

Then he strokes Cool and whispers, "Okay, I'm gonna toss you down there and I want you to run like hell."

When Cool is dropped into the open area, he sets off alarms, floodlights, and the motion sensing laser-pulse rifles, just as Luke expected. Cool easily speeds past the fusillade, leaps up and over the fence, and disappears. Luke is sad to see him go.

The lights in the rooms on the upper floor are turned on. Dark silhouettes peek out from behind curtains. He's being watched.

Luke aims and fires, taking out the rest of the webcams and floodlights, an easy feat at such close range.

The alarms are loud and shrill and alert the security detail stationed at the front gate; they immediately abandon their post, guard dogs barking, to meet the intruder at the rear of the house, but they find nobody there. Luke has jumped into the dumpster.

Still, they open fire, shooting blindly at anything that moves, mostly foliage on the ridgeline rustled by the scented breezes, but it's a waste of ammo. All they've succeeded in doing is to shred Aunt Marie's rose garden and the topiary that surrounds it. Even if the neighbors on the next estate, which is located at a considerable distance, are awakened, they know enough to mind their own business.

But the security guards are ever vigilant. They search the toolshed, cabanas, and the pool house. Luke waits until they are gathered around the diving board before he takes aim at the propane tanks that fuel the grilling stations and oxygenated chlorine tanks that filter the twenty-five-meter, eight-lane swimming pool.

One security guard bends down to tie his shoe while the others, panting and out of breath, sit on the lounge chairs, relaxing their hold on their weapons, and light cigarettes. They sure lull easily, thinks Luke, and seizes what could not be a better opportunity.

He fires at the propane tank that is closest to the security guards. The explosion sends flames high into the sky like a NASCAR crash and a shrapnel-like wave of metal in all directions. A security guard is practically incinerated on the spot.

The others flee or try to, but Luke hits another propane tank that flashes the same brilliant blast of flames followed by a mushroom cloud of smoke. They are at a loss. This is not the kind of attack they'd expected nor is it the kind of attack for which they had been trained.

Before they can make their escape, Luke aims at the oxygenated chlorine tank. This one should explode like an atom bomb. He hits it dead on and the explosion dwarfs the others, wreaking havoc in all directions. The flames are like serpent tongues, jutting out and ensnaring anything in their path. Two security guards catch fire, flail, and dive into the pool. The grass, hedgerows, shrubbery, and a large oak tree are also engulfed in orange, red, and blue flames that spread rapidly.

It's the diversion Luke needs to make a run for the house. He climbs out of the dumpster and one of the security guards, whose coat sleeve is ablaze, manages a gallant effort and takes a shot at him that misses and then jumps headlong into the Jacuzzi, sizzling and sending up a cloud of bluish smoke.

Luke can hear the crackle of gunfire in the near distance and assumes that Suggs's mission has been successful. There cannot be too many security guards left. They've decimated Uncle Paulie's little army of henchmen as well as the electronic eyes of the surveillance system. Now they can move under the cover of darkness, something that is second nature to them.

Luke makes a run for it, but despite his impressive marksmanship he has not hit all of the sensors, particularly the motion sensing laser-pulse rifles that spray bullets he barely outpaces. He's also triggered a motion sensor that turns on another blazing floodlight, but this one is accompanied by the loud barking of ferocious dogs—fake angry dogs, a hardly convincing bit of audio trickery.

Having breached the main phalanx of Uncle Paulie's security detail, he enters the house using a bump key to open the locked door that leads him down a short corridor to the garage where there is another locked door that leads into the house. The bump key doesn't work here, but a credit card does and Luke smiles at the irony of Uncle Paulie's state-of-the-art security and Internet surveillance systems that have been largely surmounted by the lowest of low-tech devices—a cat and a credit card.

There are bodyguards inside of the house, also expected, and one, a towering presence in a bulky flak vest who seems to be waiting for him, immediately opens fire. Luke ducks behind a wall for safety and, realizing that there is no time for hand-to-hand combat, exposes himself to return fire.

With one expertly placed shot he hits the bridge of the bodyguard's nose, causing him to stagger backward and collapse into a frosted glass divider. He's dead as wood.

Luke then moves cautiously down the hall and listens for voices. They will tell him a lot. The best and biggest bodyguards will be stationed outside of the room in which Uncle Paulie and his aunt will be hiding and Laura held captive.

There is no need to check the numerous guestrooms on the upper and lower floors. Or even the basement or the vast climate-controlled garage where Uncle Paulie keeps his classic car collection. Luke's hunch is that Paulie is hiding in his bedroom, the fastness of a coward.

He is confident that he can get past this last obstacle, but the challenge is to get to Uncle Paulie before he can do any more harm to Laura.

CHAPTER SIXTY-ONE

He can hear voices—loud voices crackling over walkie-talkies that emanate from the upstairs corridor at the end of which is Uncle Paulie's bedroom. The rest of the house is quiet, eerily quiet, like an abandoned bunker. As expected, that's where they have chosen to make their last stand.

"He did what?" he hears one bodyguard say, his voice panicky, confused, gruff. "The pool's on fire? How the fuck? How many dead? How could he enter the front and back simultaneously? I thought he was alone. Find him and kill him."

The remaining lights go out.

Suggs texts him. MISSION ACCOMPLISHED, SARGE. NOW WHAT?

Luke replies, BEYOND THE FOYER IS A BICAMERAL STAIRCASE. WHEN YOU GET TO THE TOP OF THE LANDING TURN RIGHT AND WALK DOWN A LONG CORRIDOR AND ENTER THE SECOND DOOR ON YOUR LEFT, A GUEST BEDROOM, WHERE THERE'S A WRAPAROUND BALCONY. FOLLOW THAT TO THE MASTER SUITE, A HUGE ROOM ABOUT TWENTY YARDS AWAY. THAT'S WHERE PAULIE IS. AND HOPEFULLY LAURA TOO. JUST COVER ME FROM THE OUTSIDE. AND DON'T ENTER UNLESS YOU HAVE TO.

"And by that you mean what?"

"If they kill me before I can kill him, you've got to finish things."

"I'm on my way."

"And watch out. There are stray security guards wandering around, though I think we got most of them."

"I mowed down a regiment," says Suggs proudly. "Unless they have another army somewhere, I think we'll be okay."

"I hope so."

Luke suddenly feels a hovering presence and then the warm muzzle of a gun on the back of his neck.

"Drop it," says a voice that seems to have come out of nowhere.

Not on your life, thinks Luke, and puts up his hands, still holding the Glock.

"I said, 'drop it,' and I won't ask you again."

Luke turns quickly, his forearm hitting the assailant's gun hand, knocking it aside. Then he pushes the heel of his hand into his nose. With one twist of the hand he acquires a new forty-five. It is not even warm in his hand before he fires it, hitting the assailant at point-blank range with a lethal blast in the forehead. He can feel a juicy splatter on his face and suit, a kind of baptismal. In a mystical moment, he hears a voice utter a passage from the Scriptures, but cannot tell if it emanates from inside or outside of himself. He is not a reader of the Bible so it seems like some kind of auditory hallucination: "…all things by the law are purged with blood: and without the shedding of blood there is no remission."

He mounts the stairs and moves silently in the direction of the voices, the real voices inside the house. He walks flush with the wall and spots two men outside Uncle Paulie's suite. He must move quickly, assuredly, precisely. It would not be unlike Uncle Paulie to kill Laura at the first inkling that he has penetrated his phalanx of flunkies, even with Paulie Jr. as a hostage.

Luke sprints with the unusual speed propelled by a sudden adrenaline rush and pounces on the two bodyguards before they can react with any proficiency. He head butts the bodyguard talking on the walkie-talkie, then knees him in the groin. The other bodyguard quickly raises his gun, but Luke pivots so that he is behind the first bodyguard and able to angle him so that he takes the bullet.

Luke draws his Glock and rips off a round with deadly accuracy, hitting them both in the head and leaving no doubt that they are out of commission, permanently, and will not cause him any further trouble. From this point on, he must be especially thorough and quick. He can't blow it now. The moment he has been waiting for has finally arrived.

CHAPTER SIXTY-TWO

Yes, he knows. He knows what lies on the other side of the door. They'll be ready for him, fully armed and expectant, so he kicks open the door and dives on the ground to avoid the predictable spray of bullets fired from Uncle Paulie's handgun.

"I've been waiting for you," says Uncle Paulie.

Luke rolls on the ground, avoiding another potshot, and fires the Glock, one bullet in each kneecap of the last and, presumably, the best bodyguard.

Laura is tied up in a chair and Aunt Marie is standing over her like a sadistic stepmother. Luke springs to his feet and shoots the gun out of Uncle Paulie's hand. It skitters across the floor and his aunt chases after it. Luke kicks her in the gut and picks up the gun.

"That's for Crissy," says Luke. "I know you were involved. And that's just for starters."

He can see Suggs's shadow on the balcony, including the outline of the AR-15 in his hands. Thankfully, he won't need him. Or so he hopes.

"Out from behind the desk," he says to Uncle Paulie who is looking at his bloody hand as if it belongs to somebody else. "And both of you. On your knees, hands behind your heads."

He focuses the gun on them and inspects Laura's condition. She is bruised and battered and barely conscious.

Luke removes the MetroCard from his pocket. He holds it

up for all to see as if it's a prized jewel. They regard it with puzzlement until he wields it, surgically slicing a large X across his aunt's right jugular vein. Uncle Paulie looks on in pained horror, fearing what's next.

"Before I kill you," he says to his uncle, "I'll let you think what it's like to live without your wife."

"You crazy fuck. You're a crazy fuck, you know that? Kill me, but not my wife. And where's Paulie Jr.? We can still make a deal. I don't care if you kill me, okay, an eye for an eye, but not them."

"I'm touched by your paternal affection." Luke looks at his watch. "He's strapped to a bomb that's due to go off in less than a minute."

"I can make you a rich man, a powerful man. Whatever you want."

"But, uncle, this is what I want," says Luke in an eerily calm voice. "I've wanted this for a long time. This is what you deserve. No, you deserve worse. You destroyed my parents, you killed my wife, and you brutalized Laura."

Choking and gasping for the last breaths she will ever take, Aunt Marie clasps her neck with both hands, an odd gesture that makes her look as if she's strangling herself. The profusion of blood gushes unstoppably through her fingers, soaking the front of her blouse, pooling up on the floor.

"I'm going to let you watch her bleed out," says Luke. "You'll know what it's like to live without your beloved wife. And it gets better. In about thirty seconds you'll hear an explosion. You'll also live to know what it's like to live without your son. And then I'll kill you."

Luke looks at his watch. "Let's wait for it together. Five, four, three, two—blast off."

Right on schedule the bomb goes off, and they can hear the

explosion, a faint rumble in the distance. Uncle Paulie bows his head, breaks down, and weeps, cursing Luke.

"You'll go to hell for this," he says.

"Won't be the first time."

CHAPTER SIXTY-THREE

"You know what I might even do?" asks Luke.

"What?" asks Uncle Paulie, his body trembling.

"I might not even kill you. I might let you spend the rest of your life with nothing, but behind bars, of course. I'll see to that. Or rather Laura here will."

Uncle Paulie gazes around the room, still looking for a way out, still hopeful that he can save himself. His optimism sickens Luke.

"You'll know what it's like to be alive but dead inside, completely without hope, in a place so dark you could never imagine it. You'll know what it was like for me, having had everything I ever loved taken away from you."

Uncle Paulie's eyes brighten. He seems relieved that Luke might actually let him live. That would be just fine.

"Do you want to live, Uncle Paulie?"

Uncle Paulie gives a sad little nod. His humiliation is so complete he is reduced to the demeanor of a spanked child.

With one eye on Uncle Paulie, Luke unties Laura, stands her up, and tenderly touches her soiled face. He grabs a blanket on the sofa, a chenille throw, and covers her with it.

She gradually begins to respond, her eyes fluttering as she regains a semblance of consciousness, enough to feel her feet beneath her, enough so that she can regain her balance. He helps her move toward the door, then abruptly stops, turns around.

"I don't think so," he says addressing his uncle as he inserts a fresh clip into the Glock. He smiles and stares, relishing the fear in Uncle Paulie's eyes, his slow comprehension of what's coming next. He knows. Yes, Uncle Paulie knows. And the look of shock registers on his face.

"No, please, don't," he begs, his hands clasped in a prayer position.

Luke takes a deep satisfied breath, his smile broadening, and empties the clip into his uncle. He continues pulling the trigger long after the clip is spent as if death has many levels and he wants to make sure that Uncle Paulie reaches them all.

His aunt turns away, slumps to the floor, the blood still spilling from the MetroCard wound, the blood making a Rorschach pattern in the carpet; a pretty floral bouquet, thinks Luke. Her gasps are feeble now and she collapses in a candy-colored red heap.

Luke savors these last images, especially the startled look in Uncle Paulie's eyes as if he expected mercy, as if he was incapable of comprehending his own mortality, even when it was a foregone conclusion.

Luke feels almost a primitive transference of power, a kind of patriarchal conversion, and savors the fruits of vengeance, a just vengeance, maybe not in the eyes of the law of the land but in his heart. It feels soulful, like a religious ritual, as if he's been born again, all of his sins expiated, and the past and the present and the future are no longer fragmented but mystically combined into a complete circle of geometric beauty, the law of angles no longer abstract but concretized.

But when he turns toward the door again, holding Laura, he hears approaching footsteps. He glances in the mirror on the wall that reflects the image in the window behind him—Suggs at the ready, his AR-15 pointed at their backs. Luke grabs Laura and they hit the floor, a fusillade flashing over their heads and blasting two armed guards who unexpectedly appear in the doorway.

Suggs breaks the rest of the glass window with the butt of the AR-15 and climbs into the room. Luke helps Laura to her feet. Suggs takes one of her elbows, Luke the other, and they move her gently but cautiously toward the exit.

"Somehow," says Suggs, "I don't think we're in the clear yet. Cops, fire department are on their way. Hear the sirens?"

"They're paid off to keep out of Uncle Paulie's business," says Luke, "But I guess you're right. They've never seen anything on this level. But I'm not worried. Follow me."

They hurry down the dimly lit corridor, the only illuminations of the lambent lights from the fires burning outside. Luke tucks the Glock into his waistband so that he can support Laura with both hands. The house is quiet and this part of the corridor is almost completely dark, except for the occasional flashes of firelight from outside. They can hear the sounds of the crackling conflagration, the snap and pop of the residual destruction wrought by Luke's forced entrance.

"She's in pretty bad shape," says Suggs, looking at Laura. "We better get her to a hospital."

Then, suddenly awakening from her stupor, she grabs the Glock from Luke's waistband and aims it at a shifting shadow lurking in the hallway. She fires, her hand miraculously steady. Both Luke and Suggs are nonplussed because they have not seen what she has managed to see, even with her left eye swollen— an assassin, no doubt the last of the bodyguards, secreted against a doorjamb, his body hidden except for the glint of his Colt Diamond .38 Special that is enough to give his position away.

Before he is able to get off a shot, Laura fires and hits him in the arm; he reels backward, drops the .38, and staggers forward, exposing himself, an easy target for Laura's second blast that hits the side of his skull, shearing off a hairy and very bloody piece of brain matter. She has saved not only her own life but also Suggs's and Luke's.

"Well, I guess, she's not in such bad shape after all," says Suggs.

But the heroic action has taken all of her strength, and she falters, wilted and wan. Suggs and Luke catch her before she collapses.

"One tough gal," says Luke admiringly. "Now, let's get the fuck out of here."

"We've got no wheels," says Suggs.

"Wheels? You want wheels?" asks Luke. "Follow me."

CHAPTER SIXTY-FOUR

Luke leads them to the climate-controlled garage where Uncle Paulie—the late Uncle Paulie—stores his beloved car collection.

Now the blare of the sirens is louder, closer.

"Take your pick," says Luke. "But hurry. Cops and fire department will arrive any second."

"Since when did that worry you?"

"Just pick one for Christ's sake!"

"My, my," says Suggs feasting his eyes on the vista of vintage automobiles that includes a 1966 red Ford Thunderbird with a white top, a 1956 Jaguar XK140, a 1970 Chevrolet Corvette, a 1966 Mustang, a 1971 Chevy Camaro, a spry 1961 MG, and a 1959 Austin-Healey. "They must be worth a fortune."

"They are. That 1961 red Porsche 356 alone is valued at around a hundred eighty thousand dollars. But all acquired by ill-gotten gains, all tainted as far as I'm concerned, all the legacy of a detestable man, and I'm gonna blow the whole damn place up—that is, after I hot-wire us some wheels if the keys aren't in the ignition; my uncle usually kept the keys in the ignition, easier to keep track of. Idiot."

For spite, Luke chooses Uncle Paulie's favorite, a roomy 1959 Ford Galaxy that has a backseat big enough to house a family of four, the perfect spot for Laura to recline in comfort. The keys are in the ignition and it starts up hesitantly, sputtering, but soon comes to life, brisk and rumbling and ready to go.

"Everybody in," says Luke, hitting the garage door opener.

He then walks to the vintage Esso gas pump and lifts the handle. He pulls the lever and sprays a sloppy line of petrol from one length of the garage to the other. Satisfied with his handiwork, he leaves the hose dangling, gasoline flowing like a nicked artery.

The Galaxy backfires, but it drives just fine. Once they're at a safe distance from the garage, Luke leans out the window, aims the Glock at the pump, and fires. The explosion is the most powerful one yet, one that would register on the Richter magnitude scale if there was a seismometer around.

A fireball erupts and soon alights the trail of gasoline that leads to the petrol tanks of the Mustang and the rest of the antique cars. The detonations are like those on a battlefield, all consuming, searing everything in their path, including the house itself.

Suggs looks as if he might break into tears. "Pyromaniac," he says. "You're a regular William Tecumseh Sherman."

"Scorched-earth policy. Exactly. Smoke screen too. The fire department and police will have their hands full, so their focus will be elsewhere. I made sure of that."

"What a shame, all those beautiful cars. What'd they ever do to you?"

"I guess I'm just mean."

"You just have a thing about blowing things up."

"True. But isn't it beautiful?" says Luke, taking one last look before he hits the gas pedal, and they exit through the front gate without a soul to stop them.

CHAPTER SIXTY-FIVE

Before they turn onto the street, they catch a glimpse of Cool sitting on top of the guardhouse railing, observing the fireworks.

"Smart cat," says Suggs. "A real survivor."

Luke slows down and Cool leaps off the fence. Luke swings open the car door and Cool scampers in, jumping into the backseat where he cuddles up against Laura as if instinctively knowing that she needs comforting.

"Don't worry, baby," says Luke to Laura. "It's all going to be okay."

In the rearview mirror Luke can see a NYFD truck, a SWAT team, and federal agents arriving on the scene, sirens blaring, lights flashing.

"Better late than never," he says. "Let them sort out the mess."

They drive onto the Verrazano Bridge where the air is cooler, the moon higher and brighter and clearer in the summer sky. Luke can feel all of his muscles relax and tensions that he never realized were there dissipate.

Laura awakens. "Hey," she says, petting Cool.

"You're back," says Luke. "How you feeling?"

"Like I've been run over by a truck."

"We're taking you to the hospital."

"I've got to call in."

"After we get you checked out."

Suggs dozes in the passenger seat.

"He's not looking so hot either," says Laura.

"We'll get him admitted too. He's lost a lot of blood."

"Your face looks like hell," says Laura, "but your suit. You could be in *GQ*."

"Not quite."

Luke reaches behind the seat and extends his hand. Laura grasps it. He squeezes gently and an intimate moment passes between them. Luke looks ahead and he can see a long, clear vista, for there is little traffic on the bridge at this time of night. The moon looks brighter, or perhaps the sky is just darker, and the cool air is soft, fragrant, sweet, an omen, he thinks, of sorts.

He feels no regrets for what he has done, no guilt, just a lessening of the rage that has sickened him. But instead of an ending, instead of a sense of finality and closure, he feels just the opposite — the intimations of a new beginning.

The emergency room at New York Hospital is overflowing, like a popular nightclub. Groups of people stand in circles outside and in the doorway, smoking cigarettes, drinking coffee, talking, texting.

All the seats in the waiting room are filled, filled with people in worse shape than Laura and Suggs. An ambulance pulls up and paramedics cart out a gunshot victim on a gurney. It's a sight he knows well, seen too many times in combat. Luke has a clear view of him, shakes his head, and thinks the guy doesn't stand a chance.

The admitting nurse is a large black woman with a scowl that seems permanently affixed to her face. Luke cuts in front of the line and approaches her, but before he can say a word she brusquely orders him to take a seat.

"She's a federal agent," he says, pointing to Laura, "and that is a war veteran. I want them seen and I want them seen now."

The admitting nurse has dealt with all kinds of tough customers, belligerent bullies, and pushy New Yorkers, probably all three types in the last hour, and has consequently developed a thick skin and a callous attitude, but there is something in Luke's tone, or maybe it's the look in his eyes, that gives her pause and sets him apart from the rabble.

"In a minute," she says.

"*Now*," says Luke firmly. She reacts promptly, a trace of fear penetrating her scowl. Luke discovers that there are other benefits of being transparently homicidal.

"Right this way," she says, her tone still just short of friendly.

Luke helps Laura to her feet, but Suggs is out of it.

"He's in shock," says Luke angrily. "Can't you see that?"

Two attendants arrive. Drifting into unconsciousness, Suggs is put into a wheelchair. Laura is offered one, but she declines, insisting that she can walk on her own.

Before she disappears behind the ER doors, she glances back at Luke and smiles trustingly, the light returning to her beautiful eyes. Luke is filled with an enormous rush of what he thinks must be a chemical reaction—interleukin, an antineoplastic drug they give to cancer patients that is also manufactured by the body in blissful moments. *Now isn't that romantic?* he thinks.

Before exiting and getting back into the Ford Galaxy, he enters the men's room and looks in the mirror, not at himself, but at his suit flecked with dried blood. He thinks about trying to remove the stains with a wet paper towel, but then thinks that he doesn't mind them. He doesn't mind them at all.

CHAPTER SIXTY-SIX

Three days later, Luke leaves his Manhattan hotel at eleven o'clock and walks up Madison Avenue. He could easily afford a cab, or even a limo, for he now has more money than he's ever had in his life—money from Fister, most of the money from Uncle Paulie, a nice pile sitting in an offshore account—but he prefers to walk. A hint of autumn is in the air and the mugginess of the last few days has been replaced with cooler temperatures and a clear sky with a strong light.

Although around two a.m. he'd had another bout with the cold sweats and a slight fever, he feels fine now. The symptoms have worsened as of late, but he is not worried or discouraged, for he has the antidote—hope and a newly regained desire to live—that he has no doubt will, combined with medical science, heal him.

Dr. Ornstein is pleased to see him.

"So, you've changed your mind about getting treatment," he says, regarding Luke a little suspiciously. After all, he's not the run-of-the-mill cancer patient, desperate for a cure, and wonders if he might have psychological problems.

Luke, almost as if he's read his mind, says, "I'm seeing a shrink. I'm working on the whole package—mind and body."

Although not given to asking personal questions, Dr. Ornstein can't resist in this case. "So," he says, "what changed your mind?"

"I've got something to live for now."

"You took up golf?" says the doctor jokingly. "Don't you have a son?"

"I do. I realize how selfish I've been. I'll be seeing him soon too. I hope."

Dr. Ornstein suddenly becomes all business and examines Luke for indications of Hodgkin's lymphoma. He finds a raised purple lump under Luke's arm, near the armpit, a swollen axillary lymph node.

"We should biopsy that."

"I hate needles," says Luke ironically. It's a kind of private joke. He's been through a lot worse, to say the least. Although he's lost track of time, he guesses that it's been over a year since the last procedure, when his mind was addled, so his recollection of it is fuzzy.

While the doctor examines his chart, Luke vaguely recalls that a needle was inserted into the lymph node and a sample removed, not exactly a painless procedure, but certainly a minor one. Given his combat background, it was a lot less painful than some of the ordeals his body has been through.

"It's been fourteen months," says the doctor, shaking his head, a gesture of chastisement. "It hasn't spread to the spleen, liver, bone marrow, or other organs. I just wish you hadn't delayed treatment."

"I feel fine," says Luke, a little chilly sitting on the examination table in a hospital gown. "I still get the night sweats, but I've got my appetite back."

"What about fatigue?"

"Feel like I could run a marathon."

Dr. Ornstein listens but doesn't respond. "We'll do more tests to determine staging."

"What's staging?"

"My guess is that you're lucky, that it hasn't spread, that you're still in Stage I, maybe Stage II. Both stages are limited and can be treated with radiation, maybe chemo, maybe both, but I'll bet radiation will be enough. We'll see how it goes."

"I'm game."

"You'll need blood chemistry tests to determine protein levels, liver and kidney function, uric acid level. CT scans of the chest, abdomen, and pelvis." Dr. Ornstein is not the warmest soul Luke has ever met, but he is thorough and that makes Luke feel that he's in good hands. "And a CBC."

"A what?"

"A CBC—complete blood count to check for anemia. I'll bet you're anemic. You look like hell. I don't know what you've been up to, but it looks like, well, you've been through another war."

"I have, sort of."

"How's the broken rib?"

"Painful, but I ignore it. I've had worse."

"Okay. Get dressed."

"So what's the prognosis?"

"Won't know until all the tests are in, but as I mentioned, it is one of the most curable forms of cancer, so count yourself lucky. At least so far."

"Oh, I do. I feel very lucky."

"But let's not get too ahead of ourselves," says Dr. Ornstein in an effort to temper what he deems is Luke's somewhat manic enthusiasm, but then he revises his judgment. The guy's in love.

CHAPTER SIXTY-SEVEN

The next day, despite still being hobbled and walking with a slight limp, Luke is feeling stronger, and he'll need every ounce of it, for it'll be a busy day. He has many stops to make, many people to see, many things to do, but he regards the list in his head not as a burden but with the cheerfulness of a man who has earned his freedom.

Still, after a few blocks his body aches, especially his bruised rib. Luke is tempted to steal a car, just because he can and just because he knows he can get away with it. Old habits die hard. But he rents one instead, a Lincoln MKZ 4-door for $89 a day at Enterprise.

Parking is a problem and he circles the block a dozen times but cannot find an empty space. Fuck it. He parks in a loading zone. The price of the ticket will probably be less than the price of parking it in a garage two blocks away and a lot more convenient.

New York Hospital is a filthy place, thinks Luke. Dingy, too, and depressing, and when he arrives he is not surprised to find that Laura is dressed and eager to depart. She is dressed in jeans and a leather jacket with a cashmere scarf loosely draped around her neck. Although the color has returned to her cheeks, the weight she has lost is evident.

"You look great," says Luke, embracing her warmly.

She smiles and says, "My Suited Hero!" She gives him a big hug and his heart leaps. His face registers a mixture of surprise and delight, the expression of a man who cannot believe he has been given a second chance.

Laura signs the discharge forms, and a nurse brings her wheelchair. Laura refuses it.

"It's policy," says the nurse politely.

"Must I?" she says.

The nurse merely smiles.

Laura rolls her eyes and sits down in the wheelchair. They reach the exit, and Laura walks on her own without any difficulty to the Lincoln, threading her arm through Luke's.

It's a simple and perhaps practical gesture, but it seems to add to his stature. It's been a long time since he's had a pretty girl on his arm. He opens the door for her and she sighs with relief.

"I am so glad to be out of there," she says.

Luke takes her to lunch at the South Street Seaport and they order glasses of wine and look out at the East River.

"Will you come to Borrego Springs with me?" he asks.

"Did you see the doctor?"

"Yes."

"How'd it go?"

"Fine. He took some tests and I'll start treatments, probably radiation, soon, if necessary. He says the cancer is in its early stages so he's sure I'll be just fine," he says, putting perhaps a more optimistic spin on his condition than Dr. Ornstein, but that's the way he feels. In fact, he knows it in his gut: he hasn't come this far just to die of cancer.

Laura regards him searchingly, as if she suspects that his optimism might be more his own than his doctor's.

"I'd like to get away for a while," he says. "With you. Even if it's a short time."

"My son," says Laura, guiltily. "I haven't seen him much."

"Bring him."

"You wouldn't mind?"

"I'll bring Jack. If you tell me where he is."

"I can't take any more time off. They want me in Clarksburg. Clarksburg, West Virginia, where the Criminal Justice Information Services Division is, as soon as possible."

"Will you at least come with me to visit Jack and my in-laws? I'm a little ashamed of my absence and what I'll find."

"Wasn't your fault. But, of course, I'll come."

"So you'll tell me where they are?"

"They're in South Salem, a small town in Westchester County, New York."

"That close? That's only what? Fifty miles from here?" says Luke, as surprised as he is excited. "Talk about hiding in plain sight. When can we go?"

"My ex has Jonathan. He'll drop him off tonight, and we can schedule something in a day or two."

"That'll be terrific!" says Luke, practically diving across the table to give her an ardent embrace and a kiss.

The waiter observes this display of affection and rolls his eyes.

They settle back into their seats and suddenly Laura's mood turns somber.

"What's the matter?" asks Luke. "I'm sorry if I embarrassed you."

"No. It's not that. It's just that . . ." She hesitates. "A life together. I'm gone a lot on assignment. Different cities. Odd hours. It broke up my first marriage. I'm just wondering if a life together is realistic at this point."

"Of course it is. Just leave it all to me."

Laura smiles at his confident reassurance. It's just what she wants to hear. Now she leans over the table to embrace and kiss him. This time the server just looks away.

CHAPTER SIXTY-EIGHT

After he makes Laura comfortable in his hotel suite, his next stop is The Rhone Addiction Institute, a rehabilitation clinic on the Upper East Side of Manhattan, where Suggs has been admitted into their alcohol detoxification program, all expenses paid by Luke.

Located in the former mansion of a New York socialite who was one of the first to insist that alcoholism should be regarded as a disease and that alcoholics deserved to be treated with respect and dignity, it is more like a resort than a hospital.

In fact, it says as much in their promotional literature. It has a heated pool and spa, a meditation garden, yoga classes, gourmet meals by a top-notch chef who had been lured away from one of Manhattan's pricey restaurants, flat-screen TVs, DVRs, and Internet connections in every room, thousand-thread-count sheets with down pillows and comforters, and—Luke can hardly believe this—turn down service. It puts the Ritz to shame. It's a long way from the shelter that he once called home. Nothing but the best for Suggs, but Luke is worried that he might never want to leave.

And that is not far from the truth. When he enters Suggs's room, he finds him in a natty robe that looks more like something Noël Coward would wear than a hospital gown, and he is sober and cheerful and enjoying the company of a new friend, a patient who resides in the room down the hall.

Luke is startled at the physical change in Suggs. In a short time, his face is leaner, his eyes clear, and he no longer has the bloated look of the sedentary lush.

"Hey, Luke! Glad to see you, buddy! Meet Chip. Chip, this is Luke Stark. He likes to blow things up."

"Don't we all," says Chip. They shake hands.

"Now Chip here," says Suggs, "is a booze writer—he writes about fancy wine and what he calls the cocktail culture. But he's an alcoholic," says Suggs cheerfully, as if introducing a member of an elite club. "Now isn't that ironic?"

"An occupational hazard," says Chip with a resigned wave of his hand. "At least in my case."

Chip is tall and handsome, with rakish floppy hair; he's in his early thirties, with an Ivy League accent and mannerisms. He holds a glass of club soda with a slightly raised pinky, a gesture that makes the simple act of sipping a nonalcoholic beverage seem smart and elegant. He sits with his legs crossed, and speaks in a soft, gracious voice as if he's addressing a highbrow colleague in an editorial meeting.

"Hey, Chip, tell Luke about some of the great people in history who were boozers."

Chip demurs, but Suggs insists.

"Almost all great historical figures were drunks," says Chip. "FDR, Hemingway, Jackson Pollock, Ulysses S. Grant, Babe Ruth, SpongeBob SquarePants, the list goes on and on. Hitler, on the other hand, was a teetotaler."

"C'mon. Tell him, tell him that story about the writers who went to Paris in the twenties."

"Ah, yes," says Chip, smoothing his pants leg as if brushing off some imaginary piece of lint. "They drank up a storm. But drinking was fun then. It didn't have the stigma it has now. It brought people together, stimulated them intellectually, created friendships, and it was a great tool for what we now call networking. They didn't sit at home in front of their televisions watching dumb reality shows and using their computers to obsessively log onto Facebook. They roamed every bar and restaurant along Paris's Left Bank. They were the best and brightest minds of the Lost Generation. Ezra Pound sipped absinthe and wrote some of the greatest poems of his generation. Ford Maddox Ford sent back a brandy four times because it wasn't to his liking. They were serious drinkers because they were serious about life.

"Of course, they were having *too* good a time. Can't have that," says Chip and Luke notices the personal note of bitterness in his tone as if he's talking about himself and not them. "Cranky critics decades later had to try to spoil the fun by saying that their excessive drinking was pathological, a form of self-medication."

Suggs smiles, chuckles, even though he's heard it before, like a kid who can't get enough of his favorite bedtime story. "Isn't that the truth," he says, shaking his head. "Tell him about Churchill."

Chip needs no encouragement to continue. He clearly likes having an audience, even a small one. "Churchill was one of the great boozers of all time, a real addict," he says. "He was drunk for most of World War II, but fearlessly lead England through the German blitzkrieg with a brandy in one hand and a stogie in the other. Booze wins wars. What was that line Lincoln said about Grant when some colonel claimed that Grant had fallen off the wagon? Oh, yes, Lincoln said, 'If drink makes fighting men like Grant, then find out what he drinks, and send my other commanders a case!'"

"Hah!" Suggs laughs uproariously. Luke is also amused, albeit skeptical. Is this really the right atmosphere to achieve long-term sobriety?

A staffer, a lithesome young woman in a lavender tank top and Capri pants, pops her head in and says, "Yoga, anybody?

Class starts in ten." Her smile is broad and shows off a set of dazzling white teeth. Her beaming good health is an intricate part of her appeal, of her beauty. "Remember. You're only as young as your spine is flexible."

After she departs, Suggs says, "The women around here are gorgeous." Suggs looks at Chip for corroboration.

"Yeah. Yoga class always has the best tail."

Luke is nonplussed. "You guys do yoga?" he asks in disbelief as if this dramatic change in hard-drinking Suggs can't be true.

"Hell yeah," says Suggs. "But we already went this morning."

"You're shittin' me."

"No. And remember," says Suggs with a mischievous grin, "you're only as young as your spine is flexible."

Both Chip and Suggs chuckle as if sharing a private joke that Luke doesn't quite get.

"Well," says Chip, "I better be going. See you at Happy Hour."

After Chip exits, Luke asks, "Happy Hour?"

"Yeah, but it is not, of course, what you think," explains Suggs. "It's something we developed. It's Happy Hour without booze. We drink Sprite with seltzer."

"Can't be much of a Happy Hour."

"Where you been staying, Luke? I know you wouldn't go back to the apartment. Or Laura's. You and Laura got some fancy new digs with all the money you made?"

"Staying at a hotel with Laura until we can figure things out."

"I think The Suited Hero's in love. Isn't that what she calls you?"

"Yeah. She's great. Anyway, I just stopped by to say hello, to see how you were doing, but I see you're doing just fine."

Luke takes a step toward the door, but Suggs stops him, says, "Shouldn't we talk?"

"About what?"

"About my money."

"Everything's all paid for. You got no worries."

Suggs's face darkens with anger. "What about my cut? You're not shafting me, are you, Luke?"

"You'll get the rest when you complete the program."

Suggs is appeased, smiles. "It better be a lot."

"More than you ever dreamed."

"I'll be clean and sober in no time. Program is great and I'm ahead of schedule. A regular star pupil."

"We'll see about that."

CHAPTER SIXTY-NINE

The next stop on his itinerary is his tailor. On his way there, out of the corner of his eye, he sees a familiar figure, a well-dressed black man, across the street, on the edge of a crowd, pedestrians in lockstep moving south as if they are in a kind of military formation. He wears a pork-pie hat, a leather jacket, and his trademark spit-shined spectator shoes. It is Billy Dee. Their eyes meet only for a moment. He was nowhere to be seen when things went down at the warehouse or Uncle Paulie's house. Luke wants to call out to him, but Billy Dee smiles and tips his hat in a congratulatory gesture and then disappears into the crowd. He has a feeling that he will never see him again.

Luke enters Busconi's, pours himself a coffee, and sits in a leather club chair, waiting for Haskell. He has the relaxed attitude of a man on vacation. He gazes out the window and watches the orderly flow of traffic and the purposeful gait of pedestrians, mostly businesspeople, on the streets outside, and seems surprised that there are no traces of the events of the summer. The normalcy is comforting and a little dull at the same time.

Haskell greets him cheerfully, ushers him into the fitting room. Haskell is a little grayer, but as spry and enthusiastic as ever about his profession, his craftsmanship, and no doubt about the size of this order. Luke has commissioned him to make not one new suit, but an entire wardrobe that will be versatile in various climates and conditions. He still has the need to keep moving and does not know where he will end up.

"Oh, it turned out marvelous, just marvelous," says Haskell, rubbing his hands together as if about to sit down to a gourmet meal. "I'll be back in a second," he says, the measuring tape dangling around his neck like a clerical necklace; he never seems to take it off. He disappears and returns with one of Luke's new bespoke suits.

Luke undresses, slips on the suit and looks admiringly at it in the mirror.

"Love the geometry," he says. "Very nice, very nice geometry."

It's the same suit as the one he's just removed, the suit that was pretty much shredded beyond repair like a uniform that had been through many battles, a two-button Glen plaid with a bluish-green overlay, no vents, with flat-front trousers.

The fit is flawless and he is delighted.

He eschews the current trend for year-round fabric weights. Each suit, each sport coat will be seasonal. This one is a heavy gauge, a sixteen-ounce with a milled finish, perfect for the coming winter weather and warm enough to be worn without an overcoat if he chooses.

It also has a few modifications, a more authoritative shoulder, a ticket pocket, and side adjusters, a kind of throwback to the past. All of his jackets have higher armholes for greater ease of movement.

Then Haskell brings the rest of the wardrobe, garments on a dozen hangers that he has looped around his index fingers. He slides them carefully onto hooks in the fitting room.

"Marvelous, marvelous," he repeats, appraising the suit Luke has on; he is all smiles today. "I told you, didn't I?"

"Oh, there's always room for improvement," says Luke,

turning to the left and then to the right to view the suit in the mirror from different angles. "I think this button needs to be moved over an eighth of an inch and the sleeves—I'm not sure they'll allow me to show enough cuff."

Haskell assures him otherwise. "Quarter of an inch of cuff," he says. "No more than that. But it's up to you, of course."

Luke gives the nod and Haskell hands him the next garment, a two-button double-breasted suit with side vents, Bemberg lining, quarter-top pockets, pick-stitched edges, and reverse pleated trousers. Double-breasted suits are not in style and Luke knows this but does not care; he does not care a damn. He likes double-breasted suits and has always wanted one and is pleased at its modern styling that he helped create with Haskell's guidance.

Next is a suit in a lighter gauge for warmer climates, a single-breasted silver number with a more athletic expression. There is also a classic two-button pinstripe, a windowpane, and a herringbone; two unconstructed and unlined blazers, one in gold and one in mocha; a checked sport coat, very casual, very comfortable; and a camel-colored cashmere sport coat. Last in the mix are several slim-cut suits reminiscent of the ring-a-ding sixties. It is an eclectic wardrobe, to say the least.

"Clothes make the man," says Luke. "Or do they? What do you think, Haskell?"

"I think they do—undoubtedly."

"Well, they sure do help."

A new suit for Luke is restorative; it brings about what he can only explain as a physiological improvement and a juicy, revivifying affect on his cognitive powers.

"Indeed, they do," he says more to himself than to Haskell. "Now which one should I wear today?"

"They all look marvelous, just marvelous."

"I'll wear the Glen plaid."

"What about the old one?"

"Burn it. And could you send the others to my hotel? I'll probably never wear them."

"You'll never wear them?" asks Haskell puzzled, almost speechless, and a bit insulted as if all of his hard work has been denigrated. "But, well—hmmm—why?"

"I guess for me it's like a uniform that works. I'm a one-suit man. And the others, well, you know how much I love clothes. I guess I'm a collector. You're an artist, Haskell." Now Haskell feels a little better, beams with pride, smiles ear to ear, but he still dislikes the idea of his garments sitting in a closet, unworn, unseen, and appreciated by only one man. "Clothes are works of art just like painting, sculpture, don't you think?"

"I've always taken great pride in my work, but never elevated them to that level. If I may beg to differ, I think they should be worn and enjoyed. Their aesthetic value should be shared with others. But, of course, to each his own."

"Yes, to each his own."

"Yet I understand, sir, I understand your point of view. And I'm flattered," says Haskell flatly, unconvincingly.

"How much do I owe you for this art collection?"

"Forty-six thousand dollars," says Haskell.

Luke writes a check.

"We also have your custom shirts. Would you like to try them on?"

"Just one to wear with this suit. White with French cuffs and a soft collar; Sea Island cotton, one hundred fifty-thread count. Send the rest over to the hotel too, will you?"

"Certainly."

Charles Tyrwhitt, a favorite menswear store in Grand Central, is where Luke picks up a few accessories—pocket handkerchiefs, argyle socks, and a pin-dot tie. Then to Church's for a pair of black calfskin Oxford cap-toe shoes. His last stop is Tiffany's where he purchases onyx cuff links.

CHAPTER SEVENTY

Luke is up early and makes the coffee. And so is Jonathan, a lively seven-year-old who has his mother's eyes. He must get his thick, black hair and dark complexion from his father. Jonathan regards him warily.

"What kind of a name is Luke?" asks Jonathan.

"It's a name given to those who have magical powers," answers Luke, pouring himself a cup of coffee.

"Really?" says Jonathan excitedly, then thinks for a second. "I never heard that."

"That's because you're too young."

"What kind of magical powers?"

"I can't tell you. They're secret."

"Ah, c'mon. *Please.* I won't tell anybody."

"Sorry. But maybe someday, if you're good."

"Luke," says Jonathan thoughtfully. "I like that name. It's sounds like someone on TV or in the movies."

"Luke Skywalker?"

"Luke who?"

"You're too young. Want some breakfast?"

"Cereal. With milk."

"I didn't think you were going to eat it dry."

"Sometimes I do," says Jonathan assertively. "My mother lets me."

Luke realizes that this is a sort of test to see if Luke will be a hard-ass like his father, who is also a federal agent with a military background—army, not navy—and Luke thinks he must be a nightmare for a kid, a strict disciplinarian with no sense of humor.

"You can have your cereal any way you like it," says Luke. "You can even have it with whiskey for all I care."

"Whiskey? In cereal?"

"Sure. I have it all the time," says Luke. "My mother lets me."

Jonathan laughs. He gets the joke. Smart kid, thinks Luke. He has the feeling they'll get along fine. He just hopes he hits it off with his own son half as well.

Laura sleepily enters the room in a bathrobe and asks, "What are you two up to?"

"We're having cereal with whiskey," says Jonathan, his gaze trained on his mother, eager to see her reaction.

"Again?" she says, playing along and the mood only brightens from here. They have been together for less than twenty-four hours and they already feel like a family.

They dress and get in the car and drive to the verdant hamlet of South Salem in the northeast part of Westchester County, the second wealthiest county in New York State, and the seventh wealthiest county nationally. The prosperity his in-laws have achieved is impressive, admirable, and the safety and serenity will surely benefit Jack, but it only points up his own dismal failure to provide for his son. This is a far cry from Brooklyn.

It is a semirural area, at least to Luke's urban way of thinking, has excellent schools, and from what he has learned from the file Laura gave him, Jack is thriving.

But this raises all kinds of questions and doubts in Luke's mind. Will his intrusion, his sudden insertion into his son's life, after a year's absence, be for good or ill? The anticipation of reuniting with Jack filled him with so much excitement last night that he hardly slept, but now he feels a sudden pang, a sense of futility, another lost chance at happiness, a bitter recrimination at his own neglect and failure.

Laura senses the change in his mood and reassures him. "They're thrilled you're coming. Just take it one step at a time. You do have a tendency to act too quickly, to want too much too soon. It's understandable. You're trying to make up for lost time."

The criticism stings Luke's pride but he knows she's right and takes comfort in the wisdom of her advice, her honesty and sincerity. With her help he won't blow this chance to make things right with Jack.

The house is a modest colonial, small but with the charm of a cottage, set back from the street with a long tree-lined drive-way that offers shade and dappled sunlight on verdant lawns. A well-tended garden is ablaze with the vibrant colors of sum-mer flowers that are still flourishing despite the onset of autumn.

Then Luke sees a bicycle and skateboard leaning against the house and his heart sinks. They are like reproaches and he de-cides that he cannot go through with this, that he should leave things well enough alone.

"I'm turning around," he says softly. This takes all the self-control he can muster because he wants to scream it, swing a fifty-mile-per-hour U-Turn, hit the gas, run, but that would only alarm Jonathan who is sitting in the backseat happily playing with his Lego blocks.

Laura reaches out to him, tenderly strokes the side of his face, draws near, and whispers, "You can do this. I know you can."

Somehow Luke conquers what he regards as a cowardly fear and drives up to the house. Before they are even out of the car, the front door opens and a towheaded little boy breaks into a run, clambers down the stairs, and yells, "Dad! Dad!"

The sight of Jack makes him vertiginous, and he staggers out of the car feeling oddly off balance. Jack slams into him with such force that he is almost tackled, knocked off his feet. Jack has changed since the last time Luke saw him, over a year ago, and the change is dramatic. He is clearly feisty, strong, and healthy, and even for a boy approaching his eighth birthday, Luke sees that he now has a more athletic build and his skin is less fair, less like Crissy's, more ruddy, manly, but he still has her grin, the slight curl of the lip she expressed during uncertain moments.

Jack looks up at him with loving eyes and says, "I hate you, I hate you, I hate you."

CHAPTER SEVENTY-ONE

Luke is at the airport with Jack waiting for their flight. He is reading a book but not absorbing one word of it. He stares at the two extra tickets in his hand as if they are cards dealt from a bad deck. Still, he looks around hopefully one last time and finally faces facts. He tears them up and tosses them into the trash bin.

Jack is quietly playing a game on his iPad. He has not said much, but they have talked about his anger and resentment, but Luke is not sure he has acquitted himself.

He does not know if his son will ever forgive his abandonment, whether it will be one of those lifelong scars that will manifest itself at different times during his life, always a sore spot, never to be fully healed. A rocky reconciliation is the best that he can do now, for he cannot undo the past and they will both have to live with that as best they can.

His in-laws, on the other hand, were a much simpler matter. They were nothing but supportive and cried when they saw him. They embraced him and welcomed him into their home. They talked about Crissy. Luke was shocked by how much they'd aged, no doubt due to the loss of their only daughter. Jack must've been a great comfort to them.

They spent many hours in the living room, a very homey living room with a beamed ceiling, hardwood floors, area rug, fireplace, and comfortable sofas where they caught up, mostly on Jack's progress at school and on the athletic field, his friends and his interests, and his past misbehavior that was getting out of hand until they sent him to a therapist who helped him understand himself and his anger in a way that they never could.

They also gave Luke the disk with all the incriminating evidence on it that Uncle Paulie wanted so badly. To him it's a worthless token of all he's been through, but he's sure Laura and her FBI colleagues will put it to good use. Or not.

Jack and Jonathan hit it off. They are about the same age and have the same interests. The coupling of their names even make them sound like brothers, all the more reason for Luke's disappointment when Laura decided to go her own way for professional obligations, at least for the time being, infuriating Luke, a reaction he now regrets.

She was indeed right about him and her words echo in his head, causing him enormous pain, "You have a tendency to want too much too soon. You're trying too hard to make up for lost time."

But maybe he'll feel better when they get to Borrego Springs, a calm oasis in the California desert, a dramatic change of scene that he hopes will prove to be a memorable adventure for Jack and a place for Luke to lie low for a while.

They'll go hiking and biking and swimming and exploring the sand dunes on ATVs. Luke will show him the off roads, the rocky terrain, the wide-open spaces, the majesty of the desert skies at night, the healing powers of the sun, and allow him to experience an area surrounded by caramel mountains, hills and valleys, the rugged landscape of the West, so different from what he has known all of his young life. They'll have a fine time.

Or maybe Jack will be bored and homesick. He'll probably miss his friends. But it'll be a singular experience for both of them, a private time to get to know each other again. There will be other kids there his age, he hopes, and it'll only be for a little more than a week, an eternity for a kid Jack's age, but Luke feels it is imperative to get away, to put as much distance, literally and figuratively, between him and the events of the recent past.

Luke has given up hope for a last-minute appearance by Laura and Jonathan, and realizes that they must go to their departing gate; the flight will be boarding in less than an hour.

But when they pass through security, he can hardly believe his eyes because Laura and Jonathan are waiting for them, tickets in hand.

"What kept you?" asks Laura. "We've been here over an hour."

"I knew you'd change your mind."

"How could I not?"

Jack and Jonathan involve themselves in their own reunion, showing each other their iPads and sharing thoughts on popular video games. They even look somewhat alike. Luke has a feeling that this might work out.

He holds Laura close and kisses her, but exercises the restraint he lacked in the restaurant. However, she does not, and gives him a fervent kiss that the kids are too busy to notice.

And there are no complaints or comments from onlookers because we are a peripatetic people, forever migrating from one destination to another, often under trying circumstances, myriad irritations, and the threat of terrorism, so the sight of a couple in love seems to be a palliative that transforms the atmosphere from one of chaos and confusion to the ideal of transportation—bringing couples and families and people happily together.

Their amorous mood seems to alter the atmosphere wherever they go. When they board the aircraft, everybody is in a cheerful mood, both passengers and flight attendants. They settle in and the kids are thrilled as only kids can be with the extra pillows and blankets and free snacks the flight attendants lavish on them.

Luke places the MetroCard in the novel he is reading and closes it. The MetroCard is now used as a bookmark.

He reaches over and grasps Laura's hand. The plane rumbles down the runway and lifts off effortlessly. It rises toward white clouds and the embrace of an infinite blue sky.

He leans back in his seat and tries to put his feelings into words audible only to himself. He thinks that he was wrong, that life is not about what you've lost or what you've left behind or what has been taken from you, but about the love you have not yet found.